12 O'Clock High!

is a magnificent novel of the United States Air Force in World War II—the story of a fighting general and the shattered bomber squadrons he led to victory in the most desperate and dangerous months of the war.

When General Frank Savage took over the 918th Bomber Group, he inherited a sick command. The 918th was the "Hard Luck" group, battered by the heaviest losses in the U.S. 8th Air Force—and now the men were licked in their own minds.

Savage offered them no pity. Instead, he lashed them with blunt truths about themselves and their jobs, drove them to perfect the skills of war, then led them relentlessly into the high and burning hell over Germany.

Taut, vivid, crackling with excitement, 12 O'Clock High! is an unforgettable human drama of the pressures of combat and the loneliness of command.

RELATED READING
IN BALLANTINE WAR BOOKS

When you have finished reading this book, you will want to read the following Ballantine Books which provide valuable information on World War II in the air:

THE FIRST AND THE LAST, Adolf Galland $.75

The rise and fall of the Luftwaffe: 1939-45, by Germany's commander of Fighter Forces. Without question the best book about German fighters in WW II. (*10th printing*)

BLACK THURSDAY, Martin Caidin $.75

The story of the Schweinfurt raid—"The 'longest day' for the B-17's in World War II. . . . Superb!"—*The New York Times*

WING LEADER, Group Captain J. E. Johnson $.75

From the Battle of Britain to the last sortie—by the top-scoring ace of the R.A.F. (*10th printing*)

STUKA PILOT, Hans Ulrich Rudel $.75

Air war on the Russian front with Germany's foremost combat pilot, veteran of six years and 2,500 sorties. (*9th printing*)

ZERO! Masatake Okumiya and
     Jiro Horikoshi with Martin Caidin $.75

The men, the planes, the combat drama of Japan's air war in the Pacific. With 8 pages of rare photographs. (*5th printing*)

TWELVE
O'CLOCK
HIGH!

Beirne Lay, Jr. and Sy Bartlett

BALLANTINE BOOKS • NEW YORK

First Printing: August, 1965
Second Printing: April, 1969

First Canadian Printing: October, 1965

Printed in the United States of America

BALLANTINE BOOKS, INC.
101 Fifth Avenue, New York, N.Y. 10003

CONTENTS

FOREWORD

Although the characters and events in this novel are fictitious, the story closely follows the actual ordeal of the real-life men with whom the authors served in England. Many are living. Many are dead.

In dedicating this novel to fighting leaders, like Frank A. Armstrong, Jr., and to all of the airmen whose tenacity proved to be America's most devastating weapon, the authors likewise wish to salute Mrs. Frank A. Armstrong, Jr. and all the wives whose fortitude during the air battles of World War II, though less spectacular, was no less heroic.

The Green Toby

In the summer of 1948, Mr. Harvey Stovall left his suite at the Hyde Park Hotel and strolled toward Piccadilly enjoying himself. First, he had just cabled good news to his partner in the firm of Stovall & Stokes, the go-gettingest legal team, he reflected, in Columbus, Ohio. Second, he was faced with a free day in which to poke about London.

Stovall paused at the intersection of Piccadilly and Bond streets, more out of curiosity than from any intent to make a purchase, and observed the latest men's hats in the window of Scott's, hatterer to his Majesty the King. That black Homburg, he thought, would certainly create a stir in Columbus, but he'd better stick to his own conservative brown Stetson. Involuntarily he appraised his reflection in the window, which mirrored a prosperous citizen, a trifle heavy about the middle, with gray hair and the shrewd, tired eyes of the overworked American businessman, a dark blue double-breasted suit, a dark red carnation in the lapel and neatly shined black shoes. He recalled with a pang that he had been leaner when last he walked these ancient streets.

Sauntering through the Burlington Arcade, he recognized the shop in which he had once bought an old silver cigarette box as a wedding-anniversary present for Martha. He was about to enter and explore the establishment when he stood suddenly transfixed, his eyes drawn by a green enameled Toby on display in the window. Vigorously modeled, with a well-formed satyr handle, the beer mug depicted a robber with a Robin Hood hat and a black mask over the eyes. Stovall hurried into the shop with such precipitance that he jostled a gnarled gnome of a man just inside the door.

7

"Wot's the bloody 'urry, mate?" said the gnome, who resembled one of the Tobies on the wall shelf behind him. "I'm the proprietor 'ere."

"Excuse me," said Stovall, making no effort to conceal his excitement. "I'd like to see that green beer mug in the front window."

"It's Tobies you're after, sir? Allow me to show you a rare salt-glaze Toby I 'ave 'ere . . ."

"No, no," said Stovall impatiently, "the one in the window, please."

"Right you are, sir." Grumbling to himself, the gnome crawled into the window and fetched the Toby, watching with evident disapproval while his customer examined it eagerly. "That one's been knocked about a bit, sir," he persisted. "Not in it with this fine collection of Staffordshire Tobies over 'ere."

"Where did you get this?" asked Stovall, running his fingertip over a scratched place where someone had defaced the Toby, adding a mustache. The proprietor searched a huge ledger.

"An auction at Archbury," he said. "After those bloody Americans left."

Stovall's eyes lighted up. "How much will you take for it?"

"I 'ates to take advantage of you, sir. Now if you'll allow me to show you a Staffordshire in perfect condition . . ."

"I want this one. How much?"

"Well, sir. Wot do you say to fourteen bob? Frankly, there's not much value to it." Instantly Stovall's expression hardened into a glare and color mounted his cheeks. Mistaking this sign for sales resistance, the proprietor added hastily: "Call it twelve bob."

"Fourteen bob is very reasonable," said Stovall quietly. He counted out the money and watched while the proprietor wrapped the jug carefully in excelsior, placed it in a box and tied it with stout cord. Then he thanked him, hurried outside and hailed a taxi, instructing the cabby to take him to the Hyde Park Hotel. It was his intention to leave the Toby in a safe place before he resumed his stroll. But halfway to the hotel he changed his mind.

"Paddington Station," he said.

Almost before his decision had fully crystallized, he found himself aboard a train bound for the village of Archbury in the Midlands. Two hours later he walked through the winding old streets of Archbury direct to a pub called the Black Swan, borrowed a bicycle from the bartender, slung his package to the handlebars and pedaled out of the village along a country road lined with hedges and shaggy houses with thatched roofs. Breaking in and out of the scudding clouds, the sun gradually thawed the chill from the air, and a light breeze cooled Stovall's forehead, moist from the exertion of pumping the bicycle up the occasional hills.

More than once he felt a little foolish and wondered whether it would not be more sensible to turn back. Certainly he, Stovall, was a methodical rather than an impulsive or emotional man. Furthermore, it annoyed him that he had brought the package along; if he took a spill he might break it. But he pedaled steadily on, glancing down now and then to insure that the metal clips were protecting his trouser cuffs. Presently he turned off on a side road, propped his bike against a hedge and strode slowly a hundred yards out onto an enormous flat, unobstructed field.

When he halted he was standing at the head of a wide, dilapidated avenue of concrete, which stretched in front of him with gentle undulations for a mile and a half. A herd of cows, nibbling at the tall grass which had grown up through the cracks, helped to camouflage his recollection of the huge runway. He noted the black streaks left by tires, where they had struck the surface, smoking, and nearby, through the weeds which nearly covered it, he could still see the stains left by puddles of grease and black oil on one of the hard-stands evenly spaced around the five-mile circumference of the perimeter track, like teeth on a ring gear. And in the background he could make out a forlorn dark green control tower, surmounted by a tattered gray windsock and behind it two empty hangars, a shoe box of a water tank on high stilts and an ugly cluster of squat Nissen huts.

Not a soul was visible, nothing moved save the cows, nor was there any sound to break the great quiet. And yet Stovall, standing there solitary against the green landscape, was no longer alone. Nor, to him, was the suit he wore still blue. Rather it was olive drab, with major's leaves on the shoulders, as befitted the adjutant of a heavy-bombardment group.

A gust of wind blew back the tall weeds behind the hardstand nearest him. But suddenly Stovall could no longer see the bent-back weeds through the quick tears that blurred his eyes and slid down the deep lines in his face. He made no move to brush them away. For behind the blur he could see, from within, more clearly. On each empty hard-stand there sat the ghost of a B-17, its four whirling propellers blasting the tall grass with the gale of its slip stream, its tires bulging under the weight of tons of bombs and tons of the gasoline needed for a deep penetration.

In the large Nissen hut used for briefing, now deserted and covered with dust, he saw foregathering a ghostly company of 250 pilots, navigators, bombardiers and gunners, encumbered with bulky flying clothes, life vests and oxygen masks, straining to hear the words of a ghostly Intelligence officer as he indicated a target on the map.

In the group commander's quarters, with its luxury of a bathroom and a sitting room and a fire grate, now rusty and cold, he saw, wandering fitfully about, two ghosts, one of whom had broken under the pressure of great events.

In the station hospital, there were no rows of beds in the ward and the operating room was vacant. But he knew that many ghosts assembled there in the small hours of the night to speak of frostbitten faces and hands, of wounds inflicted by jagged flak and exploding 20-mm. cannon shells and of the deeper wounds inflicted in the battle between a man's will and his instinct of survival.

In the adjutant's office, Stovall recognized a middle-aged ghost, himself, examining the papers that flowed across his desk telling the tale, in brief reports and in cold figures, of the ordeal of the rest of the ghosts who populated a small, self-contained universe, bounded by the limits of this deserted station, in which they had endured a terrible hour, and in which demoralization had threatened American arms with a shameful and disastrous defection.

Regaining his composure, Stovall walked back to his bicycle, perplexed at the nature of the emotion that had inspired the first real tears he could remember shedding since his youth. And then he understood. They were born, not of a sentimental wallowing in Auld Lang Syne, but of the clear realization, emerging through the perspective of time, that here on this one station America might have lost the war. That this one rotten apple, decaying at a critically early juncture, almost spoiled the barrel. Americans remembered only victories. Did they know how perilously close the sequence of events at Archbury had come to destroying in its cradle the future giant of air power which, according to its victim, was the decisive factor in Germany's plunge to defeat?

He mounted his bike, pedaled down the runway, scattering a formation of plover, turned off at the far end, and followed a narrow concrete road to an outsize Nissen hut which had been the officers' club. Seeing that the door stood ajar, he leaned his bike against the entrance and placed his hand on the rusty doorknob. He had to shove with his shoulder before the door, hanging warped on its creaking hinges, finally scraped inward, sending a hollow reverberation through the empty room. Cobwebs shrouded the windows and a layer of dust powdered the floor. Stripped of its furniture and pictures, the room was lifeless, save for a pair of rats which streaked away from Stovall and disappeared through the hole under the mantelpiece at the far end, near which was a faded square where the radio had stood against the wall.

But here, too, Stovall could see many ghosts—ghosts of the air crews who had found in the room a haven where they could relax, order a drink, shoot craps and listen to the radio. His roving eyes came to a halt on the mantelpiece. Imperceptibly his shoulders straightened and his whole body stiffened.

Abruptly he returned to his bicycle, removed his package from the handlebars, untied the cord and lifted out the shiny green Toby. He re-entered the club and strode purposefully to the mantel. With his handkerchief he cleared a spot in the thick dust. And then, with the reverence of a man laying a wreath on the tomb of the Unknown Soldier, he placed the Toby with precision on the clean patch in the center of the mantelpiece, so that the masked robber faced the room.

He walked swiftly to the door, where he turned around for a last look at the Toby, which stared back at him with a malignant leer. Once more he noticed the faded square on the wall where the radio had stood. He closed the door and mounted his bike. As he pedaled slowly away, he imagined that he could hear again a cryptic broadcast that had blared from that radio one evening in the fall of 1942.

CHAPTER ONE

The Old Man

"This is Lord Haw Haw, speaking to you from Berlin."

There was a rustle of magazines and newspapers being tossed aside by the combat crews lounging near the radio in the chilly Nissen hut, and drinks were held unsipped, as the glib voice of England's suave traitor continued its broadcast from Herr Goebbels' propaganda ministry.

"Tonight I bring a special greeting from the fighter pilots of the Luftwaffe to the suckers of the 918th Bomb Group in England. Congratulations on your safe arrival at Archbury. We've been expecting you since you left Kansas, and our U-boats have been counting your B-17's on your flight from Iceland to Prestwick, Scotland. Sorry you lost one in the drink off Bluey West Two. But the U-boat that picked up the crew reports that all of them are in good spirits . . . and most talkative.

"So here's luck on your first mission. And a friendly tip to your group commander, Colonel Keith Davenport. I say, Colonel, have your adjutant, Major Stovall, correct the clock above the radio in your officers' lounge. It's four minutes slow. Pleasant dreams, chumps, and take it easy. We'll be seeing you."

Forty pairs of eyes swung, first to the clock, then to their wrist watches and finally to the tall, bony figure of Colonel Davenport, who had been leaning on the radio cabinet and who now switched off the dial with a snap. The fatigued, mostly unshaven young faces looming above the battle jackets and flying clothes focused on him expectantly. Davenport, who likewise needed a shave, appeared more tired than anyone. Dark smudges showed under his brown eyes and his left eyelid twitched nervously as he met the questioning glance of a yellow-haired pilot who wore his crushed cap tilted back.

"How about that, Colonel?" asked the boy uncertainly. "Sounds like a gag."

"That was no gag, Bishop," said Davenport with a shrug and an awkward imitation of a smile. "The 918th has already made Goering's hit parade. Especially Major Stovall." Everyone looked at the adjutant, who stood nearby wearing a rather unhappy expression that matched a sudden craving, unprecedented in his teetotaling life, for a strong shot of whisky.

"What do you say, Harvey?" Davenport continued. "Do you keep our clock on time from now on, or do we get a new adjutant in the group?"

Disconcerted, Stovall groped for an answer amid the flurry of nervous laughs that followed Davenport's effort at humor. He led Stovall to one side.

"Let's go over to my office, Harvey," he said inconspicuously.

On their way to the door, the pair passed a heavy-set navigator with LT. HEINZ ZIMMERMANN stenciled on the breast of his flying jacket. Zimmermann had not looked up once from the red-hot stove at which he had been staring during the broadcast. After the colonel had passed, deliberately he spat on the stove.

Outside, the night was cold and damp against a man's face. Even if there had not been a trace of the fog which muffled the occasional blinks of Major Stovall's flashlight, shielded with blue tissue paper, no low-flying Ju-88 would have detected a crack of light to betray the existence of an American bomber station in the solid blackness. The two officers picked their way cautiously through the mud, past the still unfamiliar layout of the Administration Block of Nissens, past a slithering bicycle and finally past the guard who rose awkwardly to attention from behind his unpainted wooden desk in the hall of the Ops Block, shielded just inside by a blackout curtain.

As they walked down a narrow hall, hung with signs reading S-2, S-3 and ADJUTANT, Davenport spoke over his shoulder.

"What a dirty dump," he said. "They can take England and ram it and jam it."

Stovall sympathized acutely with Davenport's irritation, for he knew that it was not prompted by personal discomfort. Throughout the endless and maddening difficulties that had plagued the group during its months of training, he had never once known this conscientious West Pointer to think of himself. But he sensed that Lord Haw Haw, spokesman of an implacable enemy, sweeping everything before it toward Stalingrad and waiting across the North Sea for Davenport's green boys, had unduly disturbed the Old Man. If the colonel had a flaw, reflected Stovall, it was that he felt too much like a father toward his forty-eight air crews and that he was overidentified with his men, incessantly worrying about them. Under stress of combat, would Davenport try to spare these crews the ultimate hardships and sacrifices, would losses overly upset him and would he thereby lose his efficiency as a leader? Stovall comforted himself with the reminder that he was a civilian soldier . . . that such misgivings might well be stemming from his own inexperience.

He followed the colonel through a green door lettered C.O., groped with the blackout curtains to insure that they were tightly drawn and switched on the office light. Far away, in the little town of Archbury, the two men could hear an air-raid siren's wail, rising and falling.

"That's just what we need," grumbled Davenport. "A few bombs dumped on the 918th to prove Haw Haw wasn't fooling."

"Night intruder, maybe," said Stovall, while the colonel fished in his desk until he came up with a sealed pint of bourbon. "Snooping around over that R.A.F. airdrome near us."

Davenport unscrewed the bottle cap, sniffed the bourbon and held it toward Stovall. "Join me?"

"Afraid I still don't drink, Colonel," said Stovall and, to himself: "You're not going to find the answer to your problems at the bottom of a brown jug." Some hint of disappointment in his eyes caught Davenport's attention.

"I know what you're thinking, Harvey," he said. "Not until after our first mission, I used to say. Well, tonight I kind of feel that for us the war has begun." The siren's wail died, uncovering the distant drone of the engines in the sky as night fighters of the R.A.F. shooed the visiting Jerry away.

The colonel swallowed two swigs and wiped his mouth with the sleeve of his battle jacket. "Better have one." Davenport held out the bottle again, but the adjutant shook his head.

"If you don't mind, sir," he said.

"Okay," said Davenport. "Now, how in hell did those monkeys find out so much about us?"

Stovall scratched his head. "Well," he said, "there's the crew they picked up."

"Any nazi sympathizers on that crew?"

For a moment Stovall looked as though he hadn't understood.

"Colonel," he said in a persecuted tone, "are you still riding me about that navigator . . . Zimmermann?"

"Maybe," said Davenport. "Of course," he added, "he wasn't on that crew."

"If he isn't on the level," said Stovall, "then the F.B.I. and Counterintelligence are all wet. They couldn't have given Zimmermann a cleaner bill of health."

"And yet his old man was a big wheel in the German-American Bund."

"I'm satisfied he always hated his father. He left home when he found out about it, you know. He realizes he's suspect. He's plenty eager for combat . . . to live down the family stigma."

"He'll still have to convince me . . . with that nazi background. Maybe we'd better keep him restricted to the station and detail somebody to keep a close check on him."

"I'd recommend strongly against that, Colonel. Eventually it would attract attention, probably ruin him with the rest of the boys in the group . . . none of them knew he was ever under suspicion."

"Of course," said Davenport reluctantly, "I wouldn't want to hurt one of my boys by any hasty action." He took another shot of whisky and replaced the pint in his desk. "I've got the finest bunch of kids that ever came out of America. But you'd better issue another memorandum on security. Everybody from cooks, M.P.'s, ground crews and officers, to you and me, have got to clam up more. I don't know where you'll dig him up, but put an M.P. on the officers' club, too."

"Yes, sir."

Davenport lifted one of his green-painted phones. "Might as well see if I can work one of these scrambler phones," he said to Stovall, then, into the mouthpiece: "Get me Pinetree." There was a two-minute wait, during which Stovall studied the gloomy expression on the homely, fatherly face of his thirty-eight-year-old commander, whose cheekbones were creased from the oxygen mask he had worn on the afternoon's practice mission. It was the face of a man unable to conceal the heavy load he is carrying.

"Hello," said Davenport. "Pinetree? I want Colonel Savage." There was a pause. "Hello, Frank? This is Keith Davenport . . . thanks . . . same to you. Say, can you scramble? Okay, I'll scramble now." He waited several moments, then pressed a switch on the phone's base.

"Hello, Frank. Yes, I can understand you." Davenport's voice was traveling over the wire in garbled form, to thwart line-tapping, and was being unscrambled automatically at Savage's end. "Can you make me out? Okay? I've got a problem . . . if you're going to be there for the next half hour . . . Roger." He hung up, took his trench coat off a wall-hook, slipped it on and slung his gas mask over his shoulder.

Stovall beamed. "I see you've read that poop-sheet from headquarters I put in your basket about wearing gas masks."

"Yes. From the looks of that IN basket those cookies at Pinetree are out to win the war with mimeograph machines. It's not like Frank Savage, either; he always hated paper work."

Stovall helped Davenport adjust the straps of the mask so that it hung properly. "Memorandum thirty dash six," he said, and then, "Isn't Colonel Savage kind of low ranking for a commanding general's job?"

"He's only acting C.O. until some hot-rock general from the Pentagon shows up. Frank's strictly a stick and rudder man. But he got the dream assignment, leading the first ten missions here, and built himself a reputation back home. That was before the German fighters started playing rough." Davenport leaned against the doorway, filling his pipe, and Stovall saw that the conversation had stumbled over one of the colonel's pet subjects. "Personally," continued Davenport, "I was surprised to see General Pritchard give him that first bomb group. Savage handles men like Simon Legree."

"You've served with him, sir?" asked Stovall casually, trying to hide his eagerness for a glimpse behind the scenes of military politics.

"Off and on," said the colonel, "since we were lieutenants in the 3rd Attack Group at Barksdale Field." His expression showed that the recollection was exciting.

"What sort of a joker is he?" prompted Stovall.

"Well, to begin with he's a good-looking bastard. Part Indian. And nobody's neutral about him. You like him or you hate him. Personally, I couldn't help liking him. He's lousy at a desk job, but he's a hot pilot. Won a D.F.C. in peacetime, which takes some doing. Dames love him and I wish I had a dollar for every quart of whisky he's drunk."

"Sounds like an interesting guy to meet."

"You don't meet Frank Savage. You *collide* with him." Davenport got his pipe burning and ejected a puff like a snort. "Life is funny, Harvey. Tonight he's my boss, and yet just four years ago I was ordered down to relieve him of command of his squadron. He had been flying the boys ragged and sweating the ground personnel like a road gang. You'd of thought there was a goddam war on the way he ran that outfit. Kee-rist, were they glad to see me!"

"Is he a West Pointer?" asked Stovall. As soon as he had uttered the words he felt embarrassed, but the colonel missed the implication.

"No, he came in as a reserve officer. Finally got a regular commission." Davenport turned to leave, then added over his shoulder, "See if you can take the boys' minds off that blast from Berlin. How about cooking up a christening party for the officers' club next Sunday? Something to keep my family happy."

After the colonel had left, Stovall sat heavily on a corner of the desk and lit a cigar. He had a sense of unreality. He couldn't rid his mind of the illusion that the group was still in training, that it would always be in training. He tried to visualize the twenty-five hundred men, whose records he kept, as a finished weapon, which had been brought face to face with the enemy at the logical moment. But the picture wouldn't focus. There simply hadn't been enough time to yank youngsters off the sidewalks, throw their schoolbooks away and transform them into airplane commanders, with a quarter of a million dollars' worth of four-engine bomber and ten lives thrust into their hands. Or enough time to tap a bellhop on the shoulder and, presto, come up with a ball-turret gunner, skilled in the art of shooting to kill. Until now, he thought, I've wondered how I'd ever catch up with my work. But soon there will be decorations, missing-in-action reports, shipping home the personal effects, gathering the material for those telegrams which will read: "The Secretary of War deeply regrets to inform you . . ." I've been working harder than I ever worked in my life, and yet we haven't even started. He glanced through the connecting door to the filing cabinets in his office. There, he thought, is the first part of the story, the vital statistics. Now comes the last part. What a seat for a spectator, for the Keeper of the records, from the womb to the tomb!

The all-clear was sounding in the village as he went to his desk.

"Sergeant," he said to his chief clerk, "it may be all clear in Archbury, but I'm afraid it's going to be a long time before they sound the all-clear in this office."

"The major," said the clerk, "can say that again."

From the rear seat of his staff car, as he drove through Archbury, Colonel Davenport glanced toward the Black Swan. Four soldiers with their arms around the waists of four W.A.A.F. girls, looking particularly broad-beamed in their slate-blue R.A.F. uniforms, passed under the muffled light above the entrance and disappeared inside the pub singing "Bless them all, the long and the short and the tall." The colonel smiled to himself, and to the driver he said: "Looks as though the 918th is getting Anglo-American relations off to a fast start."

"Yes, sir," said the corporal, as the car slid forward, its shielded lights barely reflecting the doorways along the left-hand side of the cobbled street. "They tell me you've got to cultivate the local talent to get eggs with shells on. The two goes together. Dames and eggs, and eggs and dames."

But the colonel's mind, freed for the first time in days

from harassing details, had already begun to rove in broader sweeps. For the first time he was conscious of a question in his mind about the wisdom of having pulled every wire at his disposal to grab that prize plum . . . command of a bomb group. If it hadn't been for his Academy classmate, Brigadier General Ed Henderson, on duty in the Pentagon, he'd never have gotten the group. Everyone wanted the job for the prestige, for the chance to make a combat record that counted. It was nice to be the boss, and take the bows, while you were back in the States. But it cut both ways. Over here it was possible to fail, to get killed, playing guinea pig in an American bombing experiment that a lot of military minds didn't believe in. The British, for instance. They were sold on night bombing, where you had the protection of darkness. They thought the Americans were crazy to go in naked by daylight for the sake of greater bombing accuracy. Did Frank Savage up at headquarters, who had already had a taste of it, or General Spaatz, or Hap Arnold or even General Marshall really believe that the handful of B-17's, sitting on their wet hard-stands in England tonight, could challenge the skeptics with results good enough to justify building up a big air force here? Nobody knows, he told himself. It's squarely up to me, Keith Davenport, to find the answer, or fall on my face, losing most of my crews trying. In the last analysis, he reflected, I'm carrying General Marshall on my back.

Twenty minutes later the colonel stepped from his car in the driveway before a huge stone structure that resembled a castle. A crescent moon had risen, shedding enough light to illumine sweeping lawns, avenues of linden trees and a pond clustered with wild ducks and three swans. Formerly a girls' school called Wycombe Abbey, the towering, blacked-out edifice was now the headquarters of American Bomber Command, known by the code word "Pinetree."

Colonel Davenport opened the great oaken door, pushed aside the blackout curtain and found himself in a brilliantly lighted hall, high-ceilinged and austere with its Gothic arches.

So this, he told himself, is where they fight a plush war. With hot showers. And teatime at four o'clock. And lieutenants at breakfast, promoted to captains at lunch and majors by dinnertime. He showed the sentry his A.G.O. card, walked through an anteroom marked COMMANDING GENERAL, and, seeing that the door to the office was open, thrust his head in. The room was empty.

"Have a chair," said a casual voice that seemed to come from the ceiling. Davenport stepped inside and saw Colonel Savage standing precariously atop a tall bookcase from which he was reaching out to tack in place the corner of a ceiling-high map of Western Europe, mounted against the wall on beaverboard.

"Short of help around here?" asked Davenport.

"Help is short everywhere," said Savage without interrupting his hammering, "when there's a war on. You can do it yourself by the time you get hold of a corporal." He tapped the last brad into place and then, in one simultaneous movement, he tossed the hammer down at Davenport without warning and executed a spring to the floor, landing with the cushioned spring of an athlete.

Unprepared, Davenport made a grab for the hammer, but dropped it. Same old Frank, he thought; tosses the ball to you and takes it for granted that you'll catch it. Savage gave Davenport a hard handshake, pushed him toward a chair, settled himself behind his desk and confronted his visitor with a quizzical expression, predominated by friendliness and sympathy.

"Keith," he said, "I know that look—that harried look of the new group commander. As if you'd just had a barbed-wire high colonic."

"Well, anyway, I've got a problem," said Davenport.

Savage laughed and motioned toward his IN and OUT baskets. "Full of problems," he said. "I'll listen to yours if you'll give me a new one. Not shortage of spare parts. Nor generators burning out when all guns are tracking at once. Nor turbos and props running away on take-off. Nor shortage of privates for K.P. and guard duty. Nor defective tracers and machine-gun stoppages. Nor chuckholes in the runway and wheels breaking through the hard-stands. Nor powdered eggs, nor pregnant W.A.A.F.'s, nor lack of hangar space for night maintenance, nor cold shaving water, nor honey buckets instead of plumbing." He stopped for breath. "That IN basket is full of freezing oxygen masks, freezing guns, freezing plexiglass, electric flying suits that short out and burn a grid on your butt, eighteen different kinds of engine malfunctions at high altitude, gunners that can't hit anything but their own wingmen and losses that have gone up from zero to five per cent on shallow penetrations into France. That's just a sample." He grabbed the basket with both hands and flipped it upward so that the top papers fluttered back into place like a deck of cards. "Now give me a new problem."

"I've got a new one, all right," said Davenport. "A bad one. Did you hear Lord Haw Haw tonight?"

"Never listen to the son of a bitch," said Savage.

"For Christ's sake, Frank," said Davenport impatiently, "Berlin knows we're here, knows my name, even knows our clock is four minutes slow."

Savage looked with frank incredulity at the alarm written on the other man's face.

"Do you mean to tell me," he said, "that you drove through this blackout just to tell me that?"

"But, but"—Davenport was nonplussed—"what do you make of it?"

"So they've got spies," laughed Savage. "So you can't hide a bomber station. So we've got farmhouses right alongside the perimeter track. So Americans like to talk."

"Yeah, they talk," he said with a flush of guilty recollection. "And I let a few go on pass—hanging around that pub in Archbury." He arose, took a few nervous paces and lit his pipe.

There was a knock on the door and an aide stepped inside.

"A Flight Leftenant Mallory to see you, sir," said the aide.

"Please ask him to wait." Before the aide could reply, Davenport spoke up. "It's not a *him*, Frank," he said pointedly. "It's a *her*."

"Then ask *her* to wait," said Savage. When the aide had withdrawn, Savage made a wry face at Davenport.

"Why can't we fight a war over here," he said, "without having the joint loused up with babes during working hours?"

"It all depends," said Davenport, again speaking pointedly. "This babe, you haven't seen."

They exchanged glances for a moment. A twinkle came into Savage's eyes.

"An operational piece of equipment, eh?" he asked.

"If you mean is she a beautiful girl, yes."

"You've only been here three days. Where did you find her?"

"Her old man is Lord Desborough—our airdrome is on the family estate. They dropped in on me for a neighborly call."

"She's a real dish?"

"On the plus side of a knock-out. Not the kind *you* ever kept waiting in an anteroom for more than three seconds."

Savage stared at Davenport reminiscently for a moment.

"Right now," he said, "I'm not interested in dames—not even one like that. I want to know how you guys are getting along down there in the mud—what we can do to help you."

"Well—I guess we're doing okay. All except this security business. That's what's worrying me right now."

Savage stood up and walked over to the fireplace, tall, broad of shoulder, back and arm muscles showing through his battle jacket. If his easy movements suggested a former pro ball player or a man with Indian blood, it was because he was both. His crinkly hair was black, except for a fringe of gray at the edges, and his face was bronzed and much younger looking than might be expected at the age of thirty-six. As Savage turned to face him, Davenport felt a faint annoyance at this man's exceptional asset of rugged good looks and at the power of those gray eyes. One minute, when he smiled, they pulled you; a minute later they knocked you back as though he had reached out and pushed you. They were doing that now.

"You want to know about security?" The words came with emotional conviction. "Bear down on loose talk, of course. But as soon as you are operational, there will be only one kind of security that counts. Have you got a bunch of pilots that can hold a tight formation? Can the gunners shoot straight? Can you put commanders in the air who won't turn back from a target as long as the wings stay on?"

Openly irritated, Davenport ground out his cigarette in an ashtray that mounted an aluminum model of a B-17.

"Sounds like a fight talk, Frank," he said. "Do you think that's what I need?"

In spite of old rivalries, Savage had always liked Davenport personally. His expression softened.

"You're right, Keith," he said finally. "Where do I get off lecturing you? It's just that I've been over here longer, I guess. I'm sorry."

"Aw, balls, Frank," said Davenport, mollified. "I realize you've had a lot of combat experience."

Savage reached down and pulled out a bottom desk drawer. He lifted out a green Toby, modeled in the likeness of a masked robber, and set it on the desk.

"Take this old fellow along with you, Keith," he said, deliberately changing the subject. "Maybe he'll bring you as much luck as he brought me."

"Beer mug?"

"I had a better use for it. Mr. Security. He worked for me when I had the 901st Group. We stuck the mug on the mantelpiece in the club as a signal that we were alerted for a mission. The boys finished their drinks and went to bed. Any visitors hanging around were none the wiser."

"We can use that idea," said Davenport, picking up the Toby. "Thanks, Frank."

"You're welcome to it," said Savage, rising, "but don't bust it. Some day I want it back for a souvenir."

They walked together to the anteroom, where a tall W.A.A.F. officer sat with her head bent over a magazine.

"Hi there, Flight Leftenant," said Davenport. "How's everything at Desborough Hall?"

She rose and stood at attention. "Rather quiet, Colonel," she said. "But I imagine your chaps will liven things up for us a bit. Several are coming this weekend for tennis."

As the girl smiled at Davenport, Savage felt something like a shock go through him. A beautiful girl always gave him a thrill. But this girl was literally stunning.

"May I present Colonel Savage?" said Davenport. "This is Flight Leftenant Pamela Mallory." She turned her wide, violet eyes to Savage, who reached out and gave her a masculine handshake.

"Sorry I was busy," he said cordially, "but I have to make sounds in there like a commanding general until my new boss gets in. I'm pinch-hitting."

"Pinch-hitting?"

"Substituting."

"Oh—of course. Stupid of me." She hesitated. "To tell the truth, my business *was* with the commanding general, but—"

"But maybe this guy will do," interposed Davenport, who was observing with interest the difficulty with which Pamela was concealing a flustered reaction to Savage's disconcerting gaze.

She gave a little laugh. "I'm sure he does very well—as a pinch-hitter," she said.

"If you'll excuse me," said Savage, moving toward the door, "I'll be right back."

"That's perfectly all right, sir," said Pamela formally. As the two men disappeared, her eyes followed Savage's retreating figure intently for a moment, then, with a quick shift of her eyes to the aide, who looked away, she returned her attention to her magazine.

"See what I mean?" asked Davenport, as he and Savage approached the front door.

"Not bad," said Savage. "What a break for you. You're parked on the most strategic spot in England. But don't go messing around with targets of opportunity, mate. Stick to the primary."

"She's way out of my league, Frank."

Davenport extended his hand to say goodbye, then paused. "Almost forgot to ask you," he continued. "Who's the new bomber commander?"

"Ed Henderson. Left London an hour ago. Probably blundering around High Wycombe now in the blackout with a green driver."

"Henderson?" Davenport's face broke into a smile of pleased surprise. "I'll be damned."

"Yes," said Savage, drily, "your pal Ed Henderson."

Davenport felt a warm glow at this unexpected news of a friend in court. In addition to being the classmate who had used his influence to get Davenport the 918th Group, it had been Henderson who had switched Savage and Davenport in command of the 13th Attack Squadron. It was the kind of development that would have been an odd coincidence anywhere except in the Air Corps, where a small band of men, as intimate in peacetime as a family, were now running an enormous show. If you tossed any three of them together, you were sure to have similar complications, rooted in the past. But to Savage, it seemed that Henderson's arrival was carrying coincidences a little too far. He had always believed that Henderson's love of the Old School Tie had cost him the command of his squadron.

"I'd like to wait and say hello to him," said Davenport, "but I ought to get back. Give him my best. It's great news."

"Great," said Savage noncommittally, as Davenport climbed into his car. "Keep your socks up, mate."

He watched Davenport drive off, started to re-enter the Abbey, then strolled across the driveway and stood on the grass, breathing deeply of the wet night air. Through the trees he could gradually make out the church steeple in the ancient town of High Wycombe. How long, he wondered, before the steeple bell and all the bells in England, silent since they had been reserved by the government as the official warning of invasion, would ring out again in victory? If ever. This British Isle was still terribly vulnerable, a ripe apple which could be had—which the German High Command ought to invade at any price, if they understood the potential dagger that was being aimed at their heart by a few men in this old girls' school. Or, Savage asked himself, would it prove to be a rubber dagger, bending because its human metal was not hard enough?

He strode back to his anteroom and rejoined Pamela.

"Come right in, Miss Mallory," he said, showing the way to his office, but without noticing a hint of disapproval in her expression when he failed to use her military title. As she sat down by his desk, he was aware of an unmilitary scent of gardenia and he noticed that she did not cross her legs but sat rather stiffly with her feet together. Despite the camouflage of a W.A.A.F. uniform, no one could have mistaken Pamela, even at a distance, for a man. There was too much bosom, too small a waist and the race-horse ankles were too slender. Her face, straight of nose, unusually pale, and framed in chestnut-colored hair that curled in a roll above her slate-blue collar, was a rather small setting for her eyes. They were enormous, and he noticed that their whites had that bluish tinge normally seen only in small and healthy children.

"Care for American cigarettes?"

"Like anything," she said pleasantly. It was the first time he had heard this odd expression.

"Here." He reached in a drawer, taking out two packs. "I'm a cigar smoker. These are for you."

"Oh, no, thank you," she said quickly. "But may I try just one of yours, for a change?"

Savage sensed that he had touched her pride. It was the English pride, so vulnerable to the invading horde of Americans, with their abundance of cigarettes, chocolate and salted peanuts, their superior rations, their high pay, their lavish tips to London cabbies and their wealth of all material things now scarce in austere Britain. He lighted her cigarette.

"I know how busy you are, Colonel Savage," she began in a crisp, official tone, "but I came to your headquarters on a rather important matter."

"I haven't got a thing to do but listen to you," said Savage, smiling.

"You see—I'm in DDI-4-B." She saw that he was in the dark. "Signals," she amended, "radio. What we're doing is in a Secret classification that won't permit me to go into details, but perhaps that won't be necessary. The point is that I get information every day that may be very valuable to your staff."

"Sounds great." Savage looked skeptical.

"How would you like to receive accurate information on German fighter reaction to your daylight bombing strikes?"

"We'd grab at it," he said, still regarding her uncertainly. "Just how do you mean? Fighter reaction? Our crews give us pretty good reports on how the Jerries react."

"I mean a lot more than the enemy fighter tactics your crews see. I know most of the German fighter pilots by name, where they live, where they rearm and refuel, what they talk about—what they say about you."

She had Savage's rapt attention, now. "Mind telling me more?" he asked.

"Unfortunately, I can't," she said. "I think you can readily understand why security is so tight. If the enemy found out we are getting this information, the source would dry up."

"Sure. I can see that. But you've got me on the edge of my chair. I've never heard a word about—whatever it is you're doing."

"That's the way we want to keep it. Now, I can pass on our information to you, without telling you how we get it. Of course, you'll have to get an okay from Air Ministry."

"Hell, that'll take a couple of months."

"Possibly. Channels, and all that. But meanwhile, I don't see why we can't arrange something between us informally."

"I'm all for it. Nuts to the red tape."

"All right. But I'm going to need one thing from you. Otherwise, I can't be of maximum assistance to you."

"Sure. What do you want?"

"Your routes and control times, as far as possible in advance, before each of your missions."

Savage's mouth opened.

"Are you kidding?" he said.

"Of course not. It's absolutely necessary that I know your routes and times."

Savage abruptly stood up. All the early skepticism had returned to his face.

"Just a minute," he said. "That's information we don't give to anybody—except the combat units. I'd get court-martialed if I let any of it out."

"Perhaps I'd better wait and discuss this with your new general," she said.

"He'd tell you the same thing." Savage stared at the girl for a long moment, nonplussed. "I don't get it," he continued. "If the R.A.F. wants that kind of Secret dope from us, why didn't they send an officer over here to see me, Miss Mallory, instead of a—" He stopped, groping for the right word, his eyes involuntarily dropping to the unmasculine contours of her uniform jacket.

"Flight Leftenant Mallory, if you don't mind. And do I really have to remind you that *I am* an officer? I daresay that women in the W.A.A.F. have been entrusted with more confidential information during the past three years than anyone in your headquarters, Colonel Savage."

"It all sounds cockeyed," persisted Savage, in a tolerant tone, ignoring the girl's pique. "We're worried enough as it is about possible leaks on our Field Orders. Sending you a copy would be one more chance for a leak. No—I'd have to see this request in writing from Air Ministry, Miss Mallory."

"You've called me Miss Mallory twice, now, Colonel."

"Sorry."

"And I thought Americans, particularly, detested red tape. Go ahead, then, and get it in writing—a couple of months from now. Meanwhile, I'm sure I could have helped you. I'm sorry to have troubled you, sir." She rose.

"Hey, not so fast," said Savage, hurrying around his desk. "Don't get me wrong. I'm extremely interested in what you've told me, and I appreciate your coming over. I'll look into it thoroughly—get a request in for co-ordination, right away."

"Why hurry?" she asked, coolly. "Perhaps it will be a nice, long war."

Savage flushed as she gave him a brief handshake, rendered a side-wheeling R.A.F. salute and was gone. He returned slowly to his desk, sat down and stared at nothing in particular, scratching his head. Then he rang for his aide.

"Ask the communications officer to come in," he said. "Maybe he'll know what that glamor girl was driving at. She might have something."

"How do you like this layout?" asked Savage.

Shifting his small body in his easy chair, Brigadier General Edward Henderson glanced appreciatively around the quarters on the second floor which had formerly been occupied by the head mistress of Wycombe Abbey. He saw a handsomely furnished living room, large enough for entertaining his British opposite numbers with official cocktail parties, a double bedroom and guest room, a door leading into a spacious bathroom and plenty of coal in the brass scuttle handy to the blue and red flames curling in the fireplace. In their day, Gladstone and Pitt had slept in this room as guests of the viscount who had owned the historic property.

"First rate," said Henderson.

The two had just settled down with their cigars and Scotches. How easily, thought Savage, he adjusts himself to new surroundings. Already he looks as though he belongs here, and in a uniform with a star. It had not escaped Savage that although Henderson's promotion was less than a week old, his new star and shoulder patch were embroidered in silver and gold on all the uniforms and overcoats which the R.A.F. batman was carrying to the closet of the bedroom. His slacks had a straight-edge crease and the polish on his jodhpur boots glistened like glass. Even his cross-country bags, neatly stenciled with his new rank, were of special gabardine material instead of the canvas of the standard A-2 bag.

"What's the lowdown on this show?" asked Henderson briskly.

"The newspapers," said Frank, "have been putting up about a thousand bombers for me. But all I've been able to put over the target, on our biggest mission to date, is sixty-two."

"You know how it is, Frank," said Henderson with an airy wave of his hand. "It'll be months before production really starts rolling. Meanwhile we can't let people back home get discouraged. They need good news. And this is the only spot from which Americans are fighting Germans."

There was no agreement in Savage's expression. "Flak," he continued, "is getting worse. Those yellow-nosed Focke-Wulfs are pressing attacks home. Losses are running three to five per cent. And bombing accuracy is falling off."

"What is your solution?"

"Fighter cover to the target. More nose guns, or a nose turret. More bombers. And more replacement crews. Preparations for the North African show are robbing us of the build-up we need. Down at the groups, the combat crews are getting cynical about the lack of replacements, discouraged about their chances of completing a tour. They've begun to figure percentages."

"How about weather?"

"Awful. Sometimes we have to scrub a mission seven or eight times, trying to outguess the weather over the Continent. It's maddening to the crews. They fly eight missions on the ground for every one in the air. I believe that's their biggest beef, but there isn't anything we can do about it up here."

"Do you think daylight bombing from England may turn out to be a fiasco?"

Savage pondered the question before answering.

"A lot of people think so," he said finally. "But here's the way I look at it. With a big force we could get results. But if they won't give us a big force until we've proved the case for daylight bombing with sixty-two B-17's, then we're sunk. Personally, I believe we can do the job in spite of the obstacles, if we can develop the right leadership. Good group commanders are going to be your number-one problem. So far, it's been a case of a good group commander—a good group. A weak group commander—a weak group. Right there is where we'll win or lose."

"I agree with you. Incidentally, has Davenport gotten here yet with the 918th?"

"Yes, sir. Day before yesterday. He sent you his regards."

"I'll watch that outfit with a lot of personal interest. Davenport's tops at handling men."

Savage offered no comment.

"And speaking of jobs, Frank, you are the one who ought to have my job. You've earned it in combat while I've been shuffling papers in the Big House." The atmosphere between the two men became charged. Henderson's statement was literally true and they both knew it.

"I'm not kicking," said Savage quickly. "I guess I'll always be a squadron commander at heart."

"If you don't mind my saying so," said Henderson, smiling faintly, "you turned out to be a better group commander in combat than a squadron commander in peacetime."

Savage's eyes, always the color of granite, assumed the same texture. He held Henderson's glance until the latter looked away toward the fire.

"Let's call that a matter of opinion," he said.

"In any case," Henderson went on smoothly, after a pause, "I envy you. You've won everybody's admiration with the way you led the first group here. That critically important first group. Eight missions before you lost an airplane—when the British Bomber Command figured you'd lose seventy-five per cent at a crack."

"Thanks," said Savage.

"Your star is already in the mill, you know," continued Henderson. "I hope it comes through soon. You deserve it."

To himself, Savage said: "You're not kidding me, brother. There's not a dry eye in the house."

Henderson went over to the sideboard and mixed two fresh

highballs, remaining standing after he had handed one to Savage.

"Look, Frank," he said. "Quite honestly, how do you feel about serving under me—again?"

Savage was dangling his glass from his fingertips. As deftly as a man might flick a coin, and as automatically, he swung the brimming glass around in a complete loop, without spilling a drop, then looked straight into Henderson's eyes.

"I'd be a cockeyed liar," he said, "if I told you I was happy about it."

"I anticipated you'd feel that way," said Henderson, poker-faced. "I discussed it with General Pritchard. His feeling is that even if it's a shotgun wedding, we've both got to sweat it out for a while. With your experience, I'm going to need the hell out of you in Operations, and he wants you right where you are—as A-3." He sipped his Scotch. "I told him I was in complete agreement with him."

"If that's the way the Old Man wants it," Savage said casually, "that's always been good enough for me."

CHAPTER TWO

The Rate of Attrition

A woolly blanket of winter fog, lingering over the British Isles for two weeks, grounding the bombers, had finally moved east.

At Air Force Headquarters in the suburbs of London, behind a broad, glass-topped desk embellished with a polished mahogany name plaque lettered in gold with the words MAJOR GEN. PATRICK PRITCHARD, sat a grizzled, sharp-eyed man who did not need the command pilot's wings on his chest to identify him as a veteran airman. He was nearly bald from wearing a flying helmet and he had the look that accrues to some men after thousands of hours spent in a cockpit—hours that have instilled the habit of meeting emergencies resourcefully. He was dictating an unofficial report to his boss in Washington.

"By rights," he was concluding, "there should have been a constant morale problem this winter because of losses, low replacement rate, unflyable weather and rugged living conditions. On the contrary, morale is strong, even in our one Hard Luck Group, the 918th, where the rate of attrition has been higher than in the other groups."

Eighty miles away, while the general was dictating, the first Fort returning to Archbury from the day's mission to the submarine installations at Lorient was banking into its final approach. Two ambulances sped toward the end of the runway in response to a red flare from the bomber, signifying wounded aboard.

At one of the hard-stands, a crew chief and his assistant shaded their eyes toward the gliding Fort with special concern, for they had identified the number on the tail. This was their ship. With his free hand the crew chief was holding the leash of a mournful-eyed Dachshund named Corporal Kesselring. His master, Lieutenant McKesson, pilot of the incoming B-17, had started the Dachshund out as a private, but had recently promoted it to corporal, whereupon the animal had run away. The crew chief had found it that morning living with the mess sergeant.

"Boy! Will Lieutenant McKesson be glad to see Corporal Kesselring," he said to the assistant crew chief. "But," he continued, squatting down and patting the Dachshund, "I'm afraid he's going to bust you back to private, old fellow."

The dog rolled its sad eyes up to the sergeant, then returned its eager attention to the runway. The sergeant lifted the animal up to the crew chief's stand, where it could get a better view, and where he hoped the pilot would spot his mascot sooner.

The Fort settled down into a bumpy landing, rolling clean to the end of the strip, and taxied off a few yards along the perimeter track to clear the way for other B-17's in the landing pattern. Before the props stopped turning over, both ambulances were alongside the nose, on which were painted eleven bombs, one for each mission the airplane had flown since the 918th's first operation, two months previously.

Over the waist hatch was the legend: WHERE ANGELS AND GENERALS FEAR TO TREAD.

Major Don Kaiser, group flight surgeon, motioned the stretcher bearers under the nose hatch and reached up to assist as the body of the pilot, McKesson, was lowered through the opening. The job was complicated by the fact that the boy was a beefy six-footer and that he was resisting violently. The back of his head was blown off, exposing the brain.

Examining the wound quickly, while strong but tender hands restrained the boy on the stretcher, Major Kaiser turned to the navigator, Lieutenant Zimmermann, who had just dropped through the hatch.

"How long since he was hit?"

"Over two hours ago," said Zimmermann. "Feels more like two hundred to me."

The flight surgeon whistled and shook his head. "I wouldn't believe it if I wasn't looking at it," he said.

"Easy with his right leg!" snapped Zimmermann to a medical corpsman as the stretcher was lifted into the ambulance. "It's broken below the knee. And, Major—somebody'd better sit on him. I've been holding him down for the past hour."

Unheeded by the cluster of men around the ambulances, the second Fort to land came hurtling down the runway with its brakes and flaps shot out and approached the far end with no apparent deceleration. At the last moment, the pilot cut his port engines, gunned his starboard engines and ground-looped the airplane off the concrete onto the muddy turf, opposite the first B-17, where it spun completely around before coming to rest with its right wing crumpled. In a jiffy, all ten members of the crew, including Colonel Davenport, emerged.

"Everybody's in one piece!" Davenport shouted to Major Kaiser. "Don't bother about us!"

Kaiser waved back and was about to climb aboard the ambulance when Zimmermann put a detaining hand on his arm. To the flight surgeon's practiced eye, which had noted and been impressed by the navigator's stolid calm up to this point, it was obvious that something was now happening to the boy's composure. He observed the color draining from Zimmermann's swarthy cheeks and a suffering expression in the eyes, deep-set under jutting black brows and a low forehead.

"What do we do with an *arm*, Major?" he asked as though the words couldn't possibly be making sense. "We've got an arm in there—the top turret gunner's."

"Where's the rest of him?"

"In a French hospital, we hope, sir. I bailed him out."

The flight surgeon turned to a medical corpsman in the ambulance. "Give me a blanket," he said, then to Zimmermann, "We'll take care of it." He climbed up into the nose, and in a few moments reappeared. Zimmermann turned his back and looked the other way as the flight surgeon carried a long, slender object, wrapped in the blanket, to the ambulance. Then the ambulance pulled away for the hospital, followed by the second ambulance, which had picked up three frost-bitten gunners from the waist hatch.

In the cockpit, Lieutenant Jesse Bishop, copilot at the takeoff, but airplane commander at the finish, was starting up his inboard engines to taxi to his hard-stand. The assistant engineer tapped him on the shoulder.

"The truck's waiting, sir," he said. "Let me taxi her in for you."

Bishop shook his head. "I've got it, Sergeant," he said.

At the hard-stand, Bishop remained in the cockpit for several minutes, laboriously filling out the Form One, ignoring the shrill barking of Corporal Kesselring below, where the crew chief still held him by the leash. Then Bishop made his way aft from the blood-soaked flight deck, through the bomb bay, past the cluttered shell casings in the waist, tossed his chute to the ground and clambered down after it.

Zimmermann, his coveralls spattered with the drying, dark stains of another man's blood, stood waiting for him. Neither flier said a word as they walked with deathlike lethargy to a jeep which Zimmermann had flagged down.

"Let me off at the hospital," said Bishop, then, noticing the chaplain's cross on the driver's collar, he added, "Excuse me, Captain. Could you please drop me there?"

"That's right where I'm headed for myself," said Chaplain Twombley, a strong-featured officer who resembled a squadron commander more than a man of the cloth. He had made a point of being accepted as one of the boys and had succeeded rather well.

"You're always the first guy I spot," said Zimmermann as

they drove off, "out on the perimeter track when we're on the final approach."

"I believe that's where I ought to be," said the chaplain. He pointedly avoided asking any questions about the mission, waiting for his passengers to talk of their own accord.

"How did you make out in the poker game last night?" inquired Zimmermann, after a pause.

"The church," said the chaplain, "won three pounds ten." He smiled as he replied, but his thoughts were grim.

Before leaving the perimeter track, the jeep passed a Fort which was just disgorging its crew. The first man out kneeled down and kissed the earth.

Glancing back at Bishop, Chaplain Twombley said: "The ground feels pretty good, doesn't it?"

Bishop ignored the question. He had removed his helmet and the wind was ruffling through his thick yellow hair, matted above the forehead with sweat. His vividly blue eyes had a glazed stare and his young face was a gaunt mask, as if from a sudden encroachment of old age. He passed his fingers through his hair, rubbed his eyes with his balled fists and stroked the skin of his cheeks where the recent grip of the oxygen mask still itched. When he pulled a cigarette from his coveralls and tried to light it from a paper of matches, the chaplain noticed that the boy's hands began shaking with a coarse tremor. He failed to get a light after three tries, merely burning the side of the paper.

"High octane," said the chaplain, slowing down and producing a storm lighter that flamed like a torch. Bishop got his light and continued to stare blankly ahead, without thanking him, but Twombley felt rewarded that he had been able to do something, anything, for this pilot whose terrifying day's work had so visibly congealed him. To Twombley, the disheveled, unutterably weary twenty-one-year-old boy riding beside him was a sacred thing—a tragic human sacrifice, condemned by the proved superiority of his body and character to bear the maximum load that could be placed upon each.

When the jeep reached the site of large, interconnecting Nissens that comprised the station hospital, Bishop walked quickly to the door with the chaplain, disappeared inside and in less than a minute reappeared and nodded to Zimmermann.

"He's had it, Heinz," he said simply.

"Son-of-a-bitch," said Zimmermann. The words were reverent the way he spoke them.

Bishop started off down the road, hands in pockets, head down, feet shuffling.

"Hey, Jesse!" called Zimmermann. "Where you going?"

"Club." Bishop didn't turn around.

"What about Interrogation?" called Zimmermann again, in a tone which declared that a man didn't skip Interrogation any more than he would skip the Briefing for a mission, which was true.

"To hell with it," said Bishop over his shoulder.

At the club he entered the lounge, which was empty except for a corporal, who was setting out glasses at one end of the bar. As Bishop approached, the corporal smiled apologetically.

"Sorry, sir," he said. "Bar's not open for half an hour."

"Give me Scotch. A double one."

"I'd like to, Lieutenant. But there's my orders."

"On second thought," said Bishop, "make it a double-double."

"You'll have to wait, sir," persisted the soldier. He was anxious not to antagonize Bishop. "Won't be long," he added.

But Bishop showed no irritation, nor awareness of his surroundings. He leaned one elbow on the bar.

"I heard it snap, like a dry stick," he said dreamily.

"How's that, sir?" asked the corporal, puzzled.

"His leg," said Bishop.

The corporal scrutinized Bishop uncertainly. He couldn't help noticing the resemblance between the features of this dog-tired combat man in front of him and the pilot in a colored poster on the wall by the bar. The poster showed a rosy-cheeked, almost girlishly handsome, smiling youth, posing in flying clothes for an aircraft manufacturer's ad, which bore the confident slogan: "Who's Afraid of the New Focke-Wulf?" Underneath was the penciled notation: "I am," followed by the signatures of all the pilots in the 918th, with Colonel Davenport's at the top. The corporal, glancing again at the sweet-faced boy in the ad, thought: That's the way this guy must have looked back home. But look at him now.

"Pour the drink," said Bishop suddenly in a flat voice.

The corporal squinted at the clock. "That clock's been slow —once before that I know of," he said. "I guess I can take a chance." He went over and set the clock ahead a half hour. "Soda?" Bishop nodded and watched closely while the bartender poured a double-double shot into the glass, filled it with soda and handed it to him.

"I sure wish you could get ice over here," said Bishop absently. "You could hear it snap, like a stick," he continued. "I had to yank hard."

The corporal began to look a little worried.

"I just come from the sack, sir," he said. "Did we lose any this afternoon?"

"*Any?* You mean how *many* did we lose! Are you new around here?" He took a second swallow of his whisky and soda. "We lost four," he said, "four that I know of. The usual number. And everybody else caught a working-over."

"Four," said the corporal, shaking his head. "It don't hardly seem right."

Bishop carried his drink across the lounge, set it on top of a scarred, upright piano, ran his fingers over the yellow keyboard, then struck the opening crashing chords of Warsaw Concerto, a new favorite in England. While the room began to fill with the music spurting from Bishop's fingers, a captain came in, listened a moment and went over to the bar.

"I'm looking for Lieutenant Jesse Bishop," he said. "Couldn't find him at Interrogation."

"That's him."

The captain ordered a mug of beer. "From what his crew told me," he continued, "he's due for a Medal of Honor. Boy, what a story!" He paused to listen again to Bishop's playing. "And some musician, too."

"Yeah. You ought to see it when the lounge is full. They turn off the radio and everybody shuts up."

The captain walked over to Bishop and placed a hand on the boy's shoulder.

"Mind if I interrupt for a minute?" he said. Bishop struck a sharp chord in an offkey, stopped playing and looked up. The captain stuck out his hand. "Reynolds, Public Relations, Bomber Command," he said. Bishop made no move to shake hands. "I know this is no time to bother you, but they gave me a hell of a story on you at Interrogation, and if you can spare me just five minutes I can button it up. Incidentally, congratulations—"

"We've got a Group P.R.O.," said Bishop. "Talk to him."

"That's not the same. Believe me, these personal-interest stories do more good back home than—"

"We've still got a Group P.R.O." The pair locked eyes. "Listen, Lieutenant, I hate this job. But just the same it *is* my job to get your story."

Bishop reached for his glass, took a drink and swung around on his stool.

"Okay," he said, "I'll give you a story. This group is shot to hell. We've got a swell group commander, but can he turn fog, rain and clouds into weather good enough to fly formation through and bomb through? Can he order up new airplanes and fresh crews when nobody gives him any? According to my home-town paper we're making fifty thousand airplanes a year. Where are they?" He interrupted himself to glance with irritation at the beer mug which the captain had rested on the mantelpiece.

"Would you mind taking that beer mug off the mantel?"

"Sure." The captain shrugged, swallowed a draft of beer and put the mug on top of the piano.

"Give us another month," said Bishop, resuming his outburst, "and we'll have a maximum effort of one B-17."

The captain sipped his beer. "You know that's not the story I want," he said. "I understand how you feel, but—"

"You do? That's fine. Then go down and have a look at the battle damage on today's strike. Talk to the line chief, Sergeant Nero, and ask him how long it's going to take him to patch up holes you can drive a cleat track through—without enough parts, and tools and maintenance men. Just plenty of mud. Then go to the other stations and ask them if they're any better off. Then go back to your boss and ask him who dreamed up the cockeyed idea that we can bomb Europe from this cranberry bog. If you don't believe me, you ought to hear Colonel Davenport, off the record. He feels the same way."

"I tell you what," said the captain in a soothing tone. "I've got a photographer right outside. We'll forget the story now, but let me get just one shot of you."

"Why don't you drive to the hospital and get a shot of the back of Lieutenant McKesson's head?"

The captain absentmindedly placed his beer mug back on the mantelpiece.

"I asked you once," said Bishop, "to set that mug down somewhere else."

"For God's sake," said the captain, anger beginning to get the better of him, "what is this mantel? An altar, or something?"

"Just put it down somewhere else."

"You like to give orders, don't you, Lieutenant?"

"Haven't you apple-knockers got anything better to do than come down here and heckle people? Go on back to Pinetree and start a softball tournament."

"Any other suggestions?"

"Yes. Take a powder before you miss the tea hour at Bomber Command."

"All right, Lieutenant. I can get pee'd off, too. I didn't come down here to *ask* you guys for anything. I'm trying to *do* something for you—get you the recognition you deserve. But if you haven't got enough pride in your own outfit to co-operate with—"

Bishop sprang to his feet at the word "outfit."

"You've said about enough," he cried, "you silly-looking son-of-a-bitch." He drove his fist hard into the captain's jaw, knocking him back several feet.

The captain absorbed the punch without going down, flushed deep red, raised his own fists and then slowly dropped them to his sides.

"Thanks," he said slowly, "Mister Combat Fatigue." He held Bishop's burning stare for a moment before turning on his heel and walking out the door, rubbing his chin.

Bishop reached for his glass with a shaking hand, noted that it was empty, walked to the bar and ordered another drink from the wide-eyed corporal. While he was swallowing the first sip, the group's air exec, Lieutenant Colonel Ben Gately, entered the lounge, picked up Colonel Davenport's green Toby from the radio cabinet, carried it to the mantelpiece and placed it carefully in the center.

Bishop stared across the top of his raised highball at the Toby. In one lunging motion, he swept his hand the whole length of the short bar, sending glasses and bottles crashing to the floor. Gately, too startled to move, watched Bishop lurch past him, unseeing, out of the club.

Lieutenant Heinz Zimmermann, still in his flying clothes, but with his black hair slicked down with water in testimony of a hasty effort to tidy up after his summons over the Tannoy loudspeaker system to the adjutant's office, braked himself to a halt before Major Stovall's desk and uncorked a vehement salute. Stovall returned it, but did not motion Zimmermann to an empty chair, an omission which, even more than the adjutant's icy expression, told Zimmermann that his superior was boiling mad.

"Well, Zimmermann," he demanded, removing his glasses, "what's behind this brawl at the officers' club?"

Zimmermann's face, with its heavy Germanic bone structure, was capable at times of looking stupid. Now he looked positively oafish as he glowered back at Stovall.

"You mean last night, sir?" he groped. "Cobb and Dean?"

"No, I don't. I mean your roommate Bishop. A half hour ago." Zimmermann goggled back at Stovall as the latter continued. "He called a visiting officer a dirty name and socked him."

Zimmermann looked amazed. "Why, I can hardly believe it, sir," he said. "I never heard Jesse use a cuss word. He doesn't know any. He's a clean kid in every way." His voice assumed a confidential note as he sought to regain his ordinarily friendly footing with the adjutant. "Fact is, Major," he continued, "I don't think he's ever even had a piece in his life."

Stovall harrumphed, then frowned.

"I'm not interested in his sex life right now," he said. "But I am interested in why he blew his top."

"Can't understand Jesse doing a thing like that. It's not like him, sir."

"I'm getting sick and tired of these fights in the club. Half a dozen in the past week. If necessary I'm going to close that goddam bar permanently." He picked up a paper clip and bent it back and forth several times angrily between his fingers. "This one," he resumed, "I'd like to settle without bothering the colonel. He's got enough grief." He stared at

Zimmermann's honest, troubled features and felt his hot temper beginning to cool. "I don't know why I'm taking things out on you, Heinz," he said. "You didn't have anything to do with it—I just thought you could help me. Bishop flatly refused to say a word. I finally sent him back to his quarters."

"That's where I'd better go," said Zimmermann. "I never should have left him alone." He moved as if to leave.

"Not so fast," said Stovall. "Here, have a seat. Tell me what's behind that kind of outburst from the gentlest fellow in this group."

Zimmermann sat down reluctantly.

"Bishop's had three rugged ones in a row, sir," said the navigator hesitantly. "Today was the best, sir."

"The topper?"

"That's what I mean, sir."

"I heard that McKesson got it today," said Stovall. "But I don't know any of the details."

"Well, sir," said Zimmermann in a dull, tired voice, "we were crossing the enemy coast when a bunch of Focke-Wulfs hit us out of the sun from twelve o'clock high. I thought they'd gotten us on the first pass, because there was an explosion in the cockpit just above my head that shook the whole ship. I turned around in time to see the top-turret gunner slip through the flight-deck hatch and fall to the floor at the rear of my nose compartment, screaming at the pilot to land—right now." He gulped, then continued: "His right arm was blown off at the shoulder and he was spouting blood all over himself and against the side of the ship. First I tried to give him a shot of morphine, but it was forty below zero at twenty-five thousand feet when I took my gloves off. I bent the needle and couldn't get it in. I couldn't tie a tourniquet on him, either, because the arm was off too close to the shoulder, but I bandaged him the best I could. He had to have medical attention right away. No oxygen. Three hours' flying ahead. So I put the ripcord in his good hand and dumped him out the nose hatch, praying the French would rush him to a doctor. His chute opened okay."

"Did he know what it was all about?" asked Stovall.

"Yes, sir. He knew, but he was game. Mind if I smoke?"

The adjutant quickly handed him a cigarette, which Zimmermann lighted with steady fingers. Stovall waited patiently for him to continue.

"What about Bishop?" he inquired finally.

"I'm getting to that," said Zimmermann. "All this time the ship was gyrating around in the formation, but I figured it was violent evasive action. The bombardier had been busy with the nose guns and now he was getting set to toggle his bombs. The target area was pouring up smoke and we clobbered it with a few more eggs right down the middle. Then we went back to our nose guns, but most of the attacks were coming from the rear. The interphone was shot out but I learned later that all the gunners except the ball-turret had passed out from lack of oxygen when the system was shot out in the first attack. Finally, when we were starting back across the Channel, I went up to check with the pilot and look things over." Zimmermann pulled a deep drag out of his cigarette.

"I found Lieutenant McKesson slumped down in the seat with one foot jammed in the damaged pedals. He was sitting in a mess of blood and the back of his head was shot off. It had happened almost two hours previously when the FW's made the first pass. One 20 mm. had entered the right side of the windshield in front of Lieutenant Bishop, shattering it. It missed Bishop but split open the back of McKesson's skull. Flying number two in formation, he would have been looking to the left. From what Jesse told me, it happened like this:

"McKesson fell forward over the wheel, wrapping his arms around it, causing the ship to nose down sharply, smack into the middle of the low squadron. Bishop grabbed the controls from his side, avoided a collision, and pulled back into formation. He did it by plain brute force against the struggles of McKesson, who was half conscious—and McKesson's got plenty of muscle. With no interphone Bishop couldn't call for help. He thought that the waist, radio and tail gunners had bailed out because their guns had ceased firing, but he kept on toward the target. McKesson couldn't see and he didn't know what was going on, but he never stopped fighting the controls by instinct. Bishop couldn't see, either, through that shattered windshield, except straight up and out to the sides. He had kept one arm crooked through his own wheel to fly the ship and stay in formation. Meanwhile he'd been continually pulling McKesson off the controls with his other hand.

"He told me he couldn't see enough to land from his side and we'd have to move the pilot out of his seat. Took us at least fifteen minutes, with the pilot fighting all the way. Bishop finally had to reach down and jerk McKesson's leg sideways to pull it free. He couldn't help breaking the leg. Then one of the gunners revived enough to help me get McKesson down to the nose compartment. I had to hold him down until we got back to the field. Another gunner lowered gear and flaps and Bishop landed okay. Now I guess I'd better get back to the quarters—see how Jesse's making out." Zimmermann stood up.

Stovall cleared his throat twice before he could speak.

"I've been spending too much time behind this desk, Heinz," he said, returning the boy's salute. "Tell Bishop not to worry. I'll cook up some kind of official reply that will satisfy those bastards up at Pinetree."

After Zimmermann had left, Stovall leaned back in his chair feeling numb and a little nauseated. His mind tried to cope with the enormity of what he had just heard. He projected himself back to the familiar surroundings of his home in Columbus, Ohio, to a world where a man who could knock a baseball out of the park was a hero, and where the collision of an auto and a streetcar was of front-page interest. And then he tried to reconcile the coexistence of that normal world he had left with this strange world at Archbury, where the same breed of human beings lived through such utterly fantastic experiences as Bishop's this morning. He recalled the occasion in World War I when he had driven his bayonet through a German. And how he felt at the time that he had survived a supreme test of his moral fiber under stress. But how could he compare that act with the feats of Bishop during his two-hour ordeal?

He found himself thinking about Colonel Davenport in a kinder light. For some time he had been increasingly critical in his own mind of the colonel's leadership. From the standpoint of an adjutant, ever conscious of regulations and immersed in reports, the 918th had been steadily sliding downhill. Salutes were a rarity, quarters were dirty, uniforms slovenly, discipline lax, griping universal. And Davenport seemed to overlook it, failed to call the squadron commanders in and rack them back. But how could Colonel Davenport be expected to bother about things like that when he was concentrating on operations, on the desperate struggle for survival in the air? A flood of shame came over Stovall as he recalled how successfully he had insulated his thinking from the realities of operations, content to plug along in his own rut. Little wonder that the crews switched the conversation to nonflying topics when he, Stovall, the paddle-foot, the retread ground officer from another war, joined a group at the club. He told himself that he must do better.

He picked up his pen and began signing a new batch of Personal Effects inventories, nearly all of which omitted certain small items: a love letter from a girl in London, overlooked in a back pants pocket, which could stab a young widow's already broken heart; or a contraceptive, in the side pocket of a nineteen-year-old gunner's blouse, which could further sadden a mother's tragedy. These things Stovall always scrupulously removed.

At the sound of crunching tires near his window, he glanced out in time to watch Colonel Davenport climb from his car, his face darker than usual with dejected exhaustion.

Davenport had just finished a quick tour of the station, after Interrogation, during which he had inspected the bomb dumps, the worst of the battle-damaged aircraft and the repair hangars. He scraped the mud off his galoshes with a stick and went inside directly to his office, where he found the air exec and the flight surgeon waiting for him.

"The warning order just came down," said Gately. "Snafu'd as usual. It says we're low group at *nine* thousand feet."

Davenport frowned at the sheet of teletype.

"They must mean nine*teen* thousand," he said. "That's bad enough, but nine thousand is what those flak gunners dream about. I'll call Pinetree about it in a minute. Any other good news?"

"Yes," said Gately. He was a slender, sprucely uniformed West Pointer, with a thin brown mustache, liquid brown eyes and a dissipated look. "I broke your number-three iron." He indicated the golf club on the colonel's desk.

"Nice going," said Davenport. "When did you find time to do that?"

"You know me," said Gately casually. "Always get in my one hour of physical training per orders. I busted the club when Pamela beat me on the last hole this morning."

Davenport controlled his annoyance.

"I've just come from the line," he said. "Sergeant Nero thinks we can put up eighteen tomorrow, with luck. But no spares. How about crews?"

"We've got twenty-three. But half of them have been going four days in a row. They'll be asleep in the Briefing tomorrow. Isn't that right, Don?" He turned to Major Kaiser.

"Can't be helped," said Kaiser, a little curtly.

Davenport glanced from his flight surgeon to Gately.

"Better get back to the Ops room, Ben," he said. "I'll be over as soon as I find out about the altitude." After the air exec had gone, he asked Kaiser: "You think Gately's all right to fly tomorrow?"

"Yes, sir," said Kaiser. "His cold is no worse than plenty of others that are flying, but he asked to be grounded again." His voice was eloquent with disapproval.

Davenport scratched his head and tapped a pencil against his teeth, striving to reach a decision.

"What did you tell him?" he asked.

"Frankly, sir, I couldn't justify excusing him on medical grounds."

Davenport sat down heavily behind his desk, his mind busy with a battle he had fought many times. He had ample reasons for firing Gately. The man was trying to coast through an easy war, crowding in all the tennis, golf, women and social life that were consistent with a nominal discharge of his duties. Since the group's arrival in England, he had logged more hours at a card table in the club, cleaning out junior officers, than at the controls of a B-17. When Gately led missions he usually aborted with mechanical trouble or turned back on account of weather. But on the other hand, Davenport always recoiled from the prospect of relieving him. As an experienced staff officer, he was useful in many ways. Davenport admitted to himself that he didn't like to delegate much authority where operations were concerned, and Gately was not the aggressive type of air exec who might have gotten in Davenport's hair. Furthermore, there was the matter of Gately's three-star father on the Joint Chiefs of Staff. This war wouldn't last forever. There was the future to think about.

He looked up and saw the flight surgeon's eyes on him, questioning.

"Well, Don," he said, "I honestly don't know why I haven't relieved him. He's led only two missions that counted. He's weak in the air and he knows it. But he's a good staff officer and takes a big load of detail off me on the ground. Hell, if I asked for a replacement, I'd probably get some cast-off that was worse."

"If you keep him, Colonel," said Kaiser, "I don't believe it's advisable to condone his grounding himself against my repeated recommendations."

"I'll have to be the final judge of that," said Davenport shortly.

The stocky flight surgeon braced himself.

"Colonel," he said, "you and I have got to get down on the floor and wrestle this thing out. May I speak bluntly?"

"Go ahead."

"I'm a doctor and a psychiatrist. As such I am responsible to you for the mental and physical health of your combat crews. All of them are suffering from greater or lesser degrees of anxiety and stress. Acting only as a doctor it would be simple for me to remove the cause of the emotional disturbance immediately . . . by grounding the lot of them. But I am also an Army officer. I am obligated to furtherance of the military mission. Therefore, I cannot ground a man until I am convinced he has reached the limit of his capacity —or that a very little further stress will make him dangerous to the success of the next mission or to the lives and safety of his crew and aircraft. There is only one honorable way out for most of these men, except completion of a full tour of duty. And that is injury or death."

"I am aware of all that," said Davenport. "What is your point?"

"Briefly, this. I believe that the policy in this group has given too many individuals an out. They have learned that even after I have certified them fit to fly, they can trot around to the front office and be excused. As a result, we have too many men in the hospital or sick in quarters. Too many men who think they can't fly above ten thousand feet. Too many cases of frostbite—and incidentally, I am opposed to awarding any more Purple Hearts for frostbitten hands; it's too much of a temptation to a gunner who is getting shaky and sees an easy way to hospitalize himself for several months. I don't believe that my viewpoint is cold-blooded. I believe that the colonel has been overlenient. Gately is the main case in point because he sets an example for the others. I feel that it is my duty to make a stand about Gately."

Davenport, spots of color on his cheekbones, rose and paced back and forth, hands thrust deep in his pockets. He turned on Kaiser.

"Gately is my business," he said, "but Lieutenant Campbell is yours."

"What about Campbell, sir?"

"He did a swell job of leading the low squadron today," said Davenport. "But he won't lead it again. Somehow, nobody noticed he wasn't with his crew today until Interrogation was almost over. They looked for him at his quarters and at the club but couldn't find him. Finally the bombardier went back to the airplane twenty minutes ago and found him still sitting in the cockpit. He'd never left it."

"Injured?"

"No. He was whistling and singing 'Old Man River.' And he was just as happy and carefree as a bird."

Gradually the words sank in on Kaiser.

"Nuts?" he asked.

"Completely," said Davenport. "His mind was gone."

"I must take the blame for Campbell," said Kaiser in a crushed voice. "I should have seen it coming."

"That's just it!" shot back Davenport. "How can you tell?" He made another circuit of the floor. "You think I'm too lenient. But somebody's got to stand up for these boys. Up at Pinetree they're just numbers on a blackboard. To me they're flesh and blood. How can the military mission succeed if you demand the impossible of human beings?"

There was a knock at the door and an enlisted man entered with a tray bearing a coffee pot and several cups. Davenport eagerly poured two cups of black coffee and drank half of his own at a gulp.

"That's getting to be your diet, I'm afraid, Colonel," said Kaiser, glad of the interruption. "Coffee and cigarettes. Your diet last night and again tonight. And you haven't had your clothes off for three nights."

"I can take it," said Davenport. "But how long do you think these boys can take it, Kaiser? Like Lieutenant Bishop. Operations tells me he flew unassisted for two hours today with a fatally wounded pilot fighting the controls—before that Heinie navigator, Zimmermann, went up to help him."

"Yes, I know. I admit it was a miracle."

"That's what they want up at Bomber Command, isn't it?" said Davenport. "Miracles?"

"They're getting them, too," said Kaiser. "We're finding out every day that a man's tolerance for severe stress is unbelievably high."

"And I suppose you'd okay Bishop to go again tomorrow?"

"If he is medically all right in the morning, yes. Once I start grounding a man after a rugged mission, you won't be able to get a single airplane off the runway. They'd all rather go to London than to Lorient."

As Davenport listened to the flight surgeon his face grew bleaker and grayer.

"You're back on that same phonograph record," he said.

"I can't help it, sir. When we have enough replacements to keep the group up to strength, I'll favor more liberal use of rest homes. There's a lot about combat fatigue we're still learning. But if we go soft now when we need every crew, the 918th will be out of the fight."

"I know, I know," said Davenport, losing patience again. "I'm tired of arguing with you. And I've got to get on that phone, if you'll excuse me."

"Yes, sir." Kaiser stopped halfway to the door for one more try. "You'll rest up tomorrow," he said hopefully, "and send Gately?"

"Goddamit, no!" yelled Davenport. "It's a target I can't delegate to anybody else—certainly not Gately. Now beat it and let *me* run this group."

"Please try to get a little sleep tonight, then," said Kaiser placatingly as he closed the door behind him.

Davenport picked up his scrambler phone and called Colonel Savage at Pinetree.

"You mean *General* Savage?" asked the clerk at the other end.

"Since when?"

"Since yesterday, sir. One moment."

Savage came on.

"How's it feel to be a general, Frank?"

"It worries me plenty. I must have bitched something up royally to get a star for it."

"Not necessarily. But anyway, nice going. Say, Frank, I want to check an error in the Field Order. It said nine thousand."

"That's right. It's no error."

"But, Jesus Christ, Frank, that's murder. Which side are you guys fighting on?"

"We haven't been getting enough hits from high altitude. So, just once, we've got to go in low. Then we can say we've tried everything."

"You sure can!"

"We agree with you it sounds like non-habit-forming tactics. But there's only one way to find out."

"And another thing—why are we low group again?"

"A toss of the coin."

"Maybe you need a new coin." Davenport paused to pour himself another cup of coffee. "You know we got beat up again today," he continued. "I can't even put a full group in the air tomorrow." His voice rose, out of control, so that Stovall in the next room couldn't help overhearing him. "When are you going to give us a break? Nobody can keep this up. I'm asking you right now to let us stand down for a few days."

Savage didn't answer immediately. Then he said: "I admit I'd be unhappy in your shoes, Keith. But do you realize what you're saying?"

"Yes. I'm telling you there's a limit! This maximum-effort business has already gone too far!"

"Look, Keith," said Savage in a conciliatory tone, "in this

kind of a deal, if we ever get down to one B-17 and one crew left—we'll have to send it."

"That's brave talk from behind a desk."

"Now just a minute, Keith. You're talking hysterically—you don't sound like yourself. Look, Keith . . . I'll call you back."

"I'm not—" Davenport stopped, for Savage had hung up. His lips quivering, Davenport dropped the phone slowly into its cradle, then picked up the instrument and slammed it down into the wastebasket by his desk.

Ben Gately stuck his head in the door, perceived the colonel's agitation and started to withdraw.

"Now what?" snapped Davenport.

"I just wanted to ask who the colonel will fly with tomorrow," said Gately, lapsing into the formal third person.

Davenport flung himself wearily back into his chair, trying to regain his composure. He considered a moment while the unaccustomed flush in his cheeks receded, leaving the former gray pallor to accentuate the dark bags under his eyes.

"I'll lead the mission with Jesse Bishop's crew," he said.

"Very well, sir." Gately left and after a few moments Stovall appeared, standing respectfully just inside the door.

"Colonel?" he said. "If you happen to have a pint in your desk I'd like a—a snort."

Davenport looked at Stovall in amazement, then reached down and produced a bottle of whisky. He smiled sadly at the adjutant's diffident expression.

"So you finally caught a cold, Harvey," he said, opening the pint and handing it to the adjutant.

Stovall took a large swallow, coughed explosively and wiped his smarting eyes.

"Just a slight sore throat coming on," he said. He tilted the pint again—a smaller sip this time. "Heap good medicine," he said. "Better have one, Colonel."

In General Henderson's office at Bomber Command, where Frank Savage had just concluded his telephone conversation with Davenport, there was an uneasy silence. Major General Pat Pritchard, the third officer present, puffed at his cigar and peered intently through the smoke, first at Henderson and then at Savage, observing that the brand-new brigadier general had not yet exchanged his eagles for stars.

"Keith's been under a hell of a strain," said Savage finally. "Looked ninety years old the last time I saw him."

Pritchard removed his cigar and turned to Henderson. "I've kept out of this, Ed," he said. "But after hearing one end of that conversation I can't keep out of it any longer. The 918th has been a sick group—you and Frank call it a Hard Luck Group—for a long time. Perhaps you still feel that you can justify keeping Davenport. But I can't justify a weak group to my boss forever when no remedial action has been taken. Something's basically wrong. In my book that's always meant the commander."

"With the general's permission," said Henderson, "I'd like to give Davenport just a little more time. Make absolutely sure it hasn't been a long streak of bad breaks. We haven't got a group commander that works harder or flies more missions—and frankly, I'd be stumped where to find a replacement. Also, Keith is popular in the group. The crews worship him. I'm afraid of what will happen to morale if I relieve him."

"What morale?" asked Pritchard drily. "We're not staging popularity contests over here. Maybe what we need is more group commanders who aren't so popular. What do you think, Frank?"

Savage looked uncomfortably over at Henderson, who stared back noncommittally. The easiest thing, he knew, was to agree with Henderson and duck the issue. The latter's defense of his protégé had not surprised Savage, but it had disgusted him. Ostensibly, he reflected, Henderson was being loyal, but actually he was betraying a dangerously harmful flaw in his equipment as a commander. He was demonstrating that he was incapable of admitting a mistake or of rectifying it. Pritchard, on the other hand, he told himself, was a more typical West Pointer, one who could rise above his personal loyalties and think as a man fighting for his country. He watched Pritchard staring through rings of cigar smoke at the ceiling. This was the cagey old boy whom you had to get up early in the morning to fool. This was the general who had startled his West Point colleagues by bringing over a staff largely composed of newly commissioned civilians, because he believed that you could teach an intelligent man the army faster than you could teach some professional army men ability. "Pritchard's Amateurs," they had been dubbed. But in this new kind of war, where conditions changed every day and you had to throw away the book, the amateurs had been confounding the critics. This was the general who, behind that mask of his, excelled at guessing what the other fellow was thinking. Savage braced himself to answer the general's question.

"If we leave Davenport down there much longer," he said earnestly, "I'm afraid he's going to crack up. Whether it's his fault or not, the fact remains that his group always takes the worst losses. I like Keith, but I don't think it's fair to him or the group to postpone putting him out of his misery until it's too late." He glanced anxiously back and forth between his two listeners.

Pritchard noticed Henderson coloring. "I realize, Ed," he said, "that Davenport is an old classmate of yours, and that you have a lot of confidence in him. That makes it hard."

"I'm not going to let that sway me for a moment, sir," said Henderson, shifting gears smoothly into the voice of the model commander. "But there are so many factors. For instance, I have to ask myself am I partly at fault? Has my staff given the 918th all the support and co-operation it needed? Are personalities involved? I don't believe so. I think we've done our part. But just the same, I like to do a little soul searching before I kick a man out and break his back."

Now it was Savage's turn to color up. The operations of the groups were his direct responsibility, as head of A-3, and it struck him that Henderson's remarks were calculated to raise a subtle question in Pritchard's mind.

"I still have confidence," concluded Henderson, "that Davenport can pull the 918th out of the hole. If anybody can."

Pritchard sent a puff of blue smoke toward Henderson and watched it dissolve.

"We'll see how things work out tomorrow over St. Nazaire," he said. "Couple of good missions. No losses. Might put them back on their feet." He rose. "Meanwhile, I'd better get some sleep for an early start, if we're going to visit all the stations tomorrow."

Pritchard needed rest. It was a rare night that he had

been able to sleep for five uninterrupted hours since the day he had landed in England with no bases, no crews and no airplanes, carrying an order in his pocket which boiled down to: "Build an air force!"

At 2:30 A.M. many lights were burning behind the blackout curtains at Archbury. At Operations. At Intelligence. In the combat mess hall the cooks were already unpacking oranges and preparing eggs for breakfast, special premission fare, before the 3:30 briefing. But most of the station slept heavily.

Heinz Zimmermann lay awake, listening in the dark to Bishop, who was tossing and mumbling in the next bed. "Pull up!" cried Bishop sharply, jerking to a sitting position. Zimmermann thought that Bishop had awakened, but the latter slumped back, turned over on his stomach and clawed at his pillow. "Flak!" he called out. "Flak! . . . bail out, Johnny, bail out! . . . Sure, Mac, I heard you. I see him. Yellow-nose at two o'clock low . . . watch your leg, Mac. Easy now, I've got it . . . Oh, God, I didn't mean to snap it. It snapped, Mac . . . I'm your friend, Mac. You know I'm your best friend . . . there's the Channel. I swear it's the Channel."

Zimmermann smoked a cigarette, tried to doze off in spite of his roommate's mumbling, then gave it up, walked over and sat on the edge of Bishop's bed. He shook the tortured boy's shoulder. Bishop awoke with an instant startle-reaction, almost leaping from bed.

"Okay," he groaned. "I'm coming."

"No, Jesse. It's not time yet. You were having nightmares. Turning up twenty-five hundred R.P.M. That's why I woke you."

"Pulling a mission, I guess."

"You've been flying a lot of night missions lately."

"Let a guy sleep, will ya?"

"All right. But I've been thinking. I can fix it with the flight surgeon if you don't think you ought to—"

Bishop sat up, fully awake. "You crazy?" he said. "Crazy in the head?"

"Okay, okay," said Zimmermann soothingly. He returned to his own bed and pulled a pair of G.I. blankets over his chunky body, clad in coveralls. Normally a heavy sleeper, he always made it a point to retire completely dressed before a mission, with his flight gear piled neatly on a chair beside him so that he wouldn't have to grope around in the dark upon being awakened. On top of the pile was his pearl-handled revolver, which he always carried along. "They won't catch me alive," was the way he put it.

Bishop lay quietly now, but still Zimmermann couldn't drown his mind in sleep. He arose and stepped outside to the boardwalk, which was slippery with frost. His breath exhaled in plumes as he looked up at a few stars visible through rifts in the gauzelike cirrus clouds.

"What are you doing up, Heinz?" asked a voice behind him. He turned and recognized Lieutenant Butch Roby, the crew's bombardier, who lived in the next quarters. Roby flicked away a glowing cigarette.

"Can't sleep, I guess," said Heinz.

"You're slipping," said Roby, moving over to Zimmermann. "And I thought you were one of those guys with rocks in their heads that liked combat."

"I can't say I like it. I just hate those goddam nazi bastards."

"Me, I don't hate anybody. This is just a job—to get over with."

"A lot of guys feel that way. Sweating out twenty-five missions. But if it takes a hundred, that's okay with me. I never told you but I've got German blood in me on both sides."

"Everybody knows that."

"Yeah?" Zimmermann was genuinely surprised. "What do you know?"

The pair walked in silence for a while. Suddenly Roby remembered something. "Say," he said, "you forgot to pick up your personal bomb loading last night. I'll go get it."

When the bombardier returned from his quarters he was carrying a cluster of tiny incendiary bombs which Zimmermann was in the habit of tossing out over the target as an extra dividend.

CHAPTER THREE

Eggs for Breakfast

Toward noon later that morning, the traffic pattern above Archbury was empty save for a solitary Percival Q-6, which was circling to land. Major General Pritchard was at the controls of the small transport, lent by the R.A.F. until the Americans could afford the luxury of their own staff airplanes. Henderson was the only passenger, and a not too happy one.

Why, Henderson was thinking as they glided toward the runway, did the Old Man insist on flying himself? He had too much on his mind to be coping with an unfamiliar airplane. Henderson looked sideways at Pritchard's scowling face, a cigar butt clenched in his mouth, and wondered if the Old Man was satisfied with the briefing they had attended at one station and the take-off they had watched at a second. There had been raucous boos at the briefing upon the announcement that three groups were going over St. Nazaire—"flak city" to the crews—at nine, ten and eleven thousand feet, respectively, to get hits on the pin-point, concrete submarine pens. Twenty-three thousand feet would have been more to their liking. And at the second group, the taxi plan had gotten screwed up when one Fort sank a wheel in the mud just off the perimeter track and had to be hauled out by a cleat track. But the boys had managed to get off on time. The combat crews had seemed unusually on edge, and there had been a thinly veiled atmosphere of hostility toward generals, but Henderson hoped the Old Man would attribute it to the fact that the men were still full of fight.

Pritchard set the Q-6 down on the runway rather awkwardly in the slight cross wind, forestalling an incipient ground loop with a tardy, but effective, yank on the hand brake.

"When are the British going to get around to toe brakes?" he muttered, straightening out the ship's roll.

While the Q-6 trundled past the deserted hard-stands of the 918th, Henderson began to worry afresh about Davenport. The latter had been fourteen minutes late at the take-off, due to a last-minute change in the bomb loading in the Field Order. Yet the other two groups had managed to switch bombs in time. Why was the 918th always the one to get caught short? He still refused to admit, even to himself, that Davenport was incompetent—that he could so grossly have overestimated him. He hoped that Davenport had been able to make up most of the lost time by short cuts to the Wing rendezvous and could keep his losses down today. If not, how could he avoid relieving him? Things must have been in a worse mess than he realized on his last visit to Archbury, in Davenport's absence. Had that smooth-talking air exec— Lieutenant Colonel Gately—sold him a quick Persian rug? He recalled Gately's closing assurance: "Morale is very high," and how he had relayed this estimate up to General Patrick in London.

A jeep guided the Q-6 to a parking place in front of the Flying Control Tower, where the visitors were met by Major Stovall, who was concealing, behind his snappy salute, a sensation of acute discomfort. He had been notified barely in time, his shoes needed a better shine and there was a spot on his pink slacks. Furthermore, he was struggling with the novel misery of his first hangover.

"Would the general like to go up to the tower?" he asked hopefully, praying inwardly that his visitors would not ask to inspect the station.

"A little later, Major," said Pritchard cordially. "I believe we've got time to look around your station first."

"Very well, sir," said Stovall, trying to look pleased. Then, noticing that the untidy sergeant at the wheel of the waiting staff car made no move to open the door for the general, Stovall hastened to perform the courtesy himself.

"Where is your air exec?" asked Henderson as they drove off. Stovall thrust from his mind a quick mental picture of Gately's departure that morning with a tennis racket under his arm, as soon as the bombers were off.

"Wing headquarters, sir. Conference." It was only half a

lie, the adjutant told himself, for Gately had promised to drop off some reports at Wing—Pamela's house being on the same property.

"And the ground exec, Brown?" asked Henderson.

"Colonel Brown's still in the hospital, sir. I'm acting ground exec until he gets well."

Henderson frowned but lapsed into silence. Stovall's relief was short-lived, for General Pritchard turned to him.

"How many got off this morning?" he asked.

"Seventeen, sir. But I believe two aborted."

Pritchard looked at Henderson.

"Fifteen over the target," he said, "if they all get there."

A half hour later, on top of the tower, Pritchard and Henderson stood at the railing scanning the cloudless sky. Both were in a foul mood, but Pritchard wore the grimmer expression. Henderson glanced at his wrist watch.

"Any minute now, sir," he said.

"Yes," said Pritchard. He removed the cigar from his mouth. "Ed," he asked, "after what we've seen around here this morning, would you say that we still have a fighting outfit at Archbury?"

Henderson flushed. "I'm afraid, sir, they've slipped a long way." As he gripped the railing the palms of his hands were wet, moistened by the clammy tension inside an ambitious man who is suddenly conscious that his job is in jeopardy. He was able to visualize only two gleams of silver lining around the dark cloud before him. First, realizing the gravity of the situation in the 918th, Pritchard might agree to letting him send Frank Savage down to take over, in spite of the fact that the job was beneath a brigadier general's rank. Second, if Savage assumed command and whipped the outfit back into shape, a catastrophe would be averted. But Savage would be getting a thankless, almost hopeless, task; any commander who inherited the mess at the 918th could easily fall on his face. And if this happened, Henderson felt he would be rid of a competitor who was breathing hot on his neck. Either way, he told himself, it's an even swap to me. Except for one thing. How did I ever get myself into a spot where I have to pull a reverse switch on these two guys? In peacetime, I had to send Davenport down to relieve Savage.

Squirming under the irony of his reflections, Henderson looked up in time to see a cluster of specks in the distance. The specks swelled into a formation of B-17's.

"I count eight," said Pritchard.

Henderson, clenching and unclenching his fists, turned pale around the nostrils.

"Must be a few cripples down on other airdromes," he said.

"I hope so," said Pritchard gravely. "Seven would be the worst loss we've ever taken out of one group. Check the other stations and see if they've got a preliminary count yet."

"Yes, sir." Henderson went below to a telephone and returned in a few minutes.

"Twenty out of twenty-one," he said, "are in the landing pattern at the 901st, sir, and the 902nd was spotted returning with nineteen out of twenty-one."

"Thank God for that," said Pritchard. He remained silent while the eight survivors of the 918th roared over the field and broke off one by one into their landing approaches. Then he started for the stairs with a stiff, determined stride. "We'll go meet Davenport," he said, setting his jaw, so that Henderson could see the muscles stand out.

The staff car pulled away from Flying Control past a long line of spectators, resembling the sidelines of a football game. Bleary-eyed mechanics. Headquarters clerks. Cooks wearing their white chefs' caps. Every face was stricken, like the face of mourners at a funeral, but none more so than that of Harvey Stovall, sitting beside the driver. His throat had become so choked that he gave up trying to speak to the man at the wheel and gave him directions to Colonel Davenport's hard-stand with hand motions.

Presently a battered Fort, with jagged holes showing through the wings and fuselage, taxied up, swung its tail around on the small circle of concrete and cut its engines off. Pritchard got out of the car and waited patiently until an old man emerged from the waist hatch. Keith Davenport's face was shocking, indistinguishable from that of a corpse, until he caught sight of the two generals. Then fury gleamed through the exhaustion in his eyes, as the pair walked forward to meet him.

"We proved it for you," he said. "Their flak is good at nine thousand feet!"

"How bad was it, Keith?" asked Pritchard gently.

Davenport couldn't help seeing the stricken concern in his superior's eyes.

His voice lost a little of its edge.

"You see how many we've got left, sir," he said. "That's all I had with me when we left the target area."

"All flak?" asked Pritchard. "Or fighters too?"

"Flak," said Davenport. "I knew it would happen, General. I told Frank Savage so last night."

"It wasn't Savage, Keith. It was me. We had to try it."

Davenport made a great effort and kept silent. Henderson placed his arm compassionately around Davenport's shoulders. "Come on, Keith," he said. "We'll give you a lift to Interrogation."

Davenport passed Jesse Bishop and Heinz Zimmermann, who were shedding their Mae Wests near the nose. Bishop gave him a weary semblance of a salute and a wan smile, but Zimmermann looked quickly the other way.

In the car, Pritchard held a light for Davenport's cigarette, as they drove toward the Interrogation hut.

"Did you hit the aiming point?" asked Henderson.

"I think we put a few in there," said Davenport. "We were late at the I.P., after the navigation got screwed up, so we didn't have time for a good run into the target."

"I'd like to hear more about that," said Pritchard. "Let's meet in your office after the Interrogation. And bring along your group navigator."

Heinz Zimmermann stood with bowed head in Davenport's office, where the latter was concluding a critique of the mission for the two generals.

"I believe, sir," said Davenport, turning away from the wall map to which he had been referring, "that if the navigation had been better we still could have made the rendezvous on time. Then we wouldn't have caught the flak all alone. Their batteries would have been confused by three groups coming in simultaneously at different altitudes on different courses, according to plan." He glanced at Zimmermann, who was still looking at the floor. "But the responsibility, of course, is mine."

Pritchard looked from Davenport to Zimmermann. "We'd like to hear your version, Lieutenant," he said kindly.

The navigator raised his eyes to the general's. It was hard to tell whether the boy was sullen or brokenhearted.

"I did the best I could, General," he said in a low voice that sounded close to tears. "Honest I did. But I guess it was like the colonel says."

Henderson leaned forward, fixing his eyes on Zimmermann.

"Everybody makes mistakes," he said. "But it's unfortunate that navigational errors this morning had to cost the lives of seventy men."

Zimmermann turned to Davenport with pleading eyes, begging for help, for some amelioration of General Henderson's indictment. Davenport was about to speak, when General Pritchard rose from the seat he was occupying behind the desk.

"Davenport," he asked, "if your group had gotten off on time, the navigator would have been able to fly the mission as briefed. Isn't that right?"

"Yes, sir. But we still could have . . ."

"May I interrupt, sir?" said Henderson. "By the same token Keith would have gotten off on time if there hadn't been a last-minute change in the Field Order, for which my A-3 must assume responsibility."

"The other groups," said Pritchard sharply, "got off on time. I don't want Lieutenant Zimmermann to leave this room feeling that he must shoulder the whole blame."

"Neither," said Henderson, "do I feel that Colonel Davenport should take the blame for the errors of the navigator."

Zimmermann winced and shuffled his feet. Davenport faced Pritchard.

"I want to assure the general that it won't happen again," he said, "regardless of who was to blame."

"The commander," said Pritchard quietly, "is always to blame. You need a rest, Davenport, a long rest. Badly." He faced Henderson. "General, you will relieve Colonel Davenport and send someone down as soon as possible to take over."

Davenport crumpled back into a chair as though his legs

had suddenly been filled with sand, leaned forward and buried his face in his hands. His shoulders shook, out of control, and tears ran through his fingers, dripping to the floor. Henderson looked speechlessly at Pritchard. And Zimmermann, with a horrified expression, stood there watching the instantaneous and complete collapse of his commander.

Pritchard was the first to transfer his attention from Davenport, who continued to sob silently, to Zimmermann. He walked over and guided the boy with his hand to the door.

"What has happened in this room," he said, "is strictly between those who were present. I wish it could have been avoided in front of you." He patted him on the arm. "And try not to feel so badly about it."

Zimmermann saluted stiffly and closed the door behind him. He strode down the hall, setting his cap on his head crookedly, mounted his bicycle outside and rode slowly along the muddy concrete road to the combat-crew living site. He dismounted and, as he was passing the corner of the first building, encountered Stovall, whom he saluted. The adjutant passed on by without returning the salute or showing any sign of recognition. Actually Stovall was so preoccupied with his troubles, aside from being nearsighted without his glasses, that he would not have noticed Winston Churchill. But to Zimmermann it had appeared to be an intentional slight.

As Zimmermann neared his quarters, he passed an open doorway from which loud voices could be overheard, rehashing the mission. Zimmermann felt sure he had heard his name mentioned and stopped, a few steps beyond the door, to listen.

"That knuckle-headed Kraut navigator sure bitched us up today," said a voice.

"Yeah. A German ace. He can claim seven aircraft destroyed. He's won himself the Iron Cross, with bar."

Zimmermann stood frozen for a moment, then moved on. Immediately after he had left, a third voice spoke up.

"Aw, why don't you bastards quit bitching. You haven't got a navigator in your whole damn squadron that can find the seat of his pants with both hands. I'll take Zimmermann any time."

But Zimmermann was already out of earshot.

As he entered his quarters, an invigorating scent of shaving lotion spiced his nostrils.

"You look like a man in a trance," said Bishop, who had changed into a fresh uniform and was knotting his tie in front of a metal mirror. "Where in hell have you been?"

"Over at headquarters."

"Doing what?"

"Listening to a general tell me my navigation cost us seven crews today."

"Nuts. How can anybody say it was your fault when we took off so late you had to change your data in flight?"

"Just the same I won the Iron Cross. I'm a goddam German ace, that's what I am."

"You're an overconscientious, stubborn Dutchman, that's what you are. Why, the navigation was anybody's guess in that soup. The colonel was guessing right along with you. Told you to turn wrong when we hit the enemy coast."

"Maybe I misunderstood him."

"That ain't the way I heard it on the interphone. Now snap out of it. You've been needling me to pull a short mission to the Black Swan with you. Okay, I'll take you up on it right now. Throw on a clean shirt and we'll get going."

"That's not all," said Zimmermann. "I got the colonel fired. General Pritchard just relieved him for lousing up the mission."

"Fired!" Bishop whistled, then he said: "So the colonel carries out their mistakes to the letter. Then they fire him! Come on, Heinz. This *really* calls for the Black Swan."

"You go ahead, Jesse. I . . . I guess I'll hit the sack."

Bishop came over and slapped him on the back, but Zimmermann remained impassive.

"I tell you what, Heinz," said Bishop. "I've got to go over and borrow a few pounds from Major Stovall." Zimmermann turned away and moved over to the window, where he stood staring out at nothing, his lips working slowly. "When I get back, I want to find you looking pretty and smelling like a rose." He hurried out.

Heinz Zimmermann sat down heavily on the foot of the bed. "Seventy of our own guys," he said aloud. He waited until Bishop's footsteps had died away on the boardwalk.

Then he drew his pearl-handled revolver out of his belt, cocked it, pressed the muzzle against his right temple, pulled the trigger and blew his brains out.

At Wycombe Abbey, twilight glimmered across the pond, whose glassy surface was ruffled here and there by the wakes of the wild ducks and the gliding of the swans. G.I.'s, arm in arm with W.A.A.F.'s, strolled around the water's edge, tossing chunks of bread to the birds. Walking along in silence, Pritchard and Savage reached a rustic bridge across a brook running into the pond and stopped to lean on the railing. Pritchard tossed his cigar butt into the water and watched a mallard shoot toward it while he lit a fresh Havana.

"When Ed told you he'd relieved Davenport just now," he said, "did he also mention that he'd recommended you as the only man qualified to take over?"

"No, sir."

"Well, he did. And you are. But it's a step back for you right after a promotion. And it means being exposed to combat again. On the other hand, we have a group that couldn't answer a Field Order tomorrow. The blunt truth is that an American fighting outfit has quit. If it spreads to other groups, and it can, or if the truth should get out now, we might as well go home." He flicked a cigar ash down to the mallard, still circling eagerly below. "And if we fold up here, where will it stop? It could be an irreparable blow to our side, at the very time that our Allies are hanging on by a hair absorbing terrible punishment, and counting on us to live up to our big promises. We're the only force in U. S. uniforms capable of hitting the number-one enemy for a long time. But it's not just the bombing show, nor prestige that's involved, so much as the spirit that wins wars."

He turned to look squarely at Savage, his eyes glistening. "That's why I picked you to lead our first group," he continued in a husky voice. "That's why I've got to fish around in my hip pocket just once more and come up with you. It's a bigger job than Ed Henderson's got. This time I'm giving you the biggest job of the war." He paused again. "Frank, America is at stake."

Savage spoke for the first time, looking up at the thick

overcast of fog beginning to drag through the high treetops near the Abbey.

"The weather man," he said, "promises everything will be closed down for at least a week. I'm going to need that time down at Archbury, General."

CHAPTER FOUR

Shambles

Late in the afternoon, a fine drizzle was sifting down from soggy skies upon the airdrome at Archbury, glistening on the round roofs of the Nissen huts, on the runways and on the H.E. bombs stacked under thickets of dripping green leaves for concealment. Davenport had departed two days previously, leaving behind him a shambles of despair.

Whatever bond there had been to cement the men in unity —centered upon the symbol of the group and the fatherly personality of its commander—was now dissolved. Battered by the cumulative loss of friends killed in combat, by the shock of Zimmermann's tragic suicide and by the crowning blow of Davenport's collapse and dismissal, the 918th lay prostrate, psychologically defenseless against the inroads of indifference, discouragement and resentment.

Frank Savage, riding up to the south gate of Archbury in the staff car that had brought him from Pinetree, knew this, both instinctively and from combat experience. He was well aware that he was about to step out on a stage before an audience in which every member would hate him on sight. Every act of his and every word would be automatically wrong, particularly so coming from a general officer. The group would expect sympathy from him, and it would be prepared to reject this sympathy.

Savage had a plan.

Purpose showed in the hard set of his mouth and in the hot intensity of his eyes as he stared straight ahead through the rain-smeared windshield. But anyone who knew Savage well would have noted a telltale hint that alleviated the relentless expression in the eyes. Keen anticipation was there —the anticipation of a flier who loves to fly, of a leader who is born to lead and of a fighting man, waiting for the bell, who knows how to fight.

A B-17 passed low over the car—low enough so that Savage could feel the vibrations of the engines cutting through him—and skimmed toward the runway. Savage's granite eyes glowed. His heart beat faster.

When the car reached the gate, a dispirited-looking, rain-coated M.P., standing in an up-ended packing crate that served for a sentry box, tossed away a cigarette and, without saluting or coming to attention, motioned the staff car on. Savage halted his driver and jumped out.

"Do you know me, Sergeant?" he demanded of the sentry.

"No, sir."

"Then why are you admitting me to this station?"

"I seen it was an Army car, sir." The sentry was standing at attention now.

"Goering could have been inside it. Don't your orders require you to check identifications?"

"Yes, sir."

"Here's my AGO card."

The sergeant examined it, handed it back and saluted.

"This is a military base," concluded Savage, "not a zoo open to the public. Check visitors accordingly."

"Very well, General." Looking badly abused, the sentry glared down the road after the staff car.

Halfway to the administration site, Savage's slowly moving car met two G.I.'s walking in the opposite direction. Both stared directly at him in the rear seat but neither saluted. Again Savage stopped his driver and had him back up to the walking soldiers. He sprang out and halted them.

"Are you men in the United States Army?" he asked.

"Yes, sir." Belatedly the two men rendered salutes, which Savage returned with a whiplash motion.

"Take a good look at me," he said. "I'm going to be around here for a while. Even if you're a block away, God help you if you ever pass me up again!"

Through the rear-view mirror, as his car proceeded, Savage could see the pair of G.I.'s looking back at intervals, gesticulating and turning their heads toward each other in vigorous conversation.

At headquarters, after directing the driver to drop his baggage off at the C.O.'s quarters, Savage dismissed him.

"You won't see me back at Pinetree for a long time," he said. "Good luck to you, Corporal."

"Good luck to *you,* sir," said the corporal in an awed tone.

Savage strode down the hall to the adjutant's office, where the only man in sight was sitting in long-sleeved G.I. underwear at a typewriter, his shirt draped over the back of his chair.

"How do I address you?" asked Savage.

The man stood up in confusion, groping for the shirt. "I didn't rightly understand the general," he said.

"Are you a civilian? Or an Italian general? Or a rear admiral? How am I supposed to know?"

"Sergeant McIllhenny, sir," he said, flaming with embarrassment. "U. S. Army."

"You're *Private* McIllhenny now," said Savage. "Where is the air exec?"

"Colonel Gately's not on the station, sir."

"How long has he been gone?"

The man hesitated. "Two days, sir."

"Where can I reach him?"

"He didn't leave any number, sir."

"Where's the ground exec?"

"Still in the hospital, sir."

"And the adjutant?"

"Over at the club, sir."

"Get yourself dressed. Then tell the adjutant to report to me in the Ops room."

"Yes, sir!"

Savage walked swiftly down another hall until he had found the Operations room. It also was deserted save for a tech sergeant who was correcting the list of combat crews on the blackboard. Savage's eyes roved about the room, observing the litter of cigarette butts, crumpled candy wrappers and miscellaneous trash on the floor. Ignoring the sergeant, whose back was still turned, he stepped back into the hall, reached up and grabbed a fire-hose nozzle from its rack, twisted a water valve on the pipe above it and re-entered the Ops room, dragging slack hose after him.

In a moment the hose stiffened under the water pressure and a gushing stream shot across the concrete floor, splashing up against the ankles of the sergeant, who whirled around as if stabbed.

"HEY!" he yelled. "What the goddam hell do you . . ."

He stopped in mid-sentence, his jaw dropping at the sight of a brigadier general striding about the room, busily hosing the floor. Savage made a thorough job of it, directing the stream of water under the chairs, in corners and under desks, until he had swept all of the rubbish, like driftwood, out into the hall. Then he switched off the valve and replaced the nozzle on its rack.

"Looks a little cleaner in here now, doesn't it, Sergeant?"

Gaping at Savage as though undecided whether or not he had a madman on his hands, Sergeant Coulter gulped and nodded.

"If I'd known the general was coming . . ."

"Never mind that. I'm here. But I don't suppose the Operations officer is."

"Major Hollomon had to go to town, sir."

"What for?"

"I believe he's getting a haircut in London, sir."

"Do you mean he's shacked up with a babe in Thetford?"

The sergeant was dumbfounded both by the directness and the accuracy of Savage's shot in the dark. But was it, the sergeant asked himself, a shot in the dark? Hesitating in a paroxysm of indecision, he finally decided not to take a chance.

"Yes, sir," he said.

"And the squadron commanders . . . are any of them on the station?"

"Major Cobb is here, sir. Over at the club."

"Where are the others?"

"If the general will pardon the expression," said Sergeant Coulter resignedly, "I believe they are shacked up somewhere too."

"I think we're getting to understand each other, Sergeant," said Savage. He sat down on one of the desks, dug into the musette bag at his waist and hauled out a box of crackers, a tin of Nes Cafe and a can of Spam. Reaching behind him, he lifted a small, red-painted fire hatchet from the wall and split open the can of Spam with one whack. "Missed my lunch," he continued. "Do you appreciate good coffee?"

"Yes, sir."

"Fine," said Savage, tossing him the Nes Cafe. "Whip up some good coffee for both of us."

Sergeant Coulter took the can over to a hot plate and set some water on to boil.

"I take it you're the Operations chief clerk," said Savage, munching crackers and Spam.

"Yes, sir," he said. "Sergeant Coulter."

"Glad to know you, Coulter. My name is Savage. I'm taking over the group." He went over and shook hands.

While the sergeant was groping for an appropriate reply, Harvey Stovall entered, stopping just inside the door in a puddle of water, with his arm raised in a rigid salute. His eyes were bloodshot, raindrops sparkled on his nose and he was out of breath, having sprinted all the way from the club as soon as the clerk had phoned him: "There's a crazy general wants you over in the Ops room right away."

Savage returned the salute.

"Major Stovall reporting as ordered, sir," he said, glancing up and down between the water and Savage. As Savage walked over to shake hands, Sergeant Coulter came to the rescue.

"This is our new commander, Major," he said. "General Savage."

"Very glad to meet you, sir," managed Stovall, shaking hands. "We weren't notified you were arriving, sir, or . . ." He stumbled like a schoolboy losing his place in a recitation, then recovered on a new tack. "The 918th," he said with forced brightness, "never hoped to get a general." Realizing that this didn't sound quite right, either, he lapsed into painful silence.

"Been drinking, Major?" asked Savage, who had smelled Stovall's breath.

"Yes, sir. I . . . I never had a drink in my life until three days ago."

Savage turned to Coulter. "Make another cup of coffee," he said. "Strong." Then he turned back to Stovall.

"I've got two jobs for you as soon as you've drunk your coffee," he said. "Number one, cancel all leaves and passes and make sure the squadron commanders are back here tonight. Send the M.P.'s out after the air exec and bring him in to me under arrest. Number two, set up a meeting for all combat crews in the Briefing room tomorrow morning at eight o'clock."

"The general wishes Colonel Gately actually arrested?"

Savage recognized a hint of profound satisfaction in Stovall's tone.

"Exactly," he said.

The adjutant saluted, executed a clumsy about-face and was starting through the door when Savage called him back.

"Your coffee, Major," he said, taking a cup from Coulter and handing it to Stovall.

"Yes, sir," said Stovall. "Of course, thank you, sir."

While the adjutant was gulping his steaming coffee, Savage went over to the Order of Battle blackboard and began studying the chalked names and figures which summarized the group's operational status. Stovall, his eyes on the soaking wet floor, seized the opportunity to question Sergeant Coulter. "What in hell is all this water doing in here, Sergeant?" he asked in a loud whisper. "And that mess out in the hall?"

Coulter lowered his voice. "The *general*," he said, "did it."

Annoyed, Stovall stared at the sergeant in complete disbelief.

"I asked you a serious question, Coulter," he said, a bit louder than he intended.

Savage turned around. "The sergeant isn't kidding, Major," he said. "And neither was I." He resumed his scrutiny of the blackboard.

Back in his new office an hour later, after taking advantage of the failing light to drive around the station, familiarize himself with its layout and insure that airplane guards were on the job at their widely dispersed hard-stands, Savage was attending to a number of papers that required immediate signatures. His mind was already crammed with matters that must be taken up with Henderson—valuable equipment and supplies that he had just seen stored in the open, exposed to the weather, not enough bomb trailers, a score of items. He still wore his trench coat, splotched with rain, giving the impression to Stovall, who now stepped through the doorway, that the walls of this office would see the new commander only on the run.

"Colonel Gately is outside, sir," said Stovall.

"Send him in," ordered Savage.

The adjutant disappeared.

Lieutenant Colonel Ben Gately's face, as he approached the desk, followed by an M.P., betrayed no consciousness of guilt. On the contrary, there was truculence in his eyes as he raised his hand in a salute. He was smarting from the indignity of having been arrested in front of Pamela at Desborough Hall, where he had stopped for a drink on his return from a spree in London. Savage noted the slight trembling in the air exec's fingers, attributing it, correctly, to a severe hangover. Ignoring Gately's salute, Savage dismissed the M.P. with a motion of his head and pressed a buzzer, summoning Stovall.

"Bring me Gately's Sixty-six dash One," he said. "Also the squadron commanders'."

While Stovall was getting the records, Gately lowered his right hand unobtrusively to his side. The truculence in his eyes became intensified. Continuing to disregard Gately, Savage went on signing papers until the adjutant returned with the 66-1's. Savage lifted the top form off the pile and settled back in his chair, studying the compact personal entries. Two minutes passed. Gately cleared his throat.

"General," he asked, "may I ask why I was brought in here under arrest?"

"No!" The word was a bullet.

Savage proceeded to examine the records before him. Finally Gately's eyes wandered up to the clock up on the wall behind Savage. Five minutes had passed. Gately assumed a relaxed position, with his hands on his hips, and cleared his throat again.

"May I sit down, sir?" he asked.

"No," said Savage sharply. "And stand at attention!"

Gately snapped to and remained at attention. Another five minutes crawled by. He craved a cigarette. Cold sweat beaded his forehead. Occasionally, slight shudders shook his body in mute evidence of the scope of his previous night's dissipation.

When, at last, Savage glanced up and nailed Gately with his eyes, the latter had the distinct feeling that he was looking into the face of a tiger. Actually there was at all times something leonine, not in Frank Savage's close-cropped head, but in the nose and eyes.

"You're the son of Lt. Gen. Tom Gately, aren't you?" he asked.

"Yes, sir."

"Fine officer. None better."

"Thank you, sir." Gately began to look somewhat relieved.

"Gately," he continued, "you, too, are a graduate of the United States Military Academy. You have nine years' service. And you were acting commander of this station as soon as Colonel Davenport left."

"Yes, sir. And I can explain—"

"Don't interrupt. Just listen. And answer questions. You've led only two missions with this group?"

"Yes, sir, not including re-calls and aborts."

"And you have more four-engine time and more bombardment experience than anyone else in the 918th."

Savage stood up, walked around and sat down on the front of his desk, never taking his eyes off Gately. When he spoke again his voice was charged with contempt and his eyes revealed unmistakable hatred.

"Gately," he said, speaking slowly, "you've made yourself an enemy. The bitterest enemy you'll ever have as long as you live." He hit his own chest with his forefinger.

"ME!" he said. "As far as I'm concerned, you're a lousy yellow dog. You're a traitor to your country, to West Point, to the uniform that I hate to share with vermin like you, to the 918th Group and to your father."

The air exec turned the color of wet ashes. Drops of sweat rolled down from his temples. His fists contracted into knots. He started to say something, but Savage cut him short.

"It would be easy for me to transfer you out," he continued. "And saddle some unsuspecting guy with a trained, professional soldier who has been willing to let a bunch of civilian school boys carry the brunt of the fighting instead of giving them the leadership they deserve—and *need*." He began to pace the floor, still riveting his eyes to Gately's, who now occasionally looked away.

"That's what you want. A cozy berth where you can sit out the war, preferably with a combat unit, where you can steal fake glory. *But I'm not going to pass the buck.*" He stopped directly in front of Gately. "You are going to stay right here. Where I can show you how much worse I hate you than a goddam Nazi—because you're supposed to be on our side. I'm going to burn you a new butt! I'm going to make you lay square eggs! I'm going to hold your head down in the mud and trample it. I'm going to make you wish you had never been born!"

Spotty color had returned to Gately's cheeks. He was shaking all over. Never in his life had anyone talked to him remotely like this, nor had he ever experienced the scalding sensation produced by the venom in each of Savage's words. But Savage was not through, although he returned to his desk and sat down.

"Meanwhile," he said, "you're going to do a lot of flying, Gately. You're going to make every mission until further notice. You're an airplane commander now, not an air exec. I'm going to give you an airplane and I want you to paint this name on the nose: Leper Colony. I'm going to handpick you a special crew. Men who have shown a predisposition for head colds and earaches. You're going to get a co-pilot who's all thumbs, a bombardier who can't hit his plate with his fork and a navigator who can't find his own navel." He paused. "Have you anything to say?"

"Yes, sir," said Gately in a strangled voice. "I have a right to a trial. And I have a right to prefer charges against *you*, sir, for personal abuse and exceeding your lawful authority."

Savage sprang to his feet.

"Stovall!" he called.

There was the bang of a chair being overturned and the Adjutant opened the door.

"Get me General Pritchard on the phone."

"Yes, sir." Stovall quickly withdrew.

"Rights, Gately?" said Savage, his voice shaking. *"Rights?* You've got a right to cable your father. He'd be goddam

proud of you. I'd like to kill you right now with my bare
hands. But I'm going to give you a break. Explain to General Pritchard where you've been since Tuesday. Explain de-
sertion of your post at a time when a Field Order might
have come down!"

The alarm which had transformed Gately's face at Savage's
mention of Pritchard now began to resemble panic. The air
exec struggled within himself for several moments, then
came to a decision.

"General Savage," he said. "I retract my statement."

Savage stared at Gately for several seconds.

"Stovall," he called again, "cancel that call." Then he said,
"That's all, Gately."

The latter saluted, about-faced shakily and left.

Savage felt weak, almost physically ill, after the air exec
had gone. Reaction to the violent emotions which had gripped
him now left him trembling. He had always hated to humil-
iate a man, dreaded having to fire a subordinate. But
against Gately, and all the Gatelys, he felt the ferocity of an
anger that had been accumulating for many months. Upon
one man he had felt compelled to vent his personal war
against complacency in the midst of what he believed to be a
fight to the death, in the most literal sense of the words.

Stovall walked in with more papers.

"Would the general like some supper brought over?" he
asked.

"No, thanks," said Savage, still trying to quiet himself
down. "I think I'll drop by the club for a beer, though.
How about you?"

"A lot of new poop just came in, sir," he said. "Maybe
I can get over later. Er . . . excuse me, General, but the insignia must have come loose on your trench coat."

Savage looked down at his shoulders, bare of insignia.

"To tell you the truth," he said, "I haven't got enough
pairs of stars to go around. Put that on your shopping list,
will you? Next time you're in London?"

"Certainly, sir," said Stovall. "If they'll sell stars to a
major."

"Hell, you look more like a general than I do."

"A little older, anyway," said Stovall tactfully.

Savage smiled, then picked up one of the 66-1's.

"Cut an order tonight," he said, "relieving Colonel Gately."

"Very well, sir."

"There won't be any immediate replacement, though, until I've had more time. He isn't the senior squadron commander, but Major Cobb's got the most impressive record here." He tapped the forms. "The most missions, the most decorations and the best efficiency reports."

"He's a strong officer, sir."

"I want the most aggressive we've got. How does he stack up in that respect, Stovall?"

"Major Cobb is certainly aggressive, sir."

Savage studied the adjutant a moment. "You seem to have some reservations about him," he said.

"Well, sir," said Stovall, scratching his head. "He has just one fault—that you ought to know about. He goes out of his way to pick fights when he's had a drink. It's gotten so everybody's afraid to go near him in the club. He's a big bruiser."

"H'm," said Savage, tapping his fingers on the desk. "How long has this been going on?"

"Just recently, sir. It started the last month, I'd say."

Savage rose and prepared to leave. "Thanks," he said. "I'll think it over."

Outside, the rain had stopped and a full moon bathed the driveway in cold light when Savage stepped through the door. A smartly uniformed soldier stepped from the shadows and saluted.

"General Savage?"

"Yes."

"I've been assigned as your driver, sir." He motioned toward a sedan.

"Fine," said Savage. Suddenly he looked more closely at the man, whose sleeves, bare of chevrons, proclaimed that he was a buck private.

"Aren't you the clerk I met in the adjutant's office this afternoon?"

"Yes, sir. Private McIllhenny."

Savage, struck by Major Stovall's adroitness in devising this stratagem, smiled in spite of himself.

"McIllhenny," he said, "I can't have a plain dogface private driving me around. Put those three stripes back on in the morning."

"Very good, sir," said McIllhenny.

"I'll walk over to the club, Sergeant. You can follow me there a little later." He set off without asking directions, for Archbury had an arrangement of administration buildings identical with Savage's old station at Middle Heath. As he marched along he had a warm feeling of being back on his home grounds.

Entering the club, he folded his flight cap, thrust it into his trench-coat pocket and walked to the lounge. He was standing at the entrance of a low-roofed, badly lighted room, smelling of the coal burning in a stove in the center and ugly with overstuffed and lopsided leather chairs, hollowed and shaped by the backs of many men. A half dozen fliers sprawled in a semicircle of easy chairs about the stove and nearly every part of the room was crowded except for the bar, where the only customer at the moment was a tall major, built like a fullback.

As Savage walked over to the bar, he was conscious of heads swiveling around, of faces looking up and of eyes concentrating upon him. Curious eyes. Unfriendly eyes. Savage felt terribly alone. The word, he thought, had spread. I know what they're thinking . . . Zimmermann . . . Davenport . . . damn generals . . . brass hats who cancel leaves. No one approached him. No one offered him a drink.

He reached the bar and ordered a beer. The major standing near him stared into his highball without glancing up. Savage noticed at once that the officer wore a black eye and a leather jacket stenciled J. R. COBB.

Savage had drunk half his beer when Cobb finally looked over. It was obvious that the highball he was drinking was not his first. A handsome kid, thought Savage, but on the tough side.

"Have a drink," said Cobb gruffly, brushing a cowlick of red hair out of his eyes.

"Thanks," said Savage mildly, "but I've got one."

"Beer." Cobb made a sour face. "English beer. Pour it back in the cow and have a *real* drink."

"Beer is okay with me."

"Have a Scotch on me," said Cobb, his enunciation sounding a little thicker when he raised his voice.

Savage resolved to give the red-haired officer unlimited rope.

"I'm doing all right," he said. "Save your money."

"You think I can't pay for a drink?"

"Sure. I know you can."

"Well, look at that," said Cobb. He pulled a wad of crumpled, white five-pound notes from his pocket. "I can buy and sell you. Have a drink."

"I'll finish my own drink, if you don't mind."

"I do mind," he said, his face darkening with belligerence. "You don't *like* me, *do* you?" he added.

"Sure, bub. You're okay."

"Well, I don't *like you!*" He took a gulp of his highball. "And don't call me *bub.*" For the first time he noticed the absence of insignia on Savage's shoulders. "What're you? A major?"

"No."

"Captain?"

"No."

"Well, you're a plenty old-looking lieutenant. You must be awful goddam dumb."

A score of spectators had begun edging toward the bar. Savage finished his beer and set the glass down without comment.

"What's it take to insult you, anyhow?" demanded Cobb. "I s'pose if I spit in your face you'll think it's raining . . . You yellow?"

"Nope."

"You wanna fight?"

Savage smiled faintly, his eyes flickering.

"You got yourself a playmate, Cobb," he said. "There's plenty of light outside." He strode to the door, followed eagerly by Cobb and by every man in the lounge. Most of them realized that this was their new commander, but none made a move to interfere as Savage and Cobb walked to a clear space in the car-parking area out front.

"Better take off that trench coat," said Cobb.

"Just start swinging," said Savage.

Cobb took the general at his word and evidently tried to

knock his adversary's head off flush at the shoulders with his first wicked swing. But Savage's left pushed him on the chest just hard enough to spoil Cobb's aim. Then Savage stepped in closer, driving both fists to his opponent's face in two nearly simultaneous punches that traveled barely ten inches. Cobb toppled backward. No one present was ever to forget how quickly Savage managed to spring forward and catch the other man by a handful of jacket, holding up his heavy, sagging body by the sheer strength of one wrist and hand to prevent the boy's head from striking the concrete. The contest was over in six seconds.

Savage pulled Cobb back upright, dazed, the fight gone out of him. He guided the groggy boy over to his car, where McIllhenny jumped out and opened the door.

"Get in there and wait until I come back," said Savage to Cobb. As he walked back to the club, the crowd of officers quickly parted, then followed him inside. He walked over to the radio, picked up the green Toby and carried it to the mantelpiece. He turned around, facing the roomful of officers.

"Give me your attention," he called out. The murmur of voices hushed. "This station is alerted from now until our next mission. That means hit the sack. The bar is closed until further notice." He walked to the door without glancing right or left, strode to his car and climbed into the back seat with Major Cobb, who was rubbing his jaw.

"One of the boys just tipped me off, General," said Cobb ruefully. "I'm awfully sorry, sir. I guess I'm just a damn fool when I've had a couple of drinks."

"That's right," said Savage. "You are."

Cobb smoothed his hair back. "Two thousand guys on the station," he groaned, "and I have to pick on a general. Well . . . that's the way my luck's been running. I'm glad I saved my second lieutenant's bars. But I hate the idea of leaving the group."

"You think you've got a pretty fair group here?"

"If you'll excuse me, General, them's fighting words. We've got the best goddam group in England! I know we have a black eye up at Bomber Command. But all we need is half a chance . . . And I've poured mine down the drain."

"Who said anything about busting you or transferring you? You trying to run my group for me?"

"No, sir."

"I'll admit you made a horse's ass of yourself, but your Sixty-six-dash-One says you're the best squadron commander in the 918th. So, effective tomorrow, you're the air exec of this group."

"Gee," said Cobb. "Gee, sir. I don't know what to say."

"There isn't a damn thing for you to say. Just cut out your drinking entirely. You can't handle it. Save your fighting for the Jerries."

At five minutes of eight the next morning, the Briefing room was packed with the men of the combat crews. The place buzzed with conversation, most of it about Savage and most of it uncomplimentary.

"Why did they have to send a general down here?"

"Who in hell does this guy think he is? Superman?"

"Stand by, men, for a good old-fashioned fight talk."

The predominant feeling of the crews was that Davenport had been relieved, unfairly, for complaining too loudly and too often on their behalf to superiors who weren't interested in complaints.

Chaplain Twombley, who had taken the liberty of attending uninvited, sat expectantly in a front-row seat, and near the rear door was the flight surgeon, sitting next to Harvey Stovall, who was waiting anxiously to call attention as soon as Savage should appear. Stovall was nervous. He had heard about the general's unconventional encounter at the club with Major Cobb, an event which had both impressed and puzzled the witnesses. Most felt that Cobb had had it coming to him for a long time and were glad to see somebody oblige. But Stovall knew that the boys were too far gone to be won over quickly by any spectacular act on the part of the new general. He prayed that Savage would have the discretion to handle this hard-boiled crew, whose sentiments were dangerously close to mutiny, with sensitive tact.

At one minute of eight, Savage entered.

"Ten-SHUN," called Stovall.

The men rose raggedly to their feet.

"Rest," said Savage, as he walked forward to the platform.

The crews sagged back into their chairs. Savage appeared to be fresh, although he had been up all night, looking into every nook and cranny of the station and poring over reports that X-rayed the 918th's status. Over in his quarters, his bags were still unpacked.

Savage waited until the shuffling of feet and chairs had died down. Then in a clear voice that carried well, he said:

"I'm Savage. Your new C.O." His eyes swept the room slowly, giving each man the impression that the general was looking directly at him. "The local weather is going to be okay today. At eleven o'clock there will be a briefing for a practice mission." He paused until a scattering of coughs had ceased.

"I was sent down here," he resumed, "to take over what has come to be regarded as a Hard Luck Group." He paused again. "I don't believe in hard luck." Savage was reaching deep inside himself to find the words to express his feelings. It was immediately apparent to the crews that he had prepared no pat speech in advance. "Hard luck doesn't win battles," he continued. "It doesn't get bombs on the target." Pause. "I'll tell you one reason why you've had hard luck. I could see it on your faces . . . at the club last night. I can see it there now. You're *sorry* for yourselves."

Stovall winced. A faint murmur passed over the assemblage.

"Why should *you* be the fall guys, you're asking yourselves. Well, who the hell else *is* there? We're *it*. This is the front line in the dirtiest, bloodiest war in history. We're fighting the most powerful air force and the greatest land army of all time. And the most fanatical enemy. In that kind of a fight somebody's going to get hurt. Us . . . you . . . me."

An electric silence gripped the room.

"Hitler is going to whip us unless someone goes out and licks him. If we fail to lick him, then we are turning over our wives and our children to rot in nazi concentration camps just as sure as hell. That is what has happened already to the people who haven't licked him. Unless a man is willing to have that happen in America, how can he be sorry that he is sitting in this room this morning? How can he think that his own life is important?" He stopped, concentrating on his next words.

"Fear is normal," he continued. "Go ahead and be afraid. But remember that the difference between being afraid to die, and quitting, is surrender. And I'm not going to surrender while I'm C.O. of the 918th. Forget about twenty-five missions . . . and getting home. Consider yourselves already dead. If any man here wants to save his hide, then he'd better make up his mind right now. Because I don't want him in the group. He can come and see me in my office. I'll be there in five minutes."

Savage jumped from the platform and started down the center aisle, head up, gray eyes flashing. Ordinarily someone would have called attention, but the men were frozen in their seats, transfixed by a mass reaction of furious resentment, not only for the mortifying implications of his words but for the deliberately antagonistic manner in which he had said them.

Savage's eyes roved from side to side of the room as he progressed toward the door, meeting row after row of angry eyes, challenging those eyes, defying them with the sheer fire of purpose in his own. His eyes said plainly: *I dare you! I'll take you on one at a time or the whole mob!*

As the general reached the door, a voice rang out, "I'll take Colonel Davenport." There was an instantaneous roar of assent, which echoed and burned in Savage's ears as he stepped outside and walked away.

Harvey Stovall was the first to rise. He had the feeling that he had better hurry over to his office before the line started forming at a door marked "C.O."

CHAPTER FIVE

Rally Point

When Stovall entered his office, he could see Savage already at his desk, signing papers with fierce concentration. Stovall sat down and went to work on the Morning Report, trying to check it in his usual methodical manner, but every few minutes his mind wandered and he found himself glancing apprehensively out the window. Except for Sergeant McIllhenny, industriously polishing the general's car, and the passing of an occasional bicycle or jeep, there was little activity in front of headquarters. No air crew members appeared.

The adjutant began to breathe easier. He carried the Morning Report in to Savage, who gave him a searching look.

"What are you sweating about, Harvey?" Savage asked.

"For a while, sir," said Stovall, "I expected trouble."

Savage merely snorted, then began perusing the Morning Report.

As Stovall returned to his desk, he was revising his estimate of Savage's psychological approach to the combat crews. Apparently, he mused, a splash of ice water in the face has its uses—like the effect of a slap on hysterical people. Then he heard footsteps coming down the hall. Lieutenant Jesse Bishop knocked and entered.

"I'd like to see General Savage," he said firmly.

"How about me?" asked Stovall. "Won't I do?"

"The general said he'd be in his office," said Bishop pointedly.

Stovall leaned back and looked the boy over for a moment. "*You*, Jesse?" he said sadly. He fiddled with his pen, screwing and unscrewing the cap. Then he swiveled his chair toward the window behind him, and without turning around, said: "Okay. Go on in."

Bishop walked up to Savage's desk and saluted.

"Lieutenant Bishop, sir."

"Shoot, Bishop."

"Sir, the airplane commanders picked me as their spokesman. They all want a transfer. The whole lot."

Savage's face hardened into rock. He gave Bishop a long stare. He had been primed to throw the book at a few malcontents, if necessary. But this was different, worse than anything he had foreseen. This was a total emergency. Bishop stared right back at him.

"My final act, Bishop," he said, "before I left Pinetree was to forward a recommendation for your Congressional Medal —for the mission your pilot was killed on." Perhaps more than anyone in the world, Savage had been qualified fully to understand the magnitude of the deed described in the masterfully understated official language of Bishop's citation. Never had he been more moved by the act of another human being. "I can understand why they chose you to come up here, Bishop," he continued.

"Maybe the recommendation had something to do with it," said Bishop. He could have truthfully added, except that he was unaware of the fact, that he was also the most popular man in the group. "We're not quitters, General Savage. We just want transfers."

Savage drummed his fingers on the desk blotter.

"So I wasted my breath this morning," he said firmly. "You think I was talking a lot of hot air."

"We've heard better fight talks," said Bishop, "from football coaches."

Savage stood up, eyes flashing.

"Go back and tell them," he said, "to put in their requests through squadron channels. But explain this, too. Until those requests are acted on, one way or the other, all of you are still on combat duty. You'll fly."

"Yes, sir. We understand that."

"Anything else?"

"No, sir."

"That's all, then."

Bishop saluted and left.

Savage, his forehead creased, strolled slowly into the adjutant's office and sat down on a corner of Stovall's desk.

"There *is* trouble," he said.

"I couldn't help overhearing," said Stovall.

"I'm glad you did," said Savage, "because your reaction is important to me. I want to know how *you* feel about this situation—where your sympathies are."

Stovall considered carefully before answering. He removed his glasses and polished the lenses with his handkerchief.

"My sympathies," he said at length, "are where they've always been. And always will be. With the 918th." He finished polishing his glasses and folded them on the desk. "I'm just a civilian," he continued. "A lawyer, sir. I took my biggest case when I came over to England. The 918th is my client. And I aim to see my client win its case." His usually mild eyes showed slow fire. "But in any event," he continued, "my sympathies don't matter! They sent you down here! You can count on me as long as you're in command!"

Stovall noted with surprise the relief that showed in the general's face. It had never occurred to him that so impregnably self-confident a type as Frank Savage should question the automatic loyalty of his gray-haired adjutant, no matter how disturbed Savage might be about the younger boys of the combat crews. He began to realize how deeply Savage must have been shaken by the visit of Bishop.

"In that case, Harvey," said Savage, "we'll get down to cases. As you put it, winning cases. A tough case takes a little time, doesn't it?"

"Yes, sir."

"This one will take at least a week for preparation. Maybe a little more. I'll need legal assistance."

"That's my specialty, General."

"All right. How long will it take the squadron adjutants to submit all those requests for transfers?"

"It's a lot of paper work, sir. Two or three days, anyway."

"And after the papers have reached you, how long before they'll be ready for my signature?"

Stovall's eyes crinkled in a shrewd look.

"Well, let's see, General," he said. "I've got a stack of monthly reports due about now. And I believe in thorough, methodical work—taking things in order. It might be three days before I could get around to those requests." He began filling his pipe. "A couple of days more to check them through. These squadron adjutants most always make mistakes. We don't want any paper going out from this headquarters not in the proper form—bad reflection on the group. My guess is that those requests for transfer will all have to go back to the squadrons to be done over."

"How long, then," asked Savage with a faint smile, "before you can have them ready for my signature?"

"Roughly, sir," said Stovall, "about ten days."

"That," said Savage, "is a hell of a way to run a railroad. You red-tape adjutants are all alike. But"—he rose and started back toward his desk—"why should I buck the system?"

There was a twinkle in Stovall's eye as he reached for a memorandum to the four squadrons, which he had just drafted, stipulating that all official communications must be acted upon within twenty-four hours. He was tossing the memorandum into his HOLD basket, instead of the OUT basket, when Majors Cobb and Kaiser appeared. The adjutant ushered them into Savage's office, introduced the flight surgeon to the general and withdrew.

"Good morning, Doc," said Savage. "How healthy are we this morning? Any casualties besides Cobb here?"

The new air exec looked sheepish, for an overnight shiner had bloomed to match the blue and yellow discoloration beneath his other eye. But Major Kaiser seemed to find nothing amusing in the general's question.

"Psychologically," said Kaiser, frowning earnestly, "the command is far from healthy." He hesitated before adding: "As I daresay the general will agree."

Savage nodded. "Know any pills that might help?" he asked.

"At the moment," said Kaiser, "I am somewhat too far out of my depth to venture a prognosis. But I shall observe the effect of the general's recent shock treatment with close interest."

Savage considered this a moment.

"How do we stand physically?" he asked.

"Nothing unusual to report, sir. We have thirty-two cases of mild inflammation of the upper respiratory tract."

"You mean thirty-two colds?"

"Well," Kaiser coughed gently, "yes, sir. Then there's Lieutenant Colonel Brown, the ground exec, sir. I believe we'd better ship him home. He has a lung condition that won't respond to treatment."

"Okay. And see what you can do, Major, to clean out the hospital. In general, if a man is strong enough to blink his eyes, I want him returned to duty."

"Yes, sir." Kaiser's face brightened.

"And before any flying personnel are grounded, I want you to bring each case to my personal attention."

"Very well, sir." Kaiser noticed that Major Cobb was boiling with impatience. "I'll be getting along, sir," he added, saluting. He left hurriedly, like a man with an immediate purpose.

"General," said Cobb, flushing with suppressed anger, "I

did my best to cool off those hotheads after you left. I tried to stop Bishop."

"Bishop," interrupted Savage, "spoke only of airplane commanders. How about the squadron commanders?"

"They were in on it too, sir. The damn fools ought to be busted to privates."

"I want no talk of busting anybody," said Savage. "For the time being we'll just sit tight."

"All right, sir," said Cobb. But he continued to radiate indignation. "The chumps," he continued. "I told them you didn't get that Silver Star of yours with a box of Crackerjacks, but for leading the first bomb group over Europe. It was a waste of time."

"Let me do the worrying here, Joe," said Savage soothingly. "I get paid for it." He forced a smile, rose and walked with Cobb toward the door. "I'll join you in the Ops room in a minute. Get this practice mission lined up, and put me in the lead ship with Gately. You take the briefing—I'll be a spectator."

"Yes, sir," said Cobb. Halfway through the door he stopped and turned around. "Oh, I forgot to tell you about Gately," he said. "He walked out of the meeting. Washed his hands of what was going on."

"Okay, okay," said Savage, a trifle impatiently. He continued on to Stovall's office.

"Harvey," said Savage, "I haven't met all the group staff yet. Call them in at ten hundred for a short meeting."

"Yes, sir." Stovall summoned a clerk and instructed him to broadcast the order over the Tannoy system.

"And another thing," continued Savage, "that needs attention right away. I want a new adjutant." Stovall looked like a ham actor giving an exaggerated double-take. "Any ideas for the right man?" added Savage.

"Well, sir," said Stovall, groping as though he had been clubbed on the head, "there's Captain Snodgrass. The best of the squadron adjutants. I think he could swing the job." He peered at Savage's poker face in stricken bewilderment.

"Cut an order assigning Snodgrass as group adjutant."

"Yes, sir."

"And cut another order relieving Brown as ground exec. He's going home. Replace him with the next senior officer."

"But," managed Stovall, seeing the light and weak with relief, "but that's *me*, sir."

"I can't help that," said Savage. He reached out and shook hands with his ground exec.

"You've got seven holes in your head, Harvey," he said seriously. "Now listen with all seven of them. Air discipline begins on the ground. That's your bailiwick. I want ground discipline here. Until somebody upstairs tells me the rules have been changed, you're going to answer to me for a strictly military organization at Archbury, composed of soldiers —not sad sacks."

"Very well, sir," said Stovall, involuntarily sucking in his gut.

LEPER COLONY stood out in freshly painted red letters on the nose of the B-17 squatting on Ben Gately's hard-stand. While waiting for Savage to appear, Gately was performing a final visual check of the airplane. He twirled the turbo wheels of the four superchargers under the wings, testing the rim of each wheel with his fingertip for unevenness of rotation. He examined the tires for cracks, thrust his right fist against the landing-gear strut, measuring the oleo piston for proper clearance, grabbed the props and shook them to check for play in the engine mounts and inspected the control surfaces. Already he had checked everything inside the airplane—guns, bomb bay, oxygen system, radio, fuel, ammunition—double checking the previous final inspection of the copilot. Finally satisfied, he called the crew together under the nose.

To the sullen combat men who faced him, it was clear that Gately was a changed man from the handsome, debonair air exec to whom they were accustomed. He was still handsome, but there was nothing debonair in his expression nor in the pinched look about his nostrils. Baxter, the copilot, who knew him best, recognized that Gately had been suffering, but he had no means of gauging the intensity of the white heat which had consumed Gately since his interview with Savage the evening before.

"Well, fellows," began Gately, "we're a fine-looking collection, aren't we?" Baxter noticed an unnatural quiver in Gately's voice. "Are you wondering what this is all about?"

"We sure are," said a gunner amidst a general chorus of assent.

"I can't tell you more than this," said Gately, "because I don't know myself. We're the 918th's new leper colony—just like it says on the nose. We're considered deadbeats." The nine faces of the boys around him stared with breathless curiosity. "Each one of you was assigned to me on the assumption that you didn't know your jobs. Or that if you knew them, you hadn't been cutting the mustard." There was more of a shake in Gately's voice now, gripped as it was with bitter emotion. "How do you like it?"

Nobody answered.

"*I* don't like it," continued Gately after a pause. "You won't either—the first mistake you make with me, General Savage is all set to climb on our backs and ride us with a pair of spurs. There's only one way to beat that kind of a deal. The Leper Colony isn't going to give him a chance. Understand? We're going to keep that blowtorch turned the other way." He looked slowly at each man, at nine different expressions, all of which, however, told him that there was no need for anything more to be said.

As he left the group and walked to the edge of the hardstand for a smoke, Gately was filled with the things he had *not* said. His fear that he was playing right into Savage's hands. What more could Savage ask than that he, Gately, should try to "show him"? The thought had tortured him through half of a sleepless night, but where was the alternative? The trap was tight. For the first time in his life Gately was obsessed with an ambition that blotted out all else—the ambition to get even with Savage, to contrive a terrible revenge. Everything must be sacrificed to that end, even if, on the surface, it should appear that Savage had succeeded perfectly in jacking up a weak officer. But, Gately had sworn to himself, this thing was going further than Savage had calculated. He would fight this upstart general with his own weapons, with a spotlessly clean record, with superior performance in combat. Waiting. Always waiting for the day to come when he could strike back. It was the only way.

At exactly one minute before time for "Stations," a staff car drove up and Frank Savage emerged. He was wearing a flight cap and a pair of flying coveralls, open at the throat, with sleeves rolled up above his tanned forearms. Lieutenant Baxter observed that there was no hair on Savage's chest, which was also tanned. How, he wondered, did Savage stay tanned in the winter? Taking his flight gear from Sergeant McIllhenny, Savage walked up to Gately. Both men's faces were blank.

"Everything set?" asked Savage.

"Yes, sir," shot back Gately with a little more than military sharpness.

"You fly this morning, Gately," said Savage. "I'll ride behind the seats or up in the top turret where I can see."

"Radio!" called Gately.

A sergeant sprang forward.

"Rig up an extension cord to the top turret so the general can talk on the Command set."

"Yes, sir."

The man hurried into the airplane, followed by the rest of the crew. As Savage walked forward from the waist to the flight deck, his eyes took in everything. Gately and Baxter were seated when Savage assumed his station behind them, glancing at his wrist watch from time to time until it was twenty seconds before Start Engines time.

"Energize one," ordered Gately.

Baxter pressed a switch. Out on the wing an inertia starter whined. Savage watched his sweep second hand.

"Five seconds," said Gately, "four seconds, three . . . two . . . hit three!" The Fort shook as number three engine spun and caught. In quick succession, Gately ordered: "Hit four . . . Hit two . . . Hit one!" The B-17 was alive, its four props pulling at the air.

Impressed by the smooth teamwork between pilot and co-pilot, and by the dexterity with switches and throttles of the copilot, whom Major Cobb had guaranteed to be all thumbs, Savage leaned toward Baxter's ear.

"Been practicing?" he asked.

"Yes, sir," said Baxter, blushing in spite of himself. How, he wondered, did the general know that he and Gately had put in a half hour of cockpit drill after the Briefing?

The rumble of twenty-one Forts, breaking into thunder directly above Archbury, brought Master Sergeant Tony Nero out of the Aero Repair hangar at a lumbering trot. Swarthy, black of fingernail, built down close to the ground along the lines of Mr. Five-by-Five, and clutching a spanner wrench in one hand, Nero shaded his large, good-natured eyes with the other hand. He frowned critically as he watched the three boxes of the stagger formation, in which many B-17's were far out of position, until the 918th Group was out of sight.

"Lousy!" he said aloud, squirting a stream of tobacco juice on the concrete. Then he turned toward the hangar to resume supervision of the removal of a wingtip assembly from the current Hangar Queen, which he was cannibalizing to keep other airplanes operational. But Nero's dissatisfaction with the stragglers who had made the group formation look ragged was tempered with personal pride that all twenty-one had gotten off the ground without mechanical trouble. Give me a little more of this bad weather, he thought, and I'll have enough airplanes flyable to keep this new general off my neck.

Two hours later, helping with an engine change out on one of the hard-stands, Sergeant Nero again looked up to watch the group returning directly over the field from its practice mission. He rubbed his eyes.

"Look at that, fellers," he cried to the other mechanics, as he watched the spectacle of every airplane up tight in position, even in the difficult third element of the high squadron. "Well, what do you know," he added with an ear-to-ear grin. "The layoff must've done 'em good."

"More likely," said a crew chief who had been one of the two men Savage had halted for not saluting on the road to the gate, "that iron-assed general has been chewing their tails up there."

The weather broke the following afternoon. Frank Savage was sitting in the bathtub in his quarters, with rusty water swirling around his hunched-up knees, when a shaft of red sunlight broke through the clouds in the west. Shortly afterward, a jeep skidded to a halt outside and Major Joe Cobb hurried in. Savage, rubbing himself down with a towel, met Cobb in the bedroom.

"We're alerted, sir," said Cobb.

Savage's reaction was instantaneous, as though Cobb had

abruptly presented him with one million dollars. A surge of electricity seemed to pass through him, illuminating his gray eyes. He held up his thumb and forefinger, as though he were measuring a one-inch shot of whisky.

"Jest right, Joe," he said. "Jest right!" He tossed his towel on the bed and grabbed a pair of shorts. "Start her rolling. I'll be right over."

"Roger." Cobb hustled out to his jeep and drove off. By the time Savage was leaving his quarters, Cobb had already set the 918th's machinery in motion. Men of the bomb dumps, of the gas trucks, of the kitchens, of the transportation section, of the military police, of the armament, engineering, flying-control tower, intelligence and operations sections were setting about their tasks with a will. Even Chaplain Twombley was affected. He made his usual arrangements to call in a priest for an early-morning Mass.

On his way to the Ops block, Savage stopped off at the club to set the green Toby on the mantel. The room was well-filled with fliers, in spite of the closed-down bar. As he walked through the lounge and back to the door, past men reading, writing letters and playing checkers and cards, Savage encountered no smiles of recognition, no sign of softening of the stubborn animosity in the faces which glanced up and looked away. Nor had he seen any reaction of excitement to his signal that the 918th was once again alerted for a mission. "So what?" their faces seemed to say.

After Savage had left the lounge, Jesse Bishop turned to Baxter, with whom he had been discussing the group's second practice mission that morning.

"Speaking of the devil," said Baxter.

"The weather *would* break," said Bishop, "before we've had time to transfer out from under that hot rock."

"Our requests went up from the squadron today," Baxter said.

"Don't hold your breath till they're approved," advised Bishop. The pair fell silent for a moment.

"I wonder," continued Bishop, "if Savage thinks he invented formation flying?"

"Stick your wingtip in the other fellow's cockpit," quoted Baxter sarcastically. "Why doesn't he try it himself for a few hours at twenty-five thousand feet instead of riding in the top turret?" Baxter and the rest of Gately's crew had spared no effort in spreading the word that Savage had proved to be a nonflying general.

"Why did we have to get a guy," said Bishop, "who won't even shoot a landing on a practice mission?"

A thin mist hovered above the runways, and the mud was frozen hard on each side of the perimeter track just before dawn the next morning, as Savage rode from hard-stand to hard-stand, where the tense crews huddled about small fires, blowing on their hands.

To each pilot he said substantially the same thing:

"I want all twenty-one ships to drop bombs on the sub pens at La Pallice today. Likely we'll get fighters going in. Every straggler they pick off means less bombs on the target. So show me how close you can stack yourself in there."

One pilot unwittingly summed it up for the rest when he turned to his copilot, as Savage drove off, and said: "I'll stick it in there, all right. But not for General Savage. How much of this mission is he going to see, anyway, hiding out in the radio compartment?"

Savage stopped last at Jesse Bishop's B-17, which had been assigned to lead the group. It was shortly before time to take stations. The crew were already aboard, and Bishop was in the pilot's seat, when Savage approached the waist door. Noting the words painted above it, WHERE ANGELS AND GENERALS FEAR TO TREAD, he squinted at the legend with a wry smile, then made his way forward to the cockpit. He tapped Bishop on the shoulder.

"Move over, Bub," he said. "That's *my* seat."

There was no necessity for Harvey Stovall to attend the critique which took place in the Briefing room four days later, but wild horses could not have kept him away. He occupied his usual seat near the rear, cocking his eye toward the door for Savage's arrival.

"Ten-SHUN!" The voice was not Stovall's, for a pilot sitting closer to the door had beaten him to it. As one man, the crews rose to their feet. An immediate silence, broken briefly when seats were resumed while Savage mounted the platform, hushed the room.

"Give me your attention," said Savage in the customary, but

in this case superfluous, Army usage. "I'm sorry we haven't been able to hold a critique after every mission. But with missions three days in a row, like we've just had, we'll have to lump it together in one critique. In case any of you guys are getting sleepy, you'll be glad to know that we're standing down tomorrow—everything's socked in from here to Denmark." He paused. "Tonight the bar's open again." He stopped again, waiting until a prolonged murmur of approval had died down.

"A word first about these critiques. I want them to be bitching sessions," he continued. "This is the place to bitch about anything that concerns the success of a mission, whether it's your airplane, your equipment, tactics, what somebody else did or didn't do or whether you think I screwed up in the way I've been leading these missions. There's no rank in here. Everything's to be forgotten when we leave this room. Your beefs won't do any good over in your quarters. Get them off your chest here—and anything goes. Then maybe something useful can be done about them." His eyes moved about the room like a machine gun tracking a moving target.

"Okay," he resumed. "The La Pallice mission first. I haven't got much to say about that one. The bombing was good. All ships reached the target. No losses. Very little battle damage." He paused again. "You know why? Because the formation looked like the picture book. The FW's passed us up. And went after those three other groups that were strung out. They took a look at the 918th and they weren't buying any. Let's keep it that way. Of course," he added as an afterthought, "that's tough on your gunners. You didn't get a chance for many claims that day, did you?" There was a flutter of dry laughter from the enlisted men.

"Okay, the Lille mission. Not so hot." He waited until a contagious cough, spreading to several other sufferers from colds, subsided. Harvey Stovall leaned forward attentively.

"Bombing just fair," Savage said. "And we didn't lose any airplanes. But we picked up a lot of battle damage from fighters, when the high squadron lagged half a mile behind the group entering the target area." He paused. *"Pettingill!"* he called.

"Yes, sir." A chubby-faced captain stood up.

"You were leading the high squadron. Explain what happened."

"You see, General," said Pettingill, "Bishop lost number-four engine when the FW's hit us near the initial point. He couldn't keep up with his element, so I dropped back to his speed to cover him."

"In other words," said Savage, "you jeopardized the whole group for one airplane. You violated group integrity for the sake of a buddy. To save ten men you endangered all the rest. What I mean by group integrity is that every gun is needed for the defensive fire power of the formation. We didn't dream up the stagger formation because it looks pretty, but because it places every airplane in a position where it is needed to defend the group. Crippled airplanes are expendable. Let them go. Let the Jerries shoot down your own brother. The thing that's never expendable is the obligation to get bombs on the target. From past mission reports, I've discovered that there was too much of the buddy stuff in the 918th before I came down here. Maybe you guys thought it was commendable. Heroic. I think it's unforgivable." Savage stopped to blow his nose.

"Ordinarily," he resumed, "I'll give a man a second chance. But not when group integrity is involved. Pettingill, I'm relieving you of command of your squadron, right now. And I'll take action on the spot against any other man who puts his buddies or his squadron ahead of the group. We're going to operate this group as one big squadron."

Pettingill, red in the face, slowly sat down.

"Who is Colonel Gately's copilot?" called Savage.

"Here, sir." A boy stood up. "Lieutenant Baxter."

"Baxter, you're promoted out of Gately's Leper Colony. Pettingill, you're busted down to a job as Gately's copilot." Amidst the buzz of comment that arose, Gately sat motionless, his eyes fixed straight ahead. This was the first time that Savage had singled him out in public. But Gately felt no humiliation. Only a deepening of the anger that glowed within him day and night. He had been waiting for Savage to lay it on, carrying out his threat, implementing the words "I'll hold your head down in the mud and tromple it." Now he felt vaguely relieved by the manner in which the whiplash had come. He couldn't catch me off base on my job, thought Gately, so the dirty skunk had to hit me this way —from behind.

"Getting back to the mission," said Savage, picking up a pointer and indicating a spot on the map behind him, "the high squadron mistook the Brest Peninsula for Land's End and started letting down into a lot of enemy flak. Luckily you all got home, but not without excessive and unnecessary flak damage. So we've got seven men in the hospital pulling shrapnel out of their butts with flak clippers. I admit that the weather was thick. But if you'd kept up with the group, that navigation error could have been avoided. Whoever the navigator was, he gets another chance. This time. But next time Gately will receive a new navigator for the Leper Colony." He looked toward the back of the room.

"Is the ground exec here?" Harvey Stovall rose.

"Harvey," said Savage, "the Lille mission concerns you, too. Have the billeting officer work up a complete reassignment of quarters. I want everybody to get a new roommate —somebody who isn't his pal. That ought to help each man here to get used to the idea that he has only one loyalty. The group."

"Very well, sir." Stovall sat down.

"All right. Today's mission. St. Nazaire. Bombing good. No losses. Battle damage slight. Same story as La Pallice. Our formation was tight so the fighters passed us up and concentrated on the other groups. Any comments? Any questions?"

No one spoke up.

"Well, I have," continued Savage. "Bombardier trouble. Hathaway! The strike photos show that you've been toggling late three missions in a row. Your bombs have been way over, plowing up fields, instead of landing in the target area. How about it?"

Lieutenant Hathaway got up slowly, scratching his head. Embarrassed and badly flustered, he blinked at Savage for a moment.

"Could I see the general about it after the critique?" he asked finally.

"What's wrong with now?"

The boy looked at the floor, still scratching his head, then faced the general with a trace of defiance.

"Well, General," he said, "it's those civilians down there. Too many civilians around the target—and most of them aren't German, either. General . . . I don't like killing civilians and smashing cathedrals." A pregnant silence followed the young bombardier's confession. More than one other bombardier, who secretly felt the same way, waited tensely for Savage's reaction.

"I'll say this for you," said Savage. "You're honest, Hathaway. But you're also a goddam fool. A hundred and forty million Americans are working twenty-four hours a day to manufacture bombs and bombers. Nine men risk their lives riding with you for the sole purpose of putting a thousand-pounder on an enemy installation. Men who have spent their whole lives in the Air Corps have selected that installation for attack. And *you* have the gall to nullify the whole thing by electing yourself as a committee of one to select a corn field. Who gave you that right? Nobody. Do you think you're being a humanitarian? If everybody in the Eighth Air Force was your kind of humanitarian, we could save lots of time by turning the world over to the humanitarians in Berlin . . . Gately?"

Gately stood up, but without answering.

"Here's a new bombardier for you."

Gately hesitated a moment and then sat down, still without answering.

"Anybody got something to bring up?" There was silence. "Next time I want there to be plenty of squawks. A real bitching session. Okay, then, that's all."

Savage gave Stovall and Cobb a lift in his car after the critique, for the air and ground execs occupied adjoining bedrooms in the C.O.'s block. Stovall was the first to speak as they drove through the rain.

"I've been waiting for the chance to tell you some news, sir," he said. Savage, lost in thought, seemed to jerk his attention to Stovall. "About those requests for transfers I sent back to the squadrons yesterday for correction."

"They're back on your desk again?" asked Savage quickly.

"No, sir." Stovall smiled. "Two of the adjutants have notified me by phone that several of the requests have been withdrawn."

Savage broke into the widest grin that Stovall had seen the

general permit himself since coming to Archbury. Savage reached over and slapped Cobb on the knee.

"How're we doing, Joe?" he said. "How're we doing?"

Cobb grinned back. Then, with his usual bluntness, he said: "I wouldn't say you're getting exactly popular, General. But three missions without a loss don't hurt any."

"I'll be happier yet," said Savage, "when these guys stop being so loss-conscious and get more bombing-conscious."

Stovall thought to himself: I'll be happier when they start loving this great guy, the way I do, instead of giving him grudging respect. He knew from bull sessions at the club that the crews had attributed the success of the first two missions to luck. But there had been no mistaking their changing attitude in the Briefing room after today's mission. He stole a look at Savage, who looked ten years younger than on the day he had arrived. He appeared intensely alive.

The phone was ringing when the three men entered Savage's quarters. Stovall answered it, then turned reluctantly to Savage.

"I spoke a little too soon, sir," he said. "One request for transfer just came back. Only one."

"Whose?" asked Savage.

"Jesse Bishop's."

Savage's exuberance evaporated. Moodily he poured three drinks and handed one to Stovall and Cobb.

"See if you can get hold of Bishop," he said. "I'll see him here."

When Bishop appeared fifteen minutes later, Cobb and Stovall immediately picked up their drinks and withdrew. Bishop, completely at ease, his blue eyes watching Savage calmly, stood waiting.

"Have a Scotch?" asked Savage.

"No, thank you, sir."

"Have a seat, then," said Savage.

Bishop sank into a chair rather unwillingly.

"Your request for transfer just came back up to headquarters, Bishop," said Savage. "Several officers have withdrawn theirs. It occurred to me that yours might have slipped through by mistake."

"There was no mistake, sir."

Savage tossed a few lumps of coal on the grate and stirred up the fire.

"Is it personal?" he asked. "Something you've got against me?"

"No, sir."

Savage waited for the boy to amplify his statement. But he began to see that it would be pulling teeth to loosen Bishop up.

"What do you expect to gain?" asked Savage. "A pilot with your record ought to have a good future with this outfit. Why change to another? It's all the same business."

"That's right, sir," said Bishop. "The same racket. That's why I want out. Not just to another group. They can put me in a tank. Or a foxhole. Just so I'm out of the Eighth Air Force."

"You want to quit *flying?*" demanded Savage.

"Yes, sir."

Savage took a sip of his drink and stared at the fire for some seconds.

"What's good about the ground forces?" he asked presently.

"When they fight, they fight Jerries. Or Japs."

"Now wait a minute," said Savage. "Don't tell me you're going to start talking like that bombardier—Hathaway."

"He's got something," said Bishop. "I don't like bombing French civilians, either. My mother is French. Born in Lille. I've bombed it twice. But that's not the main point."

"What is the point?"

"What's the use of my trying to tell a general?"

"You don't like generals, do you?"

"No, sir. I don't."

"Ever occur to you that there are different kinds of generals? Or that I was a lieutenant once?" He peeled off his blouse and threw it on the table. "There aren't any stars on me now," he continued. "Forget I'm a general. Tell me what's eating you."

"All right," said Bishop. "I'm not afraid of flying or combat or generals. But if I'm going to get killed I want a good reason. I don't believe the generals over here know what they're doing."

"How do you mean?"

"Take today. What good did I do? Bounced a bunch of

bombs off the roof of a sub pen without hardly denting it. The crews know we're not penetrating twelve feet of concrete. Why can't a general figure that out too?"

"I'm beginning to see what you mean," said Savage. "How many of you feel that way?"

"I'd say everybody. Officers and enlisted men. We came over here to bomb Germany. We want to know why we're not doing it. Instead of piddling around making phony headlines."

Savage got up and passed a cigar box to Bishop, which he declined, lighting a cigarette instead. The general disappeared for a moment, then returned with a pair of jodhpur boots. Seating himself, he began to hone one of the boots with a dog bone—a trick he had learned from his R.A.F. batman at Pinetree, who insisted there was nothing as good as a bone to bring out the full brilliance of a shiny boot.

"So you want to bomb Germany, Bishop," he said. "I'll bet you don't want to half as much as I do. The day won't come too soon to suit me." He scratched the back of his head with the bone. "How many of our small formations do you think would get to the target? When we don't have fighter escort, yet, to go all the way in with us? And how many do you think we'd get back? Don't you see we've got to walk before we can run, Bishop? Shallow penetrations into France are teaching us to walk. And we're hurting the enemy, too. Why else would he put up his best fighters and move extra flak guns in to stop us?" He rose and stood before the fire.

"I grant you sub pens are hard to hit. So we can't penetrate concrete. Still, we're learning what kinds of bombs it *will* take. And we're doing plenty of damage to machine shops and other installations around the pens. Any damage we do reduces ship sinking on the lifeline across the Atlantic. If the subs win, England will be starved in two weeks and we'll be fresh out of aviation gasoline. Then where are we? Christ, Bishop, give these dumb generals a little time!"

"Why *haven't* we gotten enough crews and airplanes to go in deeper?" shot back Bishop.

"Because we're fighting all over the world. Because there aren't enough to go around. Because every theater commander thinks the boil on his own neck is the biggest." Savage walked over and laid his hand on Bishop's shoulder.

From the quality of his voice when next he spoke he might have been a father talking to his son. This boy, to him, had subtly become a composite of American boys. Trustworthy, but resentful of authority. Courageous, but bewildered. Capable of brilliant effort, but starved for motivation. An emotion of affection, which Savage did not recognize as such, but nevertheless a welling of pure, paternal affection, rose inside him and dammed up salt moisture behind his eyes.

"String along with me," he said, his voice actually pleading. "You've done me a lot of good. I need to know how you feel. I need you in the outfit." He paused. "Won't you string along with me?"

Bishop looked away. He seemed about to say something, but then remained silent, staring at his knees.

"Look," said Savage. "Look, Bishop. Soon—sooner than you think, we're going to be putting up a hundred B-17's for every ten we've got now. Then three times that. And they'll be going to Germany. Berlin. Every part of the Reich. Before this is over you are going to look up and see the sky black with American bombers. A solid overcast of them." He moved away toward his chair, then swung around. "That's a promise. From me to you. And don't ever forget that I told you."

Bishop rose suddenly to his feet.

"My mind's made up, General," he said. "I don't go for any more promises. There've been too many of them already. All I want is a transfer."

Savage rubbed the bone back and forth on his boot several strokes before answering. Then he looked over sadly at Bishop.

"Let's be practical, Bishop," he said. "Even if I sent your request to higher headquarters, there wouldn't be a chance of its approval. They're not spending thirty thousand dollars training an airplane commander only to ship him to the Infantry. If you transfer, it's bound to be to another bomb group."

"That's no good," said Bishop. "I'll have to request to be grounded."

Savage made an effort to control himself.

"Dammit," he said, "don't you know where that would get you? You'd meet a Flying Evaluation Board and a Medical Board. They'd find nothing wrong with you. So you'd wind up right back here for disciplinary action. And that's ugly business. Nasty business. A Congressional Medal man winding up with a dishonorable discharge. Loss of citizenship."

Bishop reached for his cap and stopped at the door.

"If that's the only solution," he said, "I'll take it."

After Bishop had disappeared into the rain-swept darkness, Savage stood for a long minute at the open door, staring out. His eyes were troubled. But in his mind he was not yet discouraged. There was still an ace-in-the-hole. Bishop's crew. Just wait, he thought, until you try to face that crew of yours, Jesse! He returned to the fire and resumed his effort to improve the already perfect shine on his boots.

Jesse Bishop confided his decision to no one, least of all to his new copilot, Baxter, or, as Savage had guessed, to the members of his crew. Nor had he been able to steel himself to interview the flight surgeon. The simplest thing, he told himself, will be just not to show up for the next mission. And let matters take their course.

Two days later the issue faced him squarely at four o'clock in the morning in the form of Baxter's flashlight shining in his face.

"Shake the lead out of your butt," said Baxter. "Breakfast in fifteen minutes."

Bishop, who had been only half asleep, struggled up on his elbows. Now! he thought. Better tell him now and get it over with. But the words didn't come.

"Roger," he said, yawning. Baxter lingered near the door, insuring that Bishop didn't drop back off to sleep. The latter cursed inwardly: Damn him, why doesn't he go away and leave me alone! But Baxter winked the flashlight at him.

"Hit the deck, Jesse," he said. "Plant the palms of both feet on the floor."

Bishop swung his legs out of bed and sat up, whereupon Baxter disappeared. Having failed to make his decision cleanly, Bishop now felt himself at sea. There must be some way to postpone the inevitable a little longer. Suddenly he thought of a compromise. Occasionally, when he hadn't been sleeping well, he had attended Briefings even though he wasn't scheduled to fly. Okay, he'd get dressed, eat breakfast with the crew, sit in at the Briefing and get himself excused afterward. That would postpone having to tell Baxter for a while.

In the combat mess, drinking black coffee and eating fried eggs with the other crew members, his brain focused more sharply on his problem. He'd skip the Briefing. It would be much less painful. He tried to shut out of his mind the fact that Baxter would have to take over with a strange copilot. And Baxter was fairly new in the group, still green. What about that? And the gunners and the rest of the crew? They all believed that he, Jesse Bishop, could fly them safely back to base with four engines shot out.

Bishop was bucking what flight surgeons came to recognize during the war as the American trait which Hitler most grossly underestimated, or failed entirely to anticipate, in his analysis of decadent, undisciplined democracy. The trait was not courage, nor patriotism nor mechanical know-how. It was the extraordinary, nearly incredible lengths, demonstrated time and again, to which Americans would go rather than fail the other members of their team, whether it were the combat crew or called by some other name.

Torn with indecision, Bishop finished his breakfast and followed the others outside to the trucks waiting in the darkness to transport the crews to the Briefing room. *Quit vacillating,* he told himself. And then, purposely separating himself from Baxter in the confusion around the trucks, he set out, unnoticed, on foot for his quarters. With each step he felt relief, now that his choice was irrevocably taken.

He stretched out on his bunk and tried to slow down the fast thumping of his heart, unseeing, unthinking. In spite of himself he stole a look at the luminous dial of his wrist watch. It said 4:56. Four minutes until Briefing. Presently he looked again, feeling that ten minutes must have passed. But the minute hand had moved only two minutes. Why couldn't it already be an hour from now? Five hours? Tomorrow?

The next time he looked, the minute hand was pointing straight up. The Briefing had begun. Abruptly Bishop sprang from the bed. He made a frantic grab for his flight gear, rushed to the door, mounted his bicycle outside and pedaled madly through the blackness.

Jumping from his bicycle, he hurried into the hall outside

the Briefing room, where he could hear Savage's voice calling the roll of airplane commanders.

"Hammet!"

"Here, sir!"

"Todd!"

"Here, sir!"

"Wieback!"

"Here, sir!"

Bishop knew that Savage was getting near his name in the roll call. He hesitated, panting from his exertion, just outside the door. *He was still in time.* But somehow he couldn't move. His mind raced back and forth like an alternating current, between the pull of pánicky emotion which had catapulted him out of his quarters and the pull of his convictions, of his mental resolve.

"Cottrell!"

"Here, sir!"

"Bishop!" After a moment he heard Savage call out more sharply: "BISHOP!" There was another pause. Bishop still stood paralyzed, his heart rising up into his throat. The sound of his name, and the timbre of Savage's voice, burned him like a hot iron.

"Is Bishop's copilot here?"

"Here, sir!" It was Baxter's voice.

"Where is Bishop?"

"He's a little late, sir." At Baxter's next words, Bishop felt something explode inside him. *"I know he'll be here in a minute."*

"Cobb," said Savage, "have a stand-by ready, just in case."

But Bishop's hand was already on the doorknob. He turned it and stepped inside, searching with his eyes for the bench on which his crew usually sat. He spotted Baxter and walked up the side aisle. As he slid into his seat, Savage caught his eye for a brief instant. To Bishop the eyes said, as plainly as if Savage had shouted: "Thank God!"

But the rest of the crews only heard Savage say, with an uncharacteristic crack in his voice:

"Cancel the stand-by for Bishop."

"Lambert?"

"Here, sir!"

The Red Cross girls knew that something unprecedented was in the wind, after the mission, when they began handing out doughnuts, coffee and cigarettes to the boisterous combat crews trooping into the Interrogation room. The men were slapping each other on the back, shouting at each other between interrogation tables. Several intelligence officers, grinning broadly, threw up their hands and temporarily postponed further questions.

Halfway across the Channel, outward-bound, with thick clouds forcing the bomber stream from base altitude down to only four thousand feet, they had heard the Recall order from higher headquarters. They had seen the four other groups turn around and set course for home base. And they had seen General Savage, in the lead ship of the 918th, continue leading them toward the enemy coast, apparently ignoring the Recall. They had seen the cloud ceiling lift until Savage eventually climbed them back to twenty-one thousand feet in time for the bombing run over the railway marshaling yards at Liége. The target had been open. They had seen their bursts mushroom about the aiming point. And then they had all come safely home.

The 918th, all alone, had gotten through to the target.

Amidst the din of jubilation, Savage was speaking on the telephone to the Operations officer at Bomber Command, giving him a flash report on the mission. Savage was leaning with his back against the wall, his cap tilted back on his head, his face weary but happy and in his hand he held a drying print of the target strike photograph, which the photo officer had just rushed over to him from the darkroom.

"From the first strike photo," Savage was saying, "it looks like we clobbered the M.P.I. . . . Yeah, about six tenths cloud cover. Five minutes later would have been too late." He listened to a question from the other end. "No, only half a dozen fighters . . . Me-109's. Soup was too thick for them, I guess." He said "yes" several times, then hung up.

"Ten-SHUN!"

The clamor in the room died away as General Ed Henderson walked in.

"Carry on!" he called, then went over to Savage. The men who had been milling around near Savage drew back a bit. But the noise did not resume its former level.

"Well, Frank," said Henderson in a voice that could be overheard, "I see you've got a picture there already." He eagerly examined the strike photo which Savage handed him. "Beautiful," he said. "Beautiful. But jumping Jesus, you shortened my life ten years! Didn't you hear the Recall?"

Savage looked Henderson straight in the eye without blinking.

"No, Ed," he said, "I didn't hear any Recall."

"Were you guarding Channel 'B'?"

"Sure. All I got was gibberish the whole way. My radio operator had trouble, too, on the Liaison set. Bad tube."

Overhearing this, Savage's radio-operator gunner recalled with an inward smile how the general had opened the receiver cabinet right after they landed and had accidentally on purpose broken a tube with his fist. Henderson glanced about the room.

"Anybody hear the Recall?" he asked in the direction of the men standing nearest.

"No, sir," answered several fliers simultaneously, shaking their heads and regarding Henderson with wide-eyed innocence.

Then Ben Gately stepped forward.

"I heard the Recall, General," he said. "Clear as a bell."

"What position were you flying?"

"Deputy leader, sir. On General Savage's wing."

"Couldn't you relay the message, Gately? Or attract his attention?"

"I tried to, sir. Several times. But I couldn't get any response."

During this conversation, Gately avoided meeting Savage's eyes, which were aimed at him like gun barrels. Jesse Bishop, who had witnessed the scene from the background, realized his coffee mug was shaking when the hot liquid spilled over and stung the back of his hand.

"Well, Gately," said Henderson, dropping his tone of interrogation, "I guess it's just one of those things." He installed a beaming smile on his face like a man putting on his hat, and confronted the sea of faces in the room.

"Congratulations to all of you," he called. "Fine job today." Then turning to Savage, he said: "Can I give you a lift to the office?"

Savage followed Henderson from the Interrogation room, looking back at the door to wave casually to the crews. They waved back with gleeful gestures, some clasping both hands above their heads.

Savage could see overt proof that his deliberate gamble in ignoring the Recall had paid off. Psychologically, the 918th had turned the corner.

Thirty minutes later, approaching the club on his bicycle, Bishop changed his direction and rode across the Admin site to headquarters. Harvey Stovall greeted him outside the general's office with a hearty handshake.

"What a day, Jesse!" he cried. "A red-letter day in the history of the 918th and the Eighth Air Force. Lord, will those other groups be burned up. I guess we showed them how to put this business on a paying basis!" He continued to pump Bishop's hand. "Great going there, boy!"

Bishop responded to the warmth in Stovall's congratulations, but his smile had reservations in it.

"Is the Old Man busy?" he asked.

"Can't you hear?" said Stovall. Even through the closed door to Savage's office, Henderson's raised voice was plainly audible.

"Goddamit!" he was saying angrily. "You might have lost the whole group. Aside from that, what am I supposed to tell the other group commanders? They obeyed orders. Then you made them look like chumps while the 918th become heroes. General Pritchard called me four times from London——half out of his mind!"

Bishop and Stovall, exchanging glances, continued to eavesdrop from the outer office.

"I can't be expected to run a big show," continued Henderson, "if my commands are ignored by a grandstand artist."

There was a considerable pause. Then Savage spoke.

"You have my official statement," he said, "that I didn't hear the Recall. And I'm getting tired of repeating it. But you might as well know *this*. Any time my judgment tells me I can get through to a target, I'm going on through, Recall or no Recall."

There was another long pause. Bishop could picture Henderson's frustration.

"Very interesting, Savage," said Henderson at last in a

lower voice. "We'll see about that." He coughed. "And one more thing," he continued. "What sort of a screwy deal is this you've been giving Colonel Gately?"

"Did he call you up?" asked Savage sharply.

"No," said Henderson. "My air inspector reports that you're carrying a regular-army lieutenant colonel in an airplane commander's job."

"The air inspector has no kick coming," said Savage, "as long as the group as a whole has no overages in grade. If I want to be technical, I can carry him temporarily unassigned."

"Your treatment of an officer of Gately's rank and background strikes me as shortsighted. You know his father's in a key spot. There can be serious repercussions. We need airplanes! To get them we need friends in Washington! Not enemies!"

"I'm responsible to you for results," snapped Savage. "As long as I give you results, my methods in this group are my own responsibility. You know that as well as I do."

"I can use Gately up at my headquarters, if you'll approve a transfer," persisted Henderson.

"Gately," said Savage, "is not available to fly a desk. He's got a job to do in this group."

The phone rang on Stovall's desk and, while Stovall talked, Bishop was unable to hear the conclusion of the conversation in the next room. But a minute later he watched Henderson come striding out and down the hall in high dudgeon. Without interrupting his phone conversation, Stovall motioned Bishop toward the general's office. When Bishop knocked, Savage looked up from his desk with a swift transition from the scowl on his face to a quizzical look of eager anticipation.

"What're you waiting on?" he called.

Bishop approached the desk self-consciously, and saluted. "General," he said, "would you mind very much kicking me in the tail?"

Deliberately he turned around and bent over. Savage immediately arose, moved around behind Bishop, swung his boot back and planted it squarely on the seat of the boy's pants. Recovering his balance, Bishop straightened up, turned around and faced Savage with a flushed smile.

"Sir," he said, "I'm awful hard to convince. I'll never know why it took until today for you to convince me. And the rest of us. But from now on you can tell me black is white . . . and I'll believe it."

"All right, Jesse," said Savage, "let's start now. I want you to be the one guy in the group that doesn't believe I'm a general. That door is always open. Any time you think I'm not doing so hot, come in and tell me. Let me know what the boys are thinking. I need you plenty, and I'll count on you to keep me straightened out. Okay, Jesse?"

At Pinetree, the chief of staff handed Henderson a teletype message which read in part: ". . . and convey my commendation to the Commander and all the members of the 918th Bombardment Group for a superb display of leadership, tenacity and skill in surmounting extremely adverse conditions to reach and bomb today's target. Signed, Pritchard."

"Shall I add the usual congratulations from us?" asked the chief of staff.

"Just forward it marked 'noted,'" said Henderson. When the officer had withdrawn, Henderson read the message once more. Then he crumpled it up and threw it into the wastebasket.

CHAPTER SIX

Pamela

When Captain Snodgrass, the adjutant, ushered two newly assigned Red Cross girls in to meet Savage, he observed that the Old Man looked rested and chipper. Savage chatted with the girls for several minutes, welcoming them to the station and agreeing with them that their first concern should be the welfare of the enlisted men, rather than with romantically inclined officers.

One of the girls was pretty, the other definitely homely, but as his visitors were leaving Savage noticed that the homely girl had interesting legs. Suddenly he remembered that for an infinity he had not once thought about a girl. It was a rediscovery of a vital part of himself that had been numbed into oblivion by the pressure of his job. A thrill, almost like a twinge of pain, shot through him, and he felt a spark of gratitude toward the homely girl with the legs for reminding him that there were still women in the world.

Later in the morning, after Savage had made a dent in the stack of IN basket papers that betrayed his recent neglect of office routine, Harvey Stovall stepped into the room from his new ground exec's sanctum.

"A flight lieutenant to see you, sir," he said.

"I'm busy as hell, Harvey. You take care of it."

"If the general insists," said Stovall blandly, "but . . ."

"I do insist," said Savage, trying not to interrupt his concentration on a new list of lead navigators.

"Very well, sir, I'll try to put her off."

Savage picked up his pencil to resume work, then slammed it down.

"Did you say *her*?" he called to the retreating Stovall.

"Yes, sir. Flight Leftenant Pamela Mallory."

"Well, for Christ sake," snapped Savage, "don't stand there! Show her in!" He stood up briskly, straightening his tie, then added, "No. Hold it. I'll be right there."

He hurried to Stovall's office, cordiality sticking out all over him. Pamela Mallory met him with a formal salute, which he returned. They shook hands.

"Come right in," he said pleasantly. "Good to see you again, *Flight Leftenant*."

"Thank you, *Colonel*." She smiled faintly.

"Don't tell me," he continued, as he showed her to a chair, "why you're here. I'm way ahead of you. Enemy fighter reactions. Or do you want a true copy of Roosevelt's directive to General Marshall?" He noticed that Stovall was still lingering at the other corner of the desk, openly admiring the girl's unmistakably aristocratic, English features, and intrigued by the suave change which had come over the general. The guy, Stovall was thinking, knows how to turn on the charm like a floodlight. I might have known it.

"Major," said Savage, "I'll ring for you if I need you." Stovall made a little bow to Pamela and strode decorously to his office.

"Actually," said Pamela, "I came on quite a different matter. But since you mention it, I have been wondering if you ever did anything about the subject of our last conversation."

"Sure I did. Got General Henderson to put out a feeler to Air Ministry next day . . ."

"And nothing came of it."

"Well—you know how it is. They shipped me down here to the sticks, so I've been kind of out of touch." He offered her a cigarette in order to change the subject.

"I feel guilty as hell," he apologized, "for not having called you at Desborough Hall. Please explain to Lord and Lady Desborough that . . ."

"They understand perfectly; we know you haven't had a spare minute. When you get a breather, they'll be delighted to see you. And so will I . . . I often get home on weekends. We've had masses of your chaps from the 918th dropping in. We're really quite fond of you."

"They're not a bad bunch," said Savage. "By the way, I understand that this airdrome is on your estate. Stovall tells me that your father had rubble from Coventry carted all the way here for our runways. I think that's swell."

He could see that she was enjoying the real tobacco in her cigarette, by contrast with wartime English brands.

"Father's not a bad type," she agreed.

"I'm convinced of that," he said pointedly. She cocked an eyebrow at him. "The runway," he added hastily, "a kind of poetic touch. No, I guess symbolic is the word. I'm really looking forward to meeting your father." He fired up the cigar that had gone out in his ashtray. "Tell him I'll think of Coventry every time I shoot a landing."

He thought he could detect that Pamela was moved. He was correct, but he did not know that Coventry held an additional significance for the girl. On the night of that raid she had lost Eric, a Beaufighter pilot. While Savage had been talking, it had occurred to her that not since Eric's death had ended their brief romance had she been so conscious of a powerful attraction to any man.

"I'm glad that you appreciate father's gesture to the Americans," she said, then adopted a more businesslike tone. "Quite apart from the social amenities," she said, "I came to see you on an official matter."

Pamela noticed the familiar look of skepticism appear in Savage's eyes.

"First," he said, laying a pack of cigarettes in her lap, "I want you to accept these. No arguments."

"Really, I shouldn't," she protested.

"Bunk!" said Savage.

"I shan't row about it," she said. "I quite understand that you're a forceful type."

Savage's eyes clouded for the first time during the interview, as the Gately incident crossed his mind.

"I'd best get on with it," she continued. "What I came to see you about is rather a delicate matter."

"Okay," he said. "I don't bruise easily."

Pamela hesitated for several seconds.

"Unfortunately," she said, "your ruddy American sergeants are much too persuasive. I sometimes think we should be better off if we'd had the damn Germans."

He shook a finger at her. "Watch that stuff," he grinned. "We send guys home on the next boat for goosing our British allies."

Pamela's eyes opened wide. "What an extraordinary expression!" she exclaimed.

"*You* know," explained Savage. "It means *needling*."

"Try me again," she said.

"Ribbing."

"One more chance?"

"Riding."

"It's no use," she said, smiling in spite of herself. "But you're putting me off. There is one of your bodies I wish they'd sent home long ago. Before . . . you see . . . one of my corporals is in serious trouble."

She regarded Savage expectantly, as though he should help her out. But he merely gazed at her politely.

"A sergeant of yours is responsible for her being P.W.O.P.," she continued.

Savage gaped at her.

"What in hell," he asked, "is P.W.O.P.?"

"It's an R.A.F. abbreviation," she said, coloring a trifle, in spite of her air of being matter of fact, "for Pregnant Without Official Permission."

The general struggled to suppress a laugh, but failed.

"You're kidding," he said. "You don't mean there actually *is* such a regulation."

"Of course," she said frostily. "And we think there is nothing humorous about it, General. Our married W.A.A.F.'s are required to apply for official permission before they can ... increase their families."

Savage pondered this a moment.

"Does our case involve a married woman?"

"No. That's the bind. Corporal Lambeth is not married."

"Then," said Savage, "I can't see how this F.O.B. regulation, or whatever you call it, applies."

Pamela stiffened. "P.W.O.P.," she corrected him.

Savage laughed afresh.

"That beats me," he said.

"Pregnancy," she said, bridling, "is not a laughing matter, General. The regulation, of course, applies whether she's married or single."

"Okay, Flight Leftenant." Then turning official in his own tone, he said: "On which of my sergeants has the Lambeth woman put the finger?"

"I beg your pardon," said Pamela coldly, nonplussed.

"Who is the guilty sergeant?" amended Savage.

"An orangutan," she said bitingly, "named McIllhenny."

"Well, I'll be damned," said Savage, startled, then added half to himself: "How does the guy find the time?"

Pamela bit her lip.

"General Savage," she said, "the child may arrive at any time. I should have taken the matter up months ago had I known the father's identity. I want you to do something about it."

"From what you tell me," said Savage, poker-faced, "there's been too much done about it already."

Now it was Pamela's turn to smother a smile.

Savage's eyes twinkled at her. "What," he asked, "do you expect me to do?"

"I think you should order him to marry her."

"H'm," said Savage, considering his fingernails. "Tell me, Flight Leftenant, was there any force involved in this case ... that a court-martial could construe as rape?"

Pamela avoided his eyes.

"On the contrary," she said, clearing her throat, "I gather that this wretched girl is very much in love with him."

"And McIllhenny?"

"He appears to be a bit shy. That's why I believe you should use your authority."

"Let's be realistic," said Savage. "I can order a man to go out and get killed. But not to marry. Don't you think that's carrying obedience too far?"

"I do not," said Pamela. "You sound as though you consider marriage a dreadful thing, General. Don't you believe in marriage?"

"I'll go with you halfway," he said. "It's okay for women."

It was hard for Savage to judge from her expression whether Pamela was merely annoyed or slightly baffled. He was enjoying himself intensely, his pulse quickening with anticipation. This girl was going to make an exciting quarry.

"I take it the general is not married," she said after a pause.

"Correct," he said.

"Never?"

"Never," he answered.

She looked at him with genuine curiosity.

"Haven't you ever been in love?" she asked.

Now it was Savage's turn to feel disconcerted by the suddenness with which his lady visitor had strayed from the main topic, and by the personal nature of the question.

"Love?" he said finally. "What is it, anyway? I wouldn't know. Frankly, I'm a very enthusiastic admirer of your sex. But I believe that ninety-five per cent of the human race would never fall in love if they hadn't heard so damn much about it."

"How clever of you," she said. "You haven't been reading Thoreau, by any chance?"

"I do my own research," said Savage.

Pamela stood up.

"This has been most instructive," she said, "but a bit beside the point. So you refuse to intervene with Sergeant McIllhenny?"

"It strikes me," said Savage, rising also, "that you're taking too dim a view, as the English put it, about this case. Millions of people are being killed every day in the war. And millions of babies are being born. Frankly I don't think a mutually agreeable roll in the hay is too important."

Inwardly, Pamela recoiled at the words. All of the emotions which had been attracting her toward Savage, all of the inner excitement of anticipation that some wonderful thing might come of their meeting, deserted her in an instant. Keen disappointment replaced these feelings—disappointment that Savage, whose personal impact had given her a brand-new experience, was just another one-night-stander.

"Is that your official attitude?" she asked.

He caught the change in her voice.

"Official and personal attitudes are hard to separate, sometimes," he said. He stood there troubled, feeling as though a warm fireplace had suddenly been doused with cold water.

"Of course," he added uncertainly, "I can bust McIllhenny, for an unseemly contribution to Anglo-American relations. That's my best offer."

"Fine lot of good that will do," she said, omitting to extend her hand in goodbye. "Although he richly deserves it. Now I must be getting along. Good day, General."

Savage accompanied her to her car, noticing that she was not quite so tall as he.

"When am I going to see you?" he asked, opening the car door and helping her in.

"The 918th," she answered, "is welcome any time at Desborough Hall. Mother is always there."

Savage stared after her car as she drove away, then returned to find Stovall placing some fresh papers on his desk. The latter looked up and regarded him with a quizzical expression.

"May I borrow a British phrase, sir?" he asked. "And remark that . . . you've had it?"

"You're an eavesdropper, Harvey."

"That door isn't soundproof, General."

"You're right," said Savage. "As of the moment, I've had it. But I still think I'd find a lot of company in the position I took."

"That's the trouble," said Stovall. "She's not interested in the ordinary." He lifted some papers from Savage's OUT basket. "You picked the wrong girl," he concluded, "to try to convince that a roll in the hay isn't important."

"Come in, Sergeant," said Savage.

McIllhenny, who in addition to his driving duties had resumed his clerical work in the adjutant's office, had just been summoned to the general's office by Stovall.

"I've had an official complaint against you, McIllhenny," he said, "from the Royal Air Force."

McIllhenny looked blank.

"Did you, or did you not," asked Savage, "knock up a W.A.A.F.?"

"I'm afraid I did, sir," said McIllhenny without hesitation. "But it was a long time ago, sir. Before I was transferred to this group."

"You should have transferred to Hawaii," said Savage. "Before I forget it, McIllhenny, I want to thank you for those eggs you scrounged for my breakfast this morning."

"Did the general find them fresh?"

"Right out of the hen."

"I am pleased that the general enjoyed them."

"Thanks. Now to get back to this business. Your offense is serious. Anything that causes friction with our Allies is serious."

"Yes, sir."

"Tell Captain Snodgrass to cut an order this morning reducing you to private."

"First class, sir?"

"You heard me. *Private!*"

"Yes, sir. I'll type the order up for the captain immediately, sir. Will there be anything else?"

"No."

"Very well, sir."

"Persons decorated," called General Pritchard, "join the reviewing party!"

Simultaneously, Harvey Stovall, facing the solid ranks of the 918th drawn up in parade formation on the ramp in front of the Aero Repair hangar, shouted the command: "Pass in review!"

Jesse Bishop, wearing the Congressional Medal of Honor around his neck, was the first to join the reviewing party, consisting of Pritchard, Henderson and a pair of high-ranking R.A.F. officers. Pamela and her family stood with a delegation from the village composed of the mayor and other local dignitaries.

Next, Savage, who had just received an Oak Leaf Cluster to his Silver Star, took his place at Bishop's left. He was followed by Major Cobb and three other officers with D.F.C.'s and several gunners with D.F.C.'s, Purple Hearts and Air Medals.

The small band made its blaring circuit past the reviewing party, and Savage's heart beat hard as the four squadrons marched smartly past. Harvey Stovall, he reflected, had done a good job of organizing a decoration ceremony on quick notice. Whatever the 918th lacked in the matter of creased slacks, it compensated for in the snap and precision which arose from its collective pride in having a Medal of Honor winner in its midst, and in the Silver Star that had been bestowed on its commander for the mission on which the 918th had been the only group to reach the target.

When it was over, Henderson was the first to rush over to Savage and shake his hand, just ahead of Pritchard.

"Keep it up, Frank," said Henderson with an edged smile on his sallow face. "Just keep this up and you'll be the most decorated man in the air forces."

Savage smiled back with a cool, detached expression that said to Henderson: Thanks for a snide crack. After accepting Pritchard's congratulations, Savage regarded Henderson through narrowed eyelids.

"By the way, Ed," he said. "We must be nearly ripe for that first strike into Germany."

Henderson glanced at Pritchard, who took the cue.

"That's right, Frank," he said. "Very soon, I think."

"In that case," said Savage to Henderson, "I want your permission, in advance, to fly that one."

Pritchard glanced from Savage over to Henderson, who saw at once that his superior was puzzled.

"Something Frank and I have discussed on the phone," Henderson explained hastily, with a disarming smile. "I've become increasingly aware, General, of my responsibility to . . . shall we say . . . protect General Savage from himself."

Pritchard studied his two subordinates alternately for a moment.

"Frank isn't to lead missions without your permission?" he asked.

"Well, sir," said Henderson smoothly, "you might say I believe it's time to put him on a ration. He won't be doing us any good as a PW in Stalagluft Three."

Pritchard reinserted the cigar fixture he had been forced, reluctantly, to remove for the decoration ceremony and lighted up.

"Perhaps that's wise," he said, then turned to Savage. "You can't make every mission, you know."

"Naturally, sir," said Savage. "Matter of fact I've skipped the last two or three. But I've got to be free to go when I think I should."

"You two," said Pritchard, "ought to be able to thresh that out. I'm sure Ed won't tie your hands, Frank. But he has a good point."

Savage felt somewhat relieved, but not entirely. He had hoped Pritchard would give clearer evidence that he knew a fighting outfit couldn't be led from behind a desk. Henderson, stroking the side of his shinily shaved chin with his fingertip, said nothing. Savage stared at him.

"Well?" he asked. "How about Germany?"

While Henderson hesitated, Pritchard slapped a hand on the bomber commander's shoulder.

"Hell, Ed," he said jovially, "we both know Frank ought to lead the air force on that first one to Germany."

"No argument about that, sir," said Henderson promptly.

As the group of three broke up, Pamela walked over to Savage, smiling rather shyly.

"Congratulations," she said, "on the gong."

"Thanks," he said.

Pamela touched the red, white and blue ribbon.

"Beautiful," she murmured. "And it really means something. Something we can both agree is important." She was looking straight in his eyes. Before he could think of an answer, she said, "Cheerio," gave him a little salute and was gone.

Driving toward the mess for lunch, Savage passed a cyclist whom he recognized through his rear window as Jesse Bishop. Savage asked Private McIllhenny to stop. Then he alighted and stood in the middle of the road, at rigid attention, with his hand raised in the salute appropriate even from a five-star general to the lowest-ranking private, if the latter wore a pale blue ribbon with white stars on it.

Bishop had thrust his Medal of Honor in a pocket of his blouse, but as he approached, it was obvious that he was as self-conscious as if he had been wearing a blinking neon sign. When he came up to Savage, Bishop raised his right hand from the handlebars to return the salute, his face smiling but scarlet with embarrassment. Savage maintained a perfectly straight face, as Bishop pedaled hastily by, almost losing control of his teetering mount.

Refreshed from a long, deep sleep, Savage arose at dawn, slipped into his bathrobe and shuffled down the hall of the C.O.'s block to the bathroom, first thrusting his head into the small bedroom assigned to Private McIllhenny. But the general's driver was already up and gone, nor was he visible in the vicinity of the car parked outside. Savage shaved leisurely, dressed quickly and, having heard Major Cobb, tapped on his door.

"Coming right up," said Cobb. A minute later the pair, preferring exercise to taking the car, set out afoot on the quarter-mile walk to the mess. A cold, butter-colored sun hit them level in the face as they strode along gulping the frosty December air, which hinted of snow.

"Maybe we'll rate a white Christmas," said Cobb, surprising Savage into the reminder that Christmas was only two weeks away.

"Sergeant Nero'd rather have a green one," he answered, thinking of the crew chiefs who had to work in freezing weather out in the open. As they walked along in step and in silence, Savage felt his blood coursing faster from the exertion, and his spirits warmed. He felt relaxed, strangely at peace, as a boxer might find precarious but nonetheless welcome peace in the time-out between the rounds. The group, he told himself, although still shaky, was at least up off its knees. And Stovall and Cobb, neither of them afraid of work or responsibility, had the makings of satisfactory deputies in the air and on the ground. Presently Cobb broke the silence.

"Sorry I spoiled your record yesterday," he said. Cobb had

lost two airplanes leading the group on a day that Savage had remained behind. It was the third mission which Savage had not accompanied. Jesse Bishop, promoted to a squadron operations officer, had led the other mission, from which one aircraft had not returned.

"I know, Joe," he said. "But what the hell. I would have lost them, too, in that kind of flak. Nobody can do anything about flak on the bombing run, sitting there straight and level."

"That's not what the boys think," said Cobb. "You've gotten yourself a reputation . . . all over the Eighth Air Force." He glanced sideways at Savage, a little bashfully. "You're supposed to be invincible," he added.

This was so forceful an admission from the laconic air exec that Savage flushed with pleasure; then he frowned, his thoughts instantly taking a more somber turn. This invincibility business could be a two-edged sword. You had to lay your championship on the line every time. One bad mission, with heavy losses, which could happen to anyone, might shatter the myth in his case into more fragments than the reviving 918th could well withstand.

"Invincible?" he repeated, partly to himself. "Wish you hadn't put it that way, Joe." Cobb waited. Savage unconsciously slowed his gait. He wondered if Cobb even vaguely suspected how vulnerable he really felt sometimes, sitting up there in that lead airplane. One thing Savage was confident of: he would never spare himself. That was the measure of his strength. The rest was in the hands of God.

"Ever stop to think, Joe," he asked, "that the Germans are already converting from bomber production to fighters? That Intelligence shows they're moving fighters from other fronts to bolster the fighter belt in Western Europe against us?"

"Yeah," said Cobb casually. "I guess we've been irritatin' 'em."

"Plenty," said Savage. "And maybe tomorrow we head into Germany. Just think how those bastards are going to react. Fatso Goering has promised them no bombs will ever fall on the soil of the Reich. When those Jerry fighter boys come up at us, they're going to be reacting the same way our guys would if enemy bombers approached Pittsburgh, or Washington, D. C., or Los Angeles. They're going to smack into us like maniacs." He paused. "They won't stop us. But not I, nor anybody, is invincible to a twenty-millimeter shell."

He returned the salute of a lone soldier who smiled straight into his eyes as he passed, reminding Savage of the change that had come over everyone at Archbury, from privates to officers who matched him for drinks at the club.

"Over Germany," he continued, "we don't want any indispensable man. That's where you, the squadron commanders, Jesse Bishop and others come in." He was thinking about the big question mark that always hovered above the head of the lonesome figure sitting in the lead ship of each large formation. Wingmen and flight leaders could be expected to cling to the formation, if only for self-preservation. They would follow where the group leader led them. Thus the success of the whole venture would depend upon the tenacity of a few key men who could press on through any hell of fighters, flak and battle damage to reach heavily defended targets. Neither Germany, in the Battle of Britain, nor the Japs had produced enough such leaders; hence their formations had been turned back many times by air opposition. Savage knew that he must develop other men in the 918th who would never turn back.

"You guys," added Savage, "are going to be the group leaders."

When next he spoke, Cobb's voice sounded worried.

"General," he asked, "you aren't thinking of leaving us?"

Immediately Savage thought of Henderson. How long, he wondered, before that politically smart stargazer would start selling General Pritchard on a new assignment for a competitor who was in a position to collect too many ribbons and headlines?

"I wouldn't worry too much about that, Joe," he said. "The big job is still ahead. I aim to stick around awhile."

Cobb looked far from satisfied.

"I hope the brass upstairs don't pull any fast ones," he said. "We're kind of getting used to you down here."

Savage remained silent. During the next dozen paces Cobb seemed to be trying to make up his mind. Finally he screwed up his courage to ask a question that had troubled him for several days, ever since he had assigned Ben Gately and his Leper Colony to the lead of a mission. Savage had studied the crew list carefully, but had offered no objection. Then Gately had aborted in mid-Channel with a bad turbo and a runaway prop, leaving Bishop, flying on his wing, to take over the lead. Although Gately had done a smooth job of returning safely to base on two engines, no mean feat, Savage had been furious. "Just what I might have expected," had been his comment.

"Sir," said Cobb, "I'd like to try letting Gately lead another mission soon."

"Why?" said Savage, making the word sound like an epithet.

"You see, sir," struggled Cobb, painfully aware that Savage was freezing up on him, "his own airplane was out for an engine change that last time. He had to rely on a spare ship that went sour on him." When Savage merely compressed his lips, saying nothing, the air exec was encouraged to continue. "General," he said, "Gately's changed to beat hell since you got here. I think he'll turn out okay."

"Assign Gately to missions," said Savage coldly, "as you see fit. But don't make excuses for him to me. I don't care to discuss him," he added, "even with you."

With Cobb smarting under the rebuff, the pair strode on, passing near the edge of the perimeter track, where a B-17 squatted, its sturdy tail rising gracefully from the dorsal fin along its spine. As always, the rugged, clean lines of the Fort reassured Savage. Here was a reliable tool. A powerful weapon to hold in your hands. He noted that the airdrome appeared nearly deserted in the early-morning light. The 918th was sleeping late. And then he heard spasmodic bursts of machine-gun fire.

Curious, the pair changed direction and walked toward the sound until they sighted a small group in the vicinity of a high mound of earth which served as a target butt. Gunners, thought Savage, bore-sighting their .50 calibers. But soon he was close enough to recognize a weird cast of characters.

Chaplain Twombley and the flight surgeon were sitting a little apart on a blanket, field-stripping their pieces. Sergeant Nero was explaining second-position stoppages to Harvey Stovall. A little distance away, Sergeant Coulter, Private McIllhenny and an armorer, whom Savage didn't recall, were firing short bursts at a target. As Savage came up the men stopped to salute.

"What's going on here, Harvey?" he asked.

Stovall seemed a little nonplussed.

" 'Morning, General," he said, wiping his brow. "I guess you might call this part of the Airdrome Defense Plan you asked me to draw up. I figure all of us paddle-feet ought to know which end of a machine gun has the hole in it—in case of emergency."

The others, especially Private McIllhenny, appeared to be relieved by the ground exec's reply. Savage had a vague feeling that there was something fishy about their expressions, as though they had been caught in some illicit act, but he merely said, "Fine, fine," and proceeded to the mess, where he and Cobb enjoyed a feast of three fresh eggs each, which the mess sergeant presented with the compliments of Private McIllhenny.

Halfway to the office, Savage was intercepted by Stovall, who leaped out of his jeep in a state of uncharacteristic excitement and handed him an envelope.

"From Pinetree," said Stovall. "By motorcycle courier. I couldn't locate you right away, so I opened it and signed for it."

Savage was seized with foreboding as he opened the letter. He had never seen Stovall so upset. The letter read:

SUBJECT: O.T.U. training in the Continental United States.

TO: Commanding General,
        918th Bombardment Group (H).

1. Effective immediately, you will refrain from further participation in combat missions without specific prior authorization from this headquarters.

2. The Commanding General, Army Air Forces, has directed the Commanding General, Eighth Air Force, to return a suitable general officer, qualified by outstanding experience in combat, to the United States for urgently important duty in connection with the training of heavy bombardment groups for combat. You are hereby advised that in the opinion of this headquarters no officer other than yourself can meet subject requirements.

3. Pursuant to par. 2, above, you will consider your-

self in readiness for reassignment to this important duty, to which you will be ordered as soon as practicable. Meanwhile you will take appropriate action relative to termination of your present duties at a reasonably early date, of which you will be advised in due course.

The letter was signed by Henderson. Savage read it through twice, then handed it back to Stovall. He turned to Cobb. "You go with Harvey," he said grimly. "I'll be over soon." When the jeep had driven off, Savage proceeded at a slow and heavy pace toward the headquarters site. His eyes burned straight ahead, his teeth were clenched and from time to time his lips moved inaudibly. Gradually his pace quickened. By the time he had reached headquarters, he was striding almost at a run. He saw his car outside. Approaching an open window of the adjutant's office, he shouted: "McIllhenny!" He had climbed into the back seat when his driver appeared.

"Pinetree!" he said. "And bend that throttle."

Savage found Henderson in his quarters at Wycombe Abbey. The latter emerged from his bathroom in a green silk dressing gown, rubbing shaving lather from his neck with a hand towel, and greeted Savage with an apologetic smile. "Had to work late last night," he explained. "What's new, Frank?"

"Nothing's new," said Savage. "I got your letter. The same ancient bottle of two-star Henderson."

Henderson reduced his smile, but continued in his manner to ignore Savage's dangerous expression.

"You're a lucky guy, Savage," he said. "Wish I could fill the bill for that assignment in the States. Means command of the Second Air Force, probably. Sunny Colorado."

"Don't fling that stuff on *me*," snapped Savage.

Henderson eyed him calmly, but no longer smilingly, the towel dangling in his hand.

"Your manner," said Henderson, "is unmilitary and, I might add, insubordinate. You've made quite a hobby of it lately."

"First of all, I want to place this discussion on a personal, not an official, basis."

"You've made it clear," said Henderson, "that we *have* no

personal relationship. I prefer to talk to you officially. We're both Army officers."

"Correct," said Savage. "And I have no apologies for my record as a soldier. However you care to construe it, this conversation is strictly personal with me."

"What do you want?" asked Henderson.

"I want you to find somebody to fly that desk at Colorado Springs. I want you to take that letter and shove it up. This is no time to railroad me."

Henderson dropped his towel on the floor and moved a little closer to Savage.

"I don't *get* this!" he said furiously.

"I'll spell it out for you. I have no military ambitions that threaten you—now, or after the war. I couldn't be less interested in another star. My job at Archbury isn't finished. And I aim to finish it."

Henderson moved still closer, until he was looking up at the taller man from only a foot away.

"This is ridiculous," he said. "I don't follow you at all. I have to comply with a directive from Washington. It says outstanding combat qualifications. That's you. And I'm sure General Pritchard will agree."

"I can't believe that General Pritchard would pull me out of the 918th now," said Savage. "You're a fast talker, Henderson, but not that fast."

"Apparently," said Henderson, "you've hypnotized yourself with the notion that I'd stoop to anything to get you out of my hair. God knows it would be a relief! But I refuse to lower myself to argue such a point with you!"

Savage grabbed Henderson by the lapels of his dressing gown with a well-muscled fist.

"Okay!" he said through his teeth. "We *won't* argue. Just forget you wrote me that letter! I'm busy, see? I've got a job of fighting to do with the 918th!"

"Take your hands off me!" snapped Henderson.

Slowly Savage released him and stepped back.

"All right," he said, his voice ringing with conviction. "But I'm giving you fair warning, here and now, on a purely personal basis." His eyes bored into Henderson. "Don't mess around with me, Henderson! Just keep the goddam hell out of my road!"

Henderson was pale with anger, trembling. The expression in his eyes had become literally murderous.

"Go ahead," he breathed. *"Go ahead, Savage, and get yourself killed!* But never say I didn't try to stop you!"

"That's better," said Savage. "A big improvement on your letter."

He turned quickly and strode out.

Driving Savage back to Archbury, Private McIllhenny was eager to unburden to the general a matter in the forefront of his mind. But the scowling, preoccupied figure in the back seat discouraged him until they were close to the base, when McIllhenny observed through the rear-view mirror that Savage seemed to have shaken off whatever was obsessing him. The boss stretched his arms in a prodigious yawn, lighted a fresh cigar and looked out of the windows with relaxed interest.

Maybe, thought McIllhenny, now is the time. He had been tipped off by Sergeant Nero that an irate family in the village was gunning for him. Yesterday a local daughter had borne twins, for which she considered McIllhenny responsible. Weighing the alternatives of marrying a girl who already had twins or the W.A.A.F. corporal who presumably would present him with only one offspring, McIllhenny had not wasted much thought in choosing the lesser evil.

"General," he said, "may I bring up a personal matter?"

"What is it, McIllhenny?"

"Sir, I've been wrestling with myself."

"Who won?"

"Well, sir, I'd like to ask your permission to get married."

"Now wait a minute," said Savage. "Maybe I had to bust you, but don't get the idea anybody's trying to coerce you into a shotgun wedding."

"It's not that, sir," he said. "I've decided I'm in love with Corporal Lambeth. I want to marry her, that's all."

Savage whistled to himself. Then he thought of Pamela. This was wonderful. Perfect. He smiled broadly.

"In that case," he said, "I wish you all the luck in the world, McIllhenny. You have my blessing."

"Thank you, sir," said McIllhenny, as much relieved as Savage. They had pulled up in front of the headquarters block. As Savage got out, his mind already racing ahead to the prospect of an early call on Pamela to break the good news, McIllhenny faced him.

"I shall do my best, sir," he said, "to make ends meet on my current pay."

Savage burst out laughing.

"All right, all right," he said. "You win. Put those stripes back on."

"Very good, sir."

Sergeant McIllhenny saluted solemnly and hurried into the adjutant's office, where he immediately inserted a sheet of paper into his typewriter.

CHAPTER SEVEN

Achtung!

"Desborough Hall," said Savage, entering his car.

"Very well, sir," said Sergeant McIllhenny.

Both the staff car and its passenger were immaculate. The sergeant had seen to the former and Savage had chosen his newest slacks and blouse and shiniest shoes to insure the latter. After a short drive through the Sunday-afternoon sunshine, they rolled up a winding driveway, through magnificent oaks, catching occasional glimpses through the trees of the ancient family seat of the Desboroughs, complete with Tudor-style architecture, croquet lawn, tennis court, boxwood hedges and flower gardens, now mostly converted to vegetables. Likewise, what formerly had been a green velvet lawn was now plowed up to the last square foot on behalf of England's impoverished larder.

A hundred yards from the mansion, an armed Tommy stepped out with a red flag and stopped the car. Savage's impatience with the delay was short-lived, for almost at once a tremendous explosion rent the air from nearby. Then the Tommy waved the car on. A fusillade of machine-gun fire rattled not far off, followed by streams of tracer bullets over-head.

"What is this, Sergeant?" exclaimed Savage. "The Fourth of July?" Before the driver could answer, both men jumped in their seats as a covey of small rockets smoked up into the sky with a great WHOOSH!

Appearing suddenly from out of nowhere, a company of middle-aged Home Guardsmen, with perspiration streaming down their beefy-red faces, charged out into the open with fixed bayonets and sprawled on their stomachs along each side of the road ahead of the car. McIllhenny applied his brakes, but the precaution was unnecessary. Before he could stop, the panting Guardsmen leaped to their feet in response to a shrill whistle from their captain and stampeded out of sight into the woods.

"Near as I can tell," said McIllhenny, as they started up again, "it's the invasion of England."

"Or the wrong place," said Savage, as they drove on to the front door.

But then Savage saw Pamela approaching casually from the tennis court on the far side of the house. She carried a racket and was wearing a thick white sweater as a concession to chilly weather for tennis. At sight of the girl, a shot of adrenalin tingled into Savage's bloodstream, akin to his reaction to emergencies in the air. To himself he said: Steady, Savage. Steady there, mate. For in her tennis costume she was a vision.

She waved and it seemed to Savage that her smile was barely polite; he was not close enough to see that the corners of her smile were unsteady. The general and the sergeant had just alighted when the ground shook with the loudest explosion yet. Both jumped. But Pamela didn't seem to have noticed, as she and Savage shook hands.

"How are you, General?" she said.

"Scared stiff," grinned Savage. "Lemme out of this flak!"

"Oh, *that;*" she said.

"Mind telling me what *that* is?"

"A land mine," she answered indifferently, "I should think."

"Don't you *know?*"

Pamela looked apologetic as they started toward the tennis court.

"I forgot you hadn't been here," she said. "They turned our place into a proving ground. Unexploded enemy bombs and mines are brought here for disposal. They test new rockets and Lord knows what else—top secret."

"Nice," said Savage. "Very soothing."

"We've gotten rather used to it," she said. They took a few paces in silence, broken by sporadic gunfire.

"I have good news for you," said Savage at length.

"Really?"

"About Sergeant McIllhenny and your W.A.A.F. I've got it all fixed. He's going to marry Corporal Lambeth."

"Thanks," she said, "very much."

Savage was disappointed at her lack of enthusiasm. As they came to the court, he noticed for the first time that the 918th was present in force. Major Cobb and Jesse Bishop were on one side of the net, Ben Gately was on the other, rallying with his opponents while waiting for Pamela. It was obvious Gately was good.

Lord and Lady Desborough were already coming down the gravel path to welcome Savage. The former had a homely face, big of nose and wrinkled with character, that caused Savage to search in vain for a resemblance to Pamela, but he saw the answer instantly in Lady Desborough, whose lovely expression and classic features proclaimed that she must have been a famous beauty. During the exchange of greetings, Lord Desborough gripped Savage's hand like a former Cambridge oarsman, which he was. Savage got the impression that Pamela's father possessed deceptive charm and ability behind his rugged Saint Bernard dog features and melancholy eyes.

Bishop and Cobb dropped their rackets, walked to the sidelines and said hello to Savage. Leaning against the net post, bouncing a ball up and down, Gately met Savage's eyes for an instant. He nodded impersonally, merely saying, "Afternoon, sir."

"Take my place," urged Pamela, "won't you, General?"

"Not today, thanks," said Savage. "You all go ahead."

"If you don't mind," said Pamela. "The boys say they have to get back after this set. Just a few more points. Father and mother would love to monopolize you, anyway."

She joined Gately and play resumed.

Pamela was clearly a competitor, heedless, in her concentration, of whether or not she was being graceful. To Savage, it seemed that her efforts to return even the hardest smashes that came off Cobb's racket made her much more attractive than some self-conscious lady performers he had watched. Bishop and Cobb played recklessly and loudly, but Gately stroked the ball back with precision and in silence until he and Pamela had come from behind to win the set. Savage begrudged the flashing smile she gave Gately, and her words: "Good show, Ben." Gately ignored Savage during the brief chatter before the three junior officers thanked their hosts and left for Archbury.

After further polite conversation, Savage and Pamela shook off the older people and found themselves before a fire in the library. A decrepit servitor appeared.

"Tea?" asked Pamela, appraising Savage through her wide, violet eyes.

"Tea is fine," said Savage, not too convincingly.

"Bring two gin and tonics, please, Benson," she said. Seeing Savage's appreciative smile, she added: "Better?"

"My favorite brand of tea," said Savage.

"Now that we are away from your office," she said, "I want to talk to you about Ben Gately." She paused, noting his reluctant expression. "Do you mind?"

He studied her a moment.

"What about Gately?" he said finally.

"Why don't you like him?"

"Not my type, I guess." Savage hoped to stay clear of the subject of Gately's official record. "Is it important?" He guessed from her expression that she must have taken Gately's attentions fairly seriously.

"It's just that I'm puzzled," she parried. "The fact that you relieved him of his old job is none of my business. But I wonder if you understand him?"

"I believe so," said Savage noncommittally.

"For instance, do you know that he's always hated the Army? Never wanted to go to West Point? Hated being forced into the family military tradition? Disliked flying, except for the higher pay?"

"What about it?" asked Savage guardedly.

Benson entered with the drinks and a plate of cucumber sandwiches. Savage touched Pamela's glass.

"God bless," she said.

"Cheers," said Savage. As Benson retired, she hastened to continue.

"It's just that we're all so fond of Ben. And he's out of place in a war. Square peg in a round hole. Terribly sensitive. But we think he's a good type . . . if given the right chance."

Savage stared into his glass, then into the fireplace.

"He's getting his chance," he said, putting a conclusive period on the subject by the tone of his voice.

Pamela sipped her drink meditatively, then set it down, stretched back her arms in a yawn and smiled across at him.

"I almost forgot," she said. "How splendid of you—inviting the village children to your group's Christmas party. They're wild with excitement."

Savage was embarrassed, for this was the first he had heard of it. The chaplain's idea, no doubt, he thought.

"Thanks," he said uncomfortably. "Glad to have them."

"You must love children," she said. To himself, Savage thought: Sure: I like them in the next county. "And you'll have the ideal Father Christmas," she continued. "Jesse will be perfect with white whiskers."

So, Savage thought, this was Bishop's idea . . . Well, I'll be damned.

"Bishop's great with kids," he said, groping, then added: "You and the family must come, too."

"Of course we shall."

They sipped their drinks in silence for a spell. Savage felt at a loss, devoid of ideas for the proper approach to this girl, helpless to prevent the precious minutes from slipping by wasted. Pamela, too, was experiencing a peculiar sense of frustration. They weren't getting anywhere, she felt; but what worried her more was that she wanted them to get somewhere. Why? she asked herself. He's callous; there's something almost inhuman about him; he's not my kind. In spite of herself she was moved by an urge to impress him— to arouse his interest.

"You seem a bit tired," she said, finally.

"Feel fine."

Relishing the surprise she had in store for him, she asked: "In spite of that bad show? Over Villecoublay last Friday at twenty-two thousand feet at 1413 hours?"

She saw at once by Savage's expression that she had scored. Leading the 918th home, he had had a vicious encounter with two *Staffeln* of FW's under the exact circumstances which she had cited. He held his glass unsipped, staring at her in astonishment.

"Been talking to the boys?"

"No."

She smiled mysteriously.

"Even if I had, I doubt that they could have told you that those FW's came all the way from Denmark and refueled at Woensdrecht before they intercepted you."

Savage set his glass down with a clink.

"What *is* your racket, anyway, Pamela?" he asked. Then, realizing he had used her first name, he corrected himself: "Flight Leftenant?"

"Pamela is better," she said. "If I may call you Frank, General."

"Okay, Pamela," he said. "Now where did you get that dope?"

"I'm afraid it's Top Secret."

"You're talking to an Allied general, aren't you?"

"A red-tape general who ought to know about it already through official channels. Although it is no secret that the Air Ministry sometimes wonders if you Americans don't talk too much."

Savage showed that he was getting nettled.

"Security's a shell game. Once I signed my life away for a Top Secret communication from the Air Ministry, with envelopes inside envelopes, which informed me that document number so-and-so was no longer classified as Secret."

Pamela laughed.

"Isn't it priceless?" she said, sympathetically. She nibbled a cucumber sandwich. "I think I shall take a chance on you. Have you never heard of RT-Intercepts?"

"Sounds vaguely unfamiliar."

"I tell you what," she said. "If you actually *are* interested, my show is on the coast, near Lowestoft. A radio monitoring station. Drop over for a visit. I think you'll find it interesting . . . and maybe even helpful in your line of work."

"The group's standing down again tomorrow," he said. "Weather. How about it?"

"Tomorrow, then," she said. "Any time . . . we work around the clock. With luck you may hear the guttural voice of a particular friend of yours. Herr Wütz Galland."

"Am I supposed to know the gent?"

"You should. He made two passes at you, head-on, last Tuesday south of Abbeville. Nearly rammed you."

Savage, completely bowled over, stared at her bug-eyed.

"I'm changing my brand of whisky," he muttered.

Pamela had another jolt ready for him.

"He doesn't like you at all," she said. "Called you a swine . . . a *schweinhund* . . . when one of your gunners chipped the corner off his windshield." She rose. "I'm afraid I'm going to be late."

Savage rose too, temporarily bereft of light conversation. England, he thought to himself, knows what it's doing; they've found out that they can trust their women with some of the damnedest jobs of the war.

Together they walked down the hall and were descending the front steps when they encountered Pamela's father, who drew Savage to one side.

"As long as you are here, General," he said, "I want you to consider this house your home. Whenever you feel like it, just pack your bag and walk in—And another thing. I went to school with Charles Portal. So if I can ever be of help to you in any matter involving the Air Ministry, I'd be only too happy." Savage thanked his host and continued down the steps.

Pamela was waiting at the car, where McIllhenny had just stepped out and was shaking hands with her.

"Corporal Lambeth," Savage was surprised to hear her saying, "is a much better choice than the girl in the village with twins. I wish you both luck."

"Thank you," said McIllhenny, blushing.

Savage experienced a bad moment of embarrassing recollection. Why in hell, he asked himself, did I have to go and tell her I'd fixed it? Pretending not to have overheard, he tried to maintain a normal expression as he shook hands with Pamela. Her eyes flashed at him in a merry smile. Looking back into her eyes, he tried to bluff it out for a couple of seconds, then broke out into a smile. He shrugged.

"Fellow can try, can't he?" he asked.

Two days later Savage attended a conference of all group commanders at Widewing, the code word for General Pritchard's headquarters in London. Detailed plans of tactical procedures for an imminent strike into Germany were at the top of the agenda. Toward the end of the long session, Savage took the floor.

"General Pritchard," he said, "I think there is one more thing that ought to be brought up at this meeting." He paused. "With General Henderson's permission," he continued, "since it lies in the province of Bomber Command rather than the group commanders." He glanced toward Henderson.

"Go ahead, Savage," said Henderson.

"We're wasting a lot of gasoline sending up a few bombers for diversionary missions on the mistaken assumption that we're drawing up enemy fighters and diverting them on a wild-goose chase." He looked about the room. "We may be fooling ourselves, but we're not fooling the Jerries. Not any longer. Worse still, we tip our hand that the main effort is directed elsewhere."

Henderson bristled, but Pritchard asked the first question.

"What makes you think so, Frank?"

"Because the R.A.F. has a wealth of information, available to us but which we have never asked for, which proves it. I visited one of the R.A.F. radio stations on the coast yesterday that monitors all Luftwaffe voice communications, twenty-four hours a day. They have German-speaking W.A.A.F.'s who have been at it so long that they know the German fighter controllers, their commanders and a lot of their pilots by their voices. They know their names. They record in minute detail how, where, when and why the Jerry fighters maneuver to meet our penetrations. They know when and why we outguess the enemy and when he outguesses us." His eyes swept around the room again, noting that Pritchard was not the only officer hanging on his words. Henderson was biting a pencil nervously.

"Our diversions are a case in point," he continued. "Those W.A.A.F.'s who listen in, monitoring RT-Intercepts as they call them, are laughing at us. So are the Jerries."

"Why?" interrupted Henderson, no longer able to contain himself.

"Because when we send bombers on diversionary missions,

ing his fingers through his hair, lost in thought. Finally Stovall spoke up.

"Will the general prepare his own indorsement to Gately?" he asked.

Savage still hesitated. He had been disturbed by the extent of the battle damage sustained by the 918th as a result of Gately's judgment, but it was hard to criticize Gately for following that military axiom: try to persuade your leader of an error, but follow him, right or wrong.

"I want to consider this a little, Harvey," he said.

Stovall withdrew. Savage had resumed his scrutiny of the bleak view beyond the windowpanes when Jesse Bishop entered, without knocking, walked up and sat down by the desk.

"Hi, Santa Claus," said Savage, relaxing into a smile. "What have you got?"

"I've got a pain," said Jesse, "from the ribbing I've been taking since I played Father Christmas."

"You were well cast," said Savage. "The kids loved you."

"Why not?" said Jesse. "They ought to love anybody that hands out a month's PX rations from two thousand men. Some party! But you didn't stay long, General."

"Kids," said Savage, "are worse than flak." His real reason for leaving early had been the absence of Pamela, who had not been able to get Christmas leave. The phone buzzed. "Excuse me, Jesse," he said. While Savage was talking, Bishop pulled open a drawer, reached in a box of cigars and lighted up.

"Have a cigar, Jesse," said Savage, as he hung up.

"Roger," said Bishop, blowing out a puff.

"How'm I doing?" continued Savage. "I can tell that you came in here to rack me back for something."

"Yes, sir, I did." He took a deep breath. "The boys think you're being too tough on Gately."

Savage frowned.

"Don't try me too far, Jesse," he warned.

"We made a deal, didn't we?"

"Okay. Go ahead."

"Well, sir. As Cobb will verify, that Leper Colony of Gately's has turned into a regular factory for lead navigators and lead bombardiers. His gunners have the most claims, too.

So the boys would think more of you if you eased up on him."

"I don't care what the boys think of me personally," said Savage evenly, "so long as they do their jobs. You can tell them to mind their own business."

"Yes, sir." Bishop looked a little crestfallen.

"But don't go off mad," amended Savage.

Bishop, realizing how busy the general was, chatted a little longer, thanked him for the cigar, saluted and left.

Savage called in McIllhenny.

"Take a First Indorsement," he said. The sergeant picked up a pencil and scratch pad from the desk. "To Lieutenant Colonel Benjamin Gately. Subject: Commendation. Paragraph One: It is always a matter of satisfaction to me to receive from another organization a communication of this kind, reflecting favorably upon a member of the 918th Bombardment Group." He paused. "For my signature, Sergeant."

Toward evening, still working at his desk in feverish concentration, Savage heard a knock and looked up to see Gately standing, ramrod stiff, at the door. It was the first time that Gately had set foot in the office since the day of Savage's arrival. He held a sheet of paper in his left hand.

"What is it?" asked Savage distantly.

Gately saluted.

"May I speak with the general?"

"Of course," said Savage, without warmth. "Come in." He allowed Gately to stand in front of him instead of offering him a chair.

"I just received the general's commendation," he said with a barely audible tremor in his voice. "I came in to thank you, sir."

"You have yourself to thank, Gately." Savage's manner still was cold. "Your work will receive the same recognition from me as anyone else's in the group." He took a puff of his cigar. "You've been doing all right, Gately."

Gately mistook these words for an overture from Savage. Conflicting emotions, springing from lingering hatred and growing respect, welled up within him. He still remembered word for word, burned into his brain, what Savage had once said to him. But as he stood there, he couldn't repress an inconsistent desire for the general to get up, come around the desk and shake his hand, burying the hatchet. His emotional stress had brought him to a crossroads.

Savage continued to regard him through inscrutable eyes. "But," he concluded, "there's still a long way to go."

Gately bit his lip, reluctant to leave the office on so inconclusive a note. Then his jaw slowly set into a harder line. He raised his hand in a salute.

"Yes, sir," he said in a choked voice. He turned quickly and departed.

Early that evening, the Green Toby leered out over a lounge that was deserted, save for a few ground officers.

Savage, wearing his flight cap and flying coveralls with the sleeves rolled above the elbows, stood before the crews in the Briefing room.

"Give me your attention!"

What little noise there had been was quickly hushed. Each face in the room was curious and tense, for the boys had come to know that when Frank Savage appeared in flying clothes they could expect bad news. Savage now led only the rugged ones. But his mere presence reassured them. The general had never failed to bring every ship back to base.

"First," he called in a penetrating voice, "I want to introduce our commander, General Henderson. He is paying us the honor of going along with us today."

There was polite applause as Henderson, bundled up in winter flying clothes, stood up and took a bow.

"Care to say anything to the crews, sir?" asked Savage, politely.

"No, thanks," said Henderson, flashing a personality smile back toward the combat men. "I'm just a crew member today." He sat down.

A ball-turret gunner nudged a tail gunner sitting next to him. "*Just* a crew member," he whispered. "What does that make *us*?"

"Gentlemen," resumed Savage, "business is picking up. Last night we all heard momentous war news. At Casablanca, the United Nations announced its policy of unconditional surrender." He smiled. "Sounds like they've heard about the 918th." His words met with a mixture of laughter and applause. "In addition," he continued, "the Russians are liquidating the trapped German forces of von Paulus around Stalingrad. And the British Eighth Army has resumed its advance westward from Tripoli." He paused while his eyes pierced to the back of the room.

"This morning," he called, "for the first time, our Intelligence officer will swing his pointer toward a target on German soil—Wilhelmshaven!"

A deep-throated cheer, lasting for many seconds, shook the room. Finally he held up his hand until quiet was restored.

"I thought you'd like it," he said, pride in his voice. "This group will lead the Eighth Air Force today. I will lead the group. Major Cobb will lead the high squadron, and General Henderson will ride with Cobb. Colonel Gately will lead the low squadron. I have only one more thing to say before the briefing officer takes over. The Jerries have been dishing it out for a long time. Let's find out today how much they like to *take* it!"

He motioned to the Intelligence officer, stepped down from the platform and took his seat beside Henderson.

Three hours later at Savage's hard-stand, after the last of the Fort's four engines had barked into life, Sergeant Mc-Illhenny quickly backed the general's car into the slipstream behind the tail, out of sight of the cockpit. He jumped out, rushed to the car's luggage compartment, yanked out a B-4 bag crammed with flying equipment, sprinted around the tail of the B-17 to the rear door and, assisted by a waist gunner, clambered aboard.

"Achtung! Feindliche Flugzeuge!" (Warning! Hostile aircraft!)

At Lowestoft, Pamela pressed the earphones closer to her head as she heard the crackling warning of ground observers to the *Jagdführer* (fighter controller), Northwest Europe. Actually, she was kibitzing, for her supervisory duties did not require her to act as an operator. For half an hour she listened to the chatter of nazi fighters taking off and forming up to intercept the American bomber force, and then she heard the first of the Messerschmitt groups make contact with the B-17's.

"Achtung! Dickeautos, Amerikanische!" (Warning! American heavy bombers!)

Her body became rigid as her mind raced forward hundreds of miles to the east to the frozen upper levels, plumed with vapor trails, where at that instant Frank Savage must be squinting through his windshield at the black specks hurtling toward him, head-on, out of the sun—from twelve o'clock high.

Reception became so poor that she was unable to judge how the battle was progressing, but occasional guttural ejaculations of glee told her that several Forts had gone down in flames. Presently, she tuned in the American bomber channel, listening for some minutes in vain. The B-17 pilots were maintaining excellent radio silence. Suddenly she heard a faint call.

"Wheelbarrow leader to Yellowjacket leader. Over." And then she recognized Savage's voice clearly in reply.

"Go ahead, Wheelbarrow."

"Give me a check with reference to course, right or left."

There was a pause of a few seconds. Then she again heard Savage's calm voice.

"Yellowjacket to Wheelbarrow. Seven miles right."

"Roger, Yellowjacket."

Then there was continued silence.

Pamela removed her earphones, lighted a cigarette with trembling fingers and walked to the window, where she stood staring out into the curling fog.

Straining their eyes upward from twenty-one hard-stands around the perimeter track at Archbury, all crew chiefs made a fast count of the formation of Forts thundering overhead, some with props feathered, others with tattered wingtips and holes big enough to be spotted at one thousand feet altitude from the ground.

"Twenty," rose from scores of lips. "One missing."

For several roaring minutes the Forts milled about the field, dropping one by one into the groove to the runway, half of them firing double red flares on the final approach as they glided swiftly to earth with wounded aboard. Gradually the din subsided as engines clanked into silence at their hard-stands.

The crew chief at Gately's empty hard-stand continued to

gaze into the sky long after the last prop had jerked to a stop. He shaded his eyes with his hand, searching the horizon for some sign of the Leper Colony as peaceful silence once more enveloped the airdrome.

In the waist of Savage's B-17, Sergeant McIllhenny was racing against time. It was his purpose to shed his bulky flying clothes and don his regular uniform in order to return to the staff car before Savage could emerge from the cockpit by the usual exit through the nose hatch. But Savage, instead, came back through the airplane to the rear door and caught McIllhenny literally with his pants down.

"Who authorized you to go on this mission, Sergeant?" he asked. His voice was weary. McIllhenny could see that the general was in no joking mood and that his nerves were on edge from the severe stress of what had proved to be a bloody struggle in and out from the target.

"No one, sir," he said apprehensively.

"You jeopardized the safety of this airplane," snapped Savage.

"Well, sir, I've checked out okay as a gunner. I hated to miss this big one."

"You overreached yourself, McIllhenny," said Savage. "From now on you stay out of airplanes. And take those stripes off. You're reduced to private, and so help me that's what you're going to stay!"

"Yes, sir," said McIllhenny despondently.

Uppermost on Savage's mind was Gately. Badly shot up, the Leper Colony had hung on with three engines until the group was starting back across the Channel, with enemy fighters still in the vicinity. Then it had lost another engine and been forced to drop out of formation. Savage had watched with alarm as the rest of the low squadron started lagging behind to cover Gately. With his thumb reaching for the mike button, prepared to blast an order at the low squadron, Savage had heard Gately beat him to it.

"Baker two!" Gately had called. "Take over the squadron! Close up on the group! . . . GODDAMIT, CLOSE IT UP!" The low squadron had quickly re-formed on the lead squadron, and Savage had watched Gately dive down to wave-crest level and drop farther and farther behind, until he was lost to view.

The Intelligence officer met Savage at the door of the Interrogation room.

"What about Gately's crew?" asked Savage at once.

"Ditched in the Channel, sir. All picked up safely. They ought to be back on the station tonight."

Savage nodded without comment, and walked on through the chattering crews, stopping to accept a cup of coffee and a doughnut from a Red Cross girl.

Henderson, jubilant, his manner suggesting the swagger of a combat veteran, was already talking excitedly on the Ops phone to Bomber Command, when Savage approached.

"Good show," he bubbled to Savage in the R.A.F. vernacular, after hanging up. "Good show!" Impulsively he shook Savage's hand.

"How did the other groups make out?" asked Savage. "I counted three ships going down."

"Pinetree says the final count is four," replied Henderson. "It could have been worse."

"Yes," said Savage drily, "it could have been worse."

After getting rid of Henderson, who seemed temporarily to have forgotten all personal grudges toward Savage in the flush of his enthusiasm at having survived his first combat mission, Savage decided to look in at the office before going to the club. He wanted a drink badly to relieve the greatest reaction of fatigue he had yet experienced after a mission. But at heart he was happy. His had been the first American bomber in World War II to cross the German coast. They had bombed the Fatherland at last.

Cobb was waiting for him.

"Got a minute, sir?"

"Sure, Joe."

"You aren't going to like this, sir," said Cobb cautiously.

"Right this minute nothing bothers me. Now what?"

"You see, sir, I understand you caught McIllhenny and busted him for stowing away."

"Yes."

"If you'll pardon me, sir, that makes things kind of complicated."

"Why?"

"The precedent, I mean, sir. We'd have to bust Captain Twombley, too."

"Jumping Jesus!" exclaimed Savage. "Don't tell me the Chaplain stowed away!"

"Yes, sir. I didn't find it out until I heard him saying the Lord's Prayer over the interphone. He was manning my left waist gun."

"I quit," said Savage, reaching for a cigar.

"I'm afraid that's not all, sir." He hesitated.

"Keep talking," said Savage, a glint creeping into his eyes.

"I might as well give it to you all at once, sir. Damn near the whole ground echelon stowed away for this mission. The flight surgeon and Harvey Stovall were at the waist guns in Jesse Bishop's ship. Even Sergeant Nero went along—with Harbold."

Savage threw up his hands, walked over to the window and turned his back on Cobb. He didn't want the air exec to see the tears that were pressing up toward his eyes. But he managed to hold the tears back. He faced Cobb.

"Any of 'em get hurt?"

"Not a scratch, sir."

Savage rubbed his head.

"So that," he said, "is what Stovall was getting at with his cooked-up Airdrome Defense Plan at the target butts that morning." He sat down again, puffing at his cigar. "I'll let it go this time, Joe," he went on. "However, I'll hold you responsible that there is no recurrence. Too risky."

"Yes, sir."

"But I'm still sore at McIllhenny. I'll bet he was at the bottom of it. Maybe he ought to sweat it out as a private . . . for a while anyway."

"I wouldn't advise it, sir."

"Why not?"

"On account of McIllhenny has just been credited officially with two FW's destroyed and one probable. He's a born gunner."

Savage gripped his head in his hands. He looked up with a helpless expression as Stovall appeared, looking distinctly sheepish and showing incongruous marks on his face from the tight oxygen mask he had worn.

"Hell of a nerve you've got, Harvey," he said. "Showing

your face in here. While you're at it, get hold of McIllhenny."

Stovall went out and returned in a moment with McIll-henny, who was wearing a shirt with plain sleeves. He saluted Savage imperturbably.

"McIllhenny," said Savage, "put 'em back on."

"Very well, sir."

"Now all of you leave me alone for a while. Give me time to pull myself together."

The three men withdrew, McIllhenny walking immediately to his desk, where he opened a bottom drawer and pulled out a shirt with sergeant's chevrons on it, into which he quickly changed, thrusting his plain-sleeved shirt back into the drawer.

A moment later Savage appeared behind him.

"I suggest, McIllhenny, that you . . ." He stopped, staring at McIllhenny's sleeves. "Skip it, Sergeant," he said, recovering himself. "I'm too late. I was going to suggest that you get yourself a set of chevrons with zippers."

Still grinning, he walked across the hall to Stovall's office, where he offered to buy the ground exec a drink at the club, effective immediately. The pair set out through the twilight on foot.

"Hit anything up there today?" asked Savage.

"I think I got a piece of one," said Stovall proudly.

"Ours or theirs?" asked Savage. "I'm surprised I haven't already had a complaint from our Spitfire escort."

"Lay off me, please, General," said Stovall plaintively. "I'm suffering from combat fatigue. But since you mention it," he added thoughtfully, "a Spit, head-on, *does* resemble an Me-109."

"Better get yourself some new glasses."

"Couldn't use 'em anyway, sir. They frosted up on me."

"Why, you nearsighted old bastard, you couldn't have hit the side of a balloon hangar!" Stovall fumbled with his pipe. "Seriously, Harvey, I'm plenty burned up with you. A gray-headed old fud like you ought to have better sense. How do you think I'd like sending your wife an MIA report on you? Besides, if I had to get a new ground exec, he might be even worse than you are." His tone was scolding, but he had placed a hand on the shoulder of his friend, and his eyes were affectionate.

"You don't seem to realize," said Stovall, "that none of us paddle-feet would have gone along with you today if we'd thought it was *dangerous*!"

"You're hopeless, Harvey," he said. But again, as in the office when he had learned about the stowaways, he was strangely moved.

Approaching the door of the club, Savage saw Chaplain Twombley walking up the side path on a collision course. He also observed that the chaplain was trying to duck him, for the latter stopped, turned around and pretended to be looking at something in the distance.

"Twombley!" called Savage.

The chaplain jumped, almost dropping the cigarette he was lighting, then, with a guilty conscience written all over his face, moved up and greeted Savage.

"Your business," said Savage sternly, "is fighting sin. Hereafter please concentrate on sin exclusively."

"I grasp the general's point," replied Twombley. "You are looking at a penitent and contrite man."

"We'll say no more about it," said Savage. "As a matter of fact I wouldn't be surprised but what your prayers came in handy more than once this morning."

"Prayer," said the chaplain, "is a wonderful source of strength, General. And I have seen some powerful praying before the take-offs since I came to Archbury. Had to make one mission in order to find out what the praying was all about."

CHAPTER EIGHT

To All Men

Rolling horses for drinks at the bar with Stovall and Cobb, the general hummed under his breath in accompaniment to "I've Got Sixpence, Jolly, Jolly Sixpence," which the swarm of officers surrounding Bishop at the piano were lustily singing, glasses held high.

Cobb lost, not too gracefully. After examining the dice critically, he handed them back to their owner, Stovall. Savage sipped his Scotch gratefully, listening to the confident ring in the voices of the men working off their tension in song. When several choruses of "Sixpence" were over, a request arose from various parts of the lounge for Bishop to hit the keys with "Warsaw Concerto." A hush descended as Jesse began to play, filling the room with music that gripped his audience. At the bar, Savage listened with one ear while conducting a low-voiced conversation with Stovall and Cobb.

"General Henderson gave us a long stand-down," he said. "At least three days."

"You can thank me," grinned Cobb. "He had to ride with me today."

"What I was thinking," said Savage, "is that now is the time to pull a short mission on London, Harvey. Fix up the maximum number of leaves and passes for the group, will you?"

"Roger, Willco and out," said Stovall fervently.

Savage smiled at this proud display of technical lingo from the ground exec in his newly acquired role of battle-scarred airman.

"Amen," said the chaplain, who was ordering a beer behind Savage and had overheard. Savage regarded the chaplain thoughtfully, glanced over toward Bishop at the piano and then brought his eyes to rest on Stovall.

"Harvey," he continued, "one thing about Jesse has been bothering me lately. He's all tense inside. Tied up in knots. I wonder if he doesn't need"—he caught himself out of deference to Twombley—"some relaxation?"

Stovall looked uncomfortable.

"If you mean blowing off steam," he observed, "on a wild tear, well, that's just not Jesse's style."

"What I'm trying to get at," said Savage, "is . . . I've got to stick around here . . . so maybe it's up to you and Joe to kind of take charge of Jesse and really show him London. The whole works."

"Sir," said Stovall, "I appreciate the compliment, but I'm just a dull family man."

"You," said Cobb, laughing rudely, "are a horny old goat,

Harvey. Tell us how many Atlantic City conventions you've lied to your wife about."

Stovall looked almost hurt. Savage intervened.

"Let's not get too personal," he said. "I just want you two reprobates to see to it, between you, that Bishop doesn't spend his leave in meditation and prayer."

"We'll do our best," said Stovall. "But I'll have to let Cobb do the navigating."

"For shame, gentlemen," said Twombley. "Remember that you are your brother's keeper. Do not tempt Bishop too far from the paths of righteousness." He sipped his beer contemplatively. "And yet," he continued, "excepting a man has seen the follies of Piccadilly, perhaps he cannot be saved." He set down his glass empty.

Bishop finished playing amidst prolonged applause and cries for more. Savage left the bar and began circulating among the boys, whereupon Chaplain Twombley turned to Stovall and Cobb.

"If I may change the subject entirely," he said speaking seriously, "I have a suggestion, Harvey. You know the American cemetery outside of London; well, there are a lot of 918th men buried there. I'd like to hold a brief memorial service." He sounded apologetic. "Do you think it would be out of place tomorrow? Interfere with the men's leave? Or do you think there might be a dozen or so who would be interested in coming?"

"We can certainly find out, Chaplain," said Stovall. "I can post a notice. Personally I think there are probably enough men who've been waiting for a chance to pay their respects. I know I'd be there."

"So would I," said Cobb.

"Please," said Twombley, "don't feel that I'm thrusting this on anybody."

"We'll see," said Stovall, "how many sign up."

At the American cemetery, Chaplain Twombley waited, prayer book in hand, against a background of white crosses, intermittently illuminated by flashes of sunlight.

Facing him, head bared, Savage stood in the center of a gathering of three hundred officers and enlisted men from

Archbury. The chaplain began reading the twenty-third Psalm.

". . . Yea, though I walk through the valley of the shadow of death, I shall fear no evil . . ." As he read on, the words registered in the minds of each man present with realistic and immediate significance. He finished in tones of forceful simplicity, dropped the prayer book to his side and looked out over the stoical expressions on the sad faces of his uniformed congregation.

"When death comes," he began, speaking extemporaneously, "as it must to all men, may God grant us the courage to meet the Unknown as bravely as have our fellow soldiers who lie buried here.

"To those of us of the 918th Bombardment Group, who live to carry on the battles yet to be fought in the skies over Germany, I shall quote the following lines: Go out into the darkness and put your hand into the hand of God. That shall be to you *better* than a light." He cleared his throat. "And *safer* than a known way. Amen."

A bugler stepped forward and sounded taps. Jesse Bishop felt a lump rising in his throat as the bugle descended, in utter finality, from the long, pleading high note.

Bishop, Stovall and Cobb checked in at Claridge's, accompanied by a telephone number named Penelope, a photogenic ambulance driver who had been recommended to Cobb by one of the boys in the group.

Fortified by a stiff Scotch and soda, and impressed by the luxurious suite of two bedrooms and a sitting room done in soft beige, Penelope got busy on the phone and crashed through with dates for all hands. Two girls, who arrived in time for the second round of drinks, were extra attractive, though not quite so pretty as Penelope. The party was soon in high gear, with all talk of dinner temporarily in abeyance after Stovall came up with a bottle of Scotch which he had in his bag. Then three other members of the 918th, whom Bishop had bumped into in the lobby, barged in, swelling the liquor supply and the feminine contingent still further.

Penelope, ignoring Cobb in favor of Jesse Bishop, was sitting in Bishop's lap and running her fingers slowly through his thick yellow hair, while she sipped her drink. Animated by the hot glow of whisky inside him, Jesse was accepting the girl's attentions with a flushed grin of pleasure, while Cobb pretended to be satisfied with the blonde curled inside his arm on the couch. Only Harvey Stovall, although he was making himself more than agreeable to a chubby girl with a saucy nose, still clung to a semblance of detached dignity. He had resolved to have a good time, but within limits.

At length Cobb left his blonde and sidled over to Bishop and Penelope.

"One side, Junior," he said insultingly to Bishop. "Make way for a grown man."

Penelope moved an arm around Bishop's shoulder, as the latter stared up at Cobb."

"Beat it, Joe," he said good-naturedly.

Cobb leaned down toward Penelope.

"You're wasting your time," he said suggestively, "robbing the cradle. Come on, babe, let's you and I start getting serious."

There was nothing good-natured about Penelope's expression.

"You bore me," she said acidly, "right off my feet. Now would you mind going away?"

Cobb straightened up, swaying slightly on his feet. He forced a grin to his face.

"There's no hurry, babe," he said. "I like 'em hard to get. I'll be back." He returned to his own girl without looking at Bishop.

Presently Cobb followed Stovall into the bathroom and closed the door on the noisy hilarity outside.

"Harvey," he said, "I'm layin' off Penelope to give Jesse a clear field. But I'm damned if I'd do it for anybody else."

"That's mighty big of you, Joe," said Stovall, who had seen Cobb's rebuff. "He doesn't need any help from you. He's all set."

"Which reminds me," said the air exec, "that it's high time the Cobb man started getting set, too." He hurried out and rejoined his girl. So engrossed had everyone become in their own drinking, arguing and pawing that Cobb was scarcely noticed when he maneuvered the blonde into one of the bedrooms and was gone for some time.

When he returned, the party had gotten louder and better. Stovall caught Cobb's eye and shook his head reproachfully, but Cobb smugly ignored him, turning to accept a highball from Bishop, who had Penelope hanging from one arm, staring up at him with an adoring expression.

Without being conspicuous, but insuring that Cobb was watching him, Bishop steered Penelope into the other bedroom, closed the door and locked it behind him.

"Too noisy in there," he said, looking self-consciously at Penelope.

"You're so right," said Penelope, looking not in the least self-conscious as she slid her arms around him and kissed him. He turned his head slightly so that the kiss landed more on his cheek than his mouth. She turned away and sat on the foot of the bed.

"Penelope," he said, sitting down in a chair and lighting a cigarette, "would you . . . would you like to do me a big favor?"

"Like anything," she said, smiling up at him demurely.

"How about staying with me for a while? In here?"

"As long as you like, Jesse, darling," she said, unzipping one side of her dress. "Why don't you take your shirt off and get nice and comfortable?"

Bishop looked embarrassed, in spite of the uninhibited complexion the evening had taken.

"Please don't get the wrong idea, Penelope," he said.

She kicked off her shoes, lay back and nestled her head on the pillow.

"But I think your idea is fine," she said. "Now you come right over here, darling, with me, and be sociable." Bishop hesitated, then went over, sat on the edge of the bed and offered her a cigarette. "Not now, darling," she whispered.

"Look, Penelope," he said uncomfortably. "I guess I must seem like a dope. But couldn't we just sit here and talk for a while . . . maybe a half hour?"

"Why? What is there to talk about?" she asked, studying him with a changed expression.

"Gee," he said. "It's hard to know just how to say it. I . . . you see . . . I've never been with a girl in my life."

Penelope shifted her head on the pillow, regarding him with tender eyes.

"Why, you sweet boy," she said slowly. "Perhaps I will have one of those cigarettes." After Jesse had lighted it for her, she continued: "There's always a first time, though, isn't there, Jesse?"

"Sure," he said, "I guess there is. But can't we just talk?"

"Of course," she said. "I'm sorry I've been so bold. Throwing myself at you. But the war is a wonderful excuse . . . so little time, and all that sort of rot."

"No, no," protested Bishop. "Please don't think that. I think you're wonderful . . . a guy'd be awfully lucky to get you."

"I believe I'm beginning to get it," she said. "You don't want your friends to think you're a sissy. You think you've got to show them."

Bishop seemed to cringe. "The truth is, Penelope," he confessed, "those guys in there, and back at the group, all kid the hell out of me—well, about not being a man."

"You look like *plenty* of man to me," she said. "What is there to be afraid of? Do *I* scare you?"

"No. Christ, no. I mean just the opposite . . . or, what I really mean is, it's something else."

"Another girl?"

"Yeah. Yeah, that's it. We grew up together. Some day I'll get home . . . and I want to marry her."

Bishop had walked over to an ashtray to extinguish his cigarette. Penelope rose, too, moved over and kissed him lightly on the cheek.

"So this is all window dressing," she said softly. "To convince those chums of yours that you're a *man*." She laughed gently. "How odd. It's really very funny. Do you know what kind of a man I think you are, Jesse?" He waited for her to answer her own question, showing in his sensitive eyes that her answer might hurt him.

"You're the kind of a man," she said, "that every woman in the whole world wants."

There was a vigorous knocking on the door, followed by Cobb's muffled voice.

"Hey, Bishop! We're all going out for dinner. Come on!"

Bishop exchanged glances with Penelope.

"What's the hurry, Joe?" he called. "I'm busy."

"I know goddam well you're busy," said Cobb, "you two-faced, horny bastard. Come on! Can't you take a little and leave a little?"

Bishop walked with Penelope to the door and opened it. Deliberately she slid the zipper back up the side of her dress in front of Cobb and the whole room.

"Really, Major," she said, "you are a drunken, bloody nuisance." Then she turned admiring eyes upward at Bishop. "What a man!" she sighed.

By the evening of the third day, the men of the 918th had straggled back to Archbury broke, hung over and happy. Savage sat in his quarters drinking a nightcap with Stovall, Cobb and Bishop, listening with vicarious enjoyment to exaggerated accounts of their adventures, including the emergence of Bishop as a dark-horse winner in the battle of the sexes. Savage noticed that Bishop was fidgety under the ribbing, for the boy was inwardly chafing as much under his new reputation as he had been under the old.

Stovall and Cobb, both looking the worse for wear, excused themselves early to hit the sack, but Bishop, who seemed comparatively fresh, lingered.

"Glad you had a good time, Jesse," said Savage when they were alone. "Wish I'd been along."

"We sure missed you," said Bishop, sliding into a chair aimlessly, as though he couldn't make up his mind whether or not to stay. Savage walked over to the hearth and poked up the fire. Bishop studied his fingernails, then fixed his eyes on the blue and red coals in the grate, seeming to find something interesting there.

"How's the weather look for tomorrow, General?" he asked presently.

"So-so," said Savage. "Seven to eight-tenths cloud cover over most of our targets, I'm afraid." After Savage returned to his chair and his glass there was another silence. Bishop still watched the fire. Savage reached for a boot and his bone, with which he began to rub the leather—a habit which had become second nature with him when mulling over a problem.

"Stick around," said Savage as Bishop made a halfhearted move to rise. "What's the rush?"

"Well, no particular hurry, I guess." He relaxed back into his chair.

It was becoming clear to Savage's observant eye that Bishop's restlessness went below the surface. The pre-weekend tension was still there in the boy. Things, he reflected, must have failed to pan out right for Jesse . . . wrong girl, maybe. He eyed the boot in his hand critically, then picked up the other boot.

Bishop leaned forward. "Sweeten that drink for you, General?"

"Haven't finished it yet, thanks." He took a sip. "You know," he went on, in a conversational tone, "dames are funny. Sometimes they get your mind off things . . . help you to blow off steam. Sometimes they make you feel worse."

"Yeah," said Bishop, noncommittally.

"But I think you guys had the right idea. Hit town, shack up, get it out of your system. Usually you come back to the station feeling a lot better."

Bishop didn't answer right away.

"All depends," he said vaguely, "how you feel about things. Okay for most guys, I guess."

So that was it. Savage perceived in an intuitive flash what must have happened. He studied the boy through sympathetic eyes.

"Got a girl back home, Jesse?"

"Yes, sir."

"Pretty nice girl, eh?"

"Yes, sir. She's really swell." He went over to the table and poured a small additional shot into his glass. "General?" he asked abruptly. "Do you think I've got anything to apologize to the rest of these guys for? Because I want to keep myself for a girl back home?"

"Jesse," said the general, "you've got me on a spot there. I'm the wrong guy to ask for advice. Hell, I've been knocking around for so many years now, taking my fun double-parked, that I'd completely forgotten a guy could feel the way you do." He turned and began a reconnaissance of the hearth, his eyes crinkled in reminiscence. "Maybe I felt that way once, I guess. When I was about eighteen. Anyway, it's been too long ago."

The revelation of Bishop's viewpoint—the honest conviction of a twenty-one-year-old boy—bothered him strangely. He searched his mind for the source of disturbance, but was unable to recognize that the source was Pamela.

"You don't think I'm . . . well, sort of a Christer, General?"

"Hell, no. Just the opposite."

Bishop's eyes flashed.

"I don't give a damn what the guys think!" he said. "If she can wait for me . . . I can wait for her!"

"Well," said Savage, "what do you say we talk about something else? Before you get me all balled up with myself."

Bad weather continued to ground the bombers. Returning through the village of Archbury next morning, from a visit to Wing Headquarters, Savage saw Pamela, carrying a shopping bag, come out of a chemist's shop near the Black Swan. He halted the car and jumped out.

"Hello, there!" called Pamela cheerily as he walked up. Immediately he realized that he was trying to analyze her smile and her voice, gauging whether they held only normal cordiality or a little more. He guessed hopefully that it was a little more.

"Hello, yourself," said Savage. "What do you say to an 'arf pint in the Black Swan?"

"Exactly what I need, my Cockney friend," she said. "I'm parched."

He led her into the gloomy interior of the ancient pub, where they seated themselves at a scarred table and ordered beers.

"How's the Luftwaffe?" asked Savage.

"Rather quiet lately. I'm sure they're grateful for the long rest your chaps have been giving them."

"Works both ways," said Savage. Their beers arrived and they touched beer mugs. He took out a cigar, then started feeling his pockets.

"Sorry I haven't any cigarettes on me," he said. "Excuse me. Be right back."

"Please don't bother," she called, as he hurried out to the car.

He returned with two packages. "You're going to take these," he said.

"In that case, I accept them." She was smiling agreeably.

"That's progress," said Savage. "Real progress. The next step is, you're having lunch with me."

"Thanks awfully," she said. "But I'm meeting Ben Gately for lunch in half an hour."

Savage tried, not very successfully, to look unconcerned. A painful, unfamiliar emotion, so unfamiliar that he barely recognized it as jealousy, disturbed him. For the first time he became aware that he didn't like the idea of Gately or any other man making time with this girl. Again he caught her scent of gardenia, noticed the sparkling clarity of her eyes, her long, slender fingers and the impression she always gave of immaculateness.

"Wish I'd known you were coming down in the middle of the week," he said, toying with his glass. "Couldn't we . . . well, couldn't you let me know?"

"You could ring me up."

"But unless I rang you up every day, I might miss you."

"Perfectly true."

Savage continued to toy with his glass, staring at it, thinking about Gately and of Pamela's unspoken implication that if Gately could take the trouble to phone often, why couldn't *he*? Savage shrugged and smiled at her.

"Just so long as it's somebody from the 918th," he said. "*We* own you and *you* own us."

"How impersonal. You make me sound like a corporation. Actually I have a very personal feeling toward you."

"Toward me?"

"Toward your group. You see, I'm really a combat crew member."

"I only wish you were."

"But I am. I go along on every mission." She accepted another pint of beer from the barmaid. "Yellowjacket to Wheelbarrow," she said, imitating Savage's voice without too much difficulty, for hers was low. "Goddam it to hell, Joe, close it up!"

Shaking his head, Savage blushed and touched her beer

mug. "Roger, Yellowjacket," he said. "I promise to guard my language from now on. You're a full-fledged crew member. I may even make you a squadron commander, if you work hard."

"You really think I'd have a future under you . . . under your command?" She saw that Savage had not missed her slip of the tongue. Flushing a trifle, she took out a compact from her gas-mask container and powdered her nose.

"I'm ashamed of you," he said. "Cosmetics in gas masks are contrary to regulations."

She gave him a quick, furtive smile.

"Please don't turn me in," she said. "I have enough trouble already disciplining my girls for doing the same thing."

Savage knocked a long ash from the end of his cigar, braced himself and fastened his eyes on Pamela's.

"Look, Pamela," he said tensely. "Let's quit fooling around. There's been too much of it already, and it's my own damn fault."

Pamela returned his gaze steadily, expectantly. He noticed the tiniest tremor at the corner of her half smile and plunged ahead.

"Whether you like it or not," he said, "and you'd *better* like it, it has suddenly occurred to me that I'm in love with you."

Pamela's reaction was the last one that he had been prepared for. She stared at his eyes so long and so intently that he felt as though the two of them were locked together in some kind of death struggle. Slowly her eyes filled with tears until they brimmed over, then she quickly averted her head and partly shielded her face in her hand.

Savage became conscious of the ticking of the small clock on a wall shelf above them, as the seconds slipped past. He sat there, stricken and stunned, not only by the girl's reaction to his words, but by the violence of the bomb which had exploded inside him, blasting the words out of him. Words which he had never said before. Words which, even now, he found it difficult to believe he had uttered. But he knew beyond any question that they were true.

Helplessly, unable to remove his eyes from her averted head and her slightly quivering shoulders, he slid his hand into hers. She started to move her hand, then gripped back hard with her fingers.

She reached in her gas mask until she had found a handkerchief, then dabbed at her nose and eyes. Finally she turned and looked up at him from under damp eyelashes.

"Do I look dreadful?" she asked.

"No. You look the way you always do. Beautiful. Only more so."

"This is perfectly awful. Give me a cigarette, quick."

He handed her a cigarette and fumbled with the lighter so clumsily that, between them, it was three tries before she got her light.

"I'm horribly ashamed," she said. "Making such a fool of myself."

They were staring at each other in growing wonderment, in mutual disbelief. Their tense faces began to relax into shaky smiles. "Man came up and hit me on the head," continued Savage. "From behind. What hit you?"

"You!" she said, her voice sounding on the edge of hysteria. "Something you said. Something insane. Something I've been dreading ever since I met you."

"It was nothing insane. I'll repeat it. I said I loved you. What's dreadful about that?"

"Don't keep saying it . . . Oh, damn it all, I don't know what I'm saying."

"Relax, Pam," he said. "Just relax."

"If only you'd made passes at me. I could have brushed you off. That would have been easy. But how can I brush off a man who breaks me down right in front of his eyes? You've made things so abominably difficult."

"Let's make it still more difficult. I'm asking you to marry me." For a moment he thought she was going to cry again.

"*When*, Frank?" she asked breathlessly. The question was barely out before she caught herself. "What in the world am I saying? I must be delirious. You, too. We're both absolutely crazy."

"I liked the way you started that speech better."

"Let's face up to it, Frank. We'd be a miserable combination . . . we wouldn't have a chance. We mustn't even talk about it."

"We've got to."

"But we don't believe in the same things. Love. Marriage."

"I admit I don't believe in love. But dammit, I'm *in* love. And it's the first time in my life that I've said it."

"But it's too quick . . . much too quick, Frank."

"Lightning strikes quick, too. For keeps."

"But you'd make a wretched husband. The other woman and all that. I couldn't bear it."

"*You're* the other woman." He squeezed her fingers tightly. "*All* the other women. Wrapped up in one package."

They sat for a few moments, catching their breaths, just looking at each other, as though for the first time.

"How does a girl know?" she asked. "Until too late?"

"You'll find out. After we've been married sixty years." There was rare beauty in her eyes as she watched his face closely. She saw the jaw muscles moving under his skin. "This job I've got won't last forever. They'll give me some new assignment eventually . . . where I can offer you something better than a Nissen hut."

"Frank, you've got to stop talking that way. It's all simply out of the question."

Savage twisted his beer mug slowly around and around between his fingers.

"Damn Bishop," he muttered, as though talking to his beer mug. "He got me into this. It's all Bishop's fault."

Pamela frowned.

"What on earth has Jesse Bishop to do with us?"

"Sorry," he said. "Just rambling. I couldn't explain it . . . even to myself."

Suddenly Savage became aware of McIllhenny motioning to him from the door, and beyond McIllhenny, a jeep from the 918th.

"Afraid that man is here again, Pam," he said, rising. "I'm A.W.O.L. Never can tell what this weather's going to do." He reached for his cap.

"And I have to go back to Lowestoft this afternoon."

"Dammit. Anyway, I'll call you from the field."

"Perhaps you won't have to, dear," she said. "Since we are getting a little better acquainted, would you think me too forward if I should ring *you* up?"

For answer, he seized her arm and guided her toward the door, stopping at a large phone booth, hidden away in the privacy of a dark corner beneath a staircase. He backed her into the booth and closed the door behind them. Instantly their lips crushed together. He held her tightly for a long time.

"You're hurting me, Frank," she said finally. He continued to hold her. "You're *really* hurting me."

At last he released her, stepped back and held up his thumb and forefinger a half inch apart.

"Just right!" he said. "And remember, Pam. No cold feet. No backsliding."

"But Frank . . . wait . . . I didn't really . . nothing's settled."

"Everything's settled. You and I are going on through to the target. There isn't any turning back."

He slapped his cap on his head and strode to the door.

Savage walked about the Ops room feeling like a stranger, as he helped lay on the next day's mission. The blackboard was strange, Cobb was strange, the whole room was strange. For minutes, lost in concentration, he could regain his old self. And then Pamela would flash across his mind like a white light, filling his insides with an indescribable warmth.

He was summoned to the phone in his office. It was Pamela.

"I have to leave right off," she said, and the sound of her voice pierced through his heart like a rapier. "Say something to me, Frank. Talk to me."

"When can I see you?"

"When can you come?"

"Will you be home for the weekend?"

"It's never certain. Could you come to Lowestoft? Before then?"

"If we get a stand-down. Even if I have to crawl."

"Flying is faster."

"I'll fly." There was a pause, as both of their minds raced.

"Well?" she asked.

"Well . . . what about the cold feet? How are they doing?"

"Come up and see." Her voice was almost a whisper. "God bless. I really must dash now, darling."

"Goodbye . . . darling." After he hung up, the word lingered in his mouth as though he had just discovered it.

CHAPTER NINE

Missing in Action

Satisfied that everything was shaping up properly for the next day's mission to Kassel, Germany, Savage left the Ops room and walked over to the club for a late dinner. A few paddle-feet officers and a handful of fliers not scheduled for the mission sat around the lounge drinking. Major Kaiser came over and offered to buy Savage a beer.

"Thanks, Doc," said Savage. "But I'm leading this one tomorrow. Beer makes me dopey."

Kaiser looked concerned.

"Speaking as a flight surgeon," he said, "that reminds me of a question I've been wanting to ask the general. I hope you don't plan to lead *all* the missions, sir."

Savage laughed.

"How much is too many?"

"It's a medical fact, sir, that this high-altitude-bombing business is twice as hard on a man in his thirties as youngsters in their twenties."

"Hell, Doc. I never felt better in my whole life. Agrees with me."

"I wouldn't guarantee that, sir. I don't want to sound alarming in any sense, but I've been keeping an eye on you since that last mission. I know the first signs of overstrain when I see them."

Savage laughed heartily and slapped the flight surgeon on the back.

"I've been watching you too, Doc. Kinda noticed a coarse tremor in your drinking hand lately."

"But I'm serious, General."

Savage fetched Kaiser another, and harder, clap on the back. He felt half drunk on the intoxication of Pamela's phone call.

"Jesus Christ, Don, you quacks tickle the hell out of me. Why don't you psychoanalyze yourselves instead of worrying about phlegmatic guys like me?" He held out his fingers. "Look at that. Like a rock."

Kaiser regarded the general with a protesting smile.

"I'm really very serious, sir," he persisted. "Any man, no matter how strong, may succumb to a war neurosis if the stress reaches his threshold."

"All double-talk to me." Savage shook with mirth. "Neurosis. Thresholds. Hell, I can toss that lingo around too. But any time I get flak-happy, Doc, I promise to take a rest. Now, anything more important bothering you?"

"No," said Kaiser, swallowing the rest of his beer. His glance happened to fall on Gately, who was reading the *Stars and Stripes* in a corner. "Oh, another matter, sir," he continued. "Colonel Gately spoke to me awhile ago. About the mission. He seemed reluctant to see you personally."

"Yes?"

"He's complained about his back, sir. It's been troubling him since that ditching . . ."

"He wants you to ground him tomorrow?"

"Well, sir, he's not sure whether he's safe to go."

"So now it's his back. Used to be head colds." Savage's face hardened. "Hell, no. He'll go as scheduled."

He noticed a bare suggestion of a shrug in the flight surgeon's shoulders.

A week later, Savage stood atop the control tower watching the bombers of the 918th approaching the field from a strike against Oschersleben, Germany. He had been on the tower for nearly an hour, trying not to let thoughts of his frustration about Pamela creep into the emptiness of the waiting period. Due to a freak spell of clear weather, with missions coming thick and fast, it had been out of the question for him to go to Lowestoft since the day the roof had fallen in on him at the Black Swan. But at sight of the Forts, all else was swept from his mind, and, as always, he suffered greater anxiety from being on the ground than in the air.

Cobb was leading today, to give Savage a breather after two missions in a row in which, despite fierce air battles and heavy damage, Savage's record of losing no crews was still intact. But on one of the other missions, led by a squadron commander, the group had lost three. This, coupled with the increasing losses many groups had been sustaining since the inception of strikes into Germany, had convinced Savage anew that the Eighth Air Force's critical problem was still that of combat leadership. The 918th, he knew, would need him for a long time yet.

His tired, bronzed face tensed up as he counted the ships in the formation. Three missing. Then, off in the distance he spotted two stragglers, down low, heading for the field, one of them trailing black smoke. He waited a minute longer, scanning the horizon in vain for a third straggler, then hurried below to his car. He drove directly to Cobb's hardstand.

As soon as the props had come to a stop, he called up to Cobb, who thrust his head out of the cockpit window.

"Hit it?" Savage asked.

"Clobbered it, I think, sir."

"Who's missing?"

"Bishop."

Savage's heart sank like a stone. He felt wobbly in the knees. But he gave no sign. Instead of asking questions, he waited stolidly until Cobb left the cockpit, swung down out of the nose hatch and walked over.

"Didn't look too good, General," he said, lighting a cigarette. "Jesse got a direct burst right over Oschersleben. No chutes seen by our crew. Went into a vertical dive toward the deck . . . disappeared into low clouds."

Savage listened to Cobb's recital attentively, but his eyes did not falter once. Cobb, on the other hand, looked close to tears.

"The best damn little son-of-a-bitch in the whole group," concluded Cobb.

"Hate to lose anybody, Joe," said Savage impassively. "But it could have been lots worse. One crew. Don't let it get you down."

Back in his office, Savage relayed Cobb's firsthand mission report by phone to General Henderson, who expressed official satisfaction with the damage assessment indicated by the strike photographs, but grumbled to Savage about the severe losses two other groups had taken. The 918th had been the lead group, and Cobb had admitted having gotten slightly off course going into the target. Savage immediately stood up for Cobb; it was easy, he reminded Henderson, to lead a good mission from the ground. Henderson hastily agreed and changed the subject.

"By the way, Frank," he said. "General Barker is visiting from Washington. He'd like to come down and make a mission with your group. Shall I send him on?"

"How much does he weigh?"

Henderson was undecided whether or not Savage was joking.

"Oh, about a hundred and eighty, I guess."

"I wish General Barker had brought a hundred and eighty pounds of armor plate with him from Wright Field . . . that I've been begging for to save our crews the trouble of pulling flak out of their butts. How about doing me a favor and sending him somewhere else?"

"He specified your group."

"Hell, I thought the waiting list had dropped to zero lately. Since we started going to Germany."

"It's slumped, all right. But Barker wants to go."

"To be honest with you, sir, it's a damn nuisance. These V.I.P.'s worry the crew they fly with. And what's worse, they hurt morale."

"News to me. How?"

"By coming back from one ride as a passenger, trussed up in two chutes, climbing out at the hard-stand and bumping right into a Silver Star that's waiting for them."

Savage knew that Henderson's blood pressure was taking a jump, for the latter had been awarded a Silver Star after his lone mission.

"I didn't ask for that ribbon they gave me," said Henderson, tartly.

"I'm referring," said Savage, "to visiting firemen. And believe me, it's a real problem . . . one that the other group commanders have hesitated to bring up."

"What am I supposed to tell Barker?"

"Tell him we've got scarlet fever down here."

"All right, all right, we'll skip it. Number two: how soon do you think you can wind up your job there?"

Savage almost clenched his teeth clear through his cigar. He waited so long to reply that Henderson clicked his receiver to see if they had been cut off.

"I'm still here," said Savage. "But your question is a little baffling. I'll leave the day I have air leaders experienced enough to keep the group out of trouble. It was my impression that we had reached an understanding."

"That's just fine. It settles everything except the fact that *I* don't have an understanding with the Pentagon Building. I've got to fill that OTU training assignment. Pritchard's saving it for you. Seems to think it's about time you were available."

"He's been misinformed."

"Well. You think it over. And congratulations on staying on the ground today for a change." He rang off.

Savage rose wearily to his feet, perturbed, and began to pace the floor, resisting an impulse to call Pritchard, whom he had not conversed with privately since their conversation by the duck pond at Wycombe Abbey. But he knew Pritchard had been snowed under beneath the mountainous problems confronting his fast-growing air force. He'd cross this particular bridge, he decided, when he had to. Quickly he forgot Henderson under the pressure of an emotion with a higher priority.

Jesse Bishop forced his way into the general's consciousness, filtering into his feelings through the anesthetic which had frozen him against the first shock of the news. But now the anesthetic had worn off. Savage was face to face with his pain. He hated the pain, not only because it was there, but because he dared not acknowledge it, even to himself. It had no place here at Archbury. Terribly unforgiving of weakness in others, demanding by his own example that his men be harder than the metal of their B-17's, Savage now combatted with his whole strength against any indulgence of his own personal feelings.

Pamela. There was another threat. Bishop. Pamela. Henderson. A three-way tension tore at his mind and feelings, turning his face bleak.

Stovall came in, carrying some papers, but stopped halfway across the room when he saw Savage's face. The skin was the color of dough.

"Excuse me, sir," he said quickly. "Got the wrong papers here . . ." He turned and left, after noting the instant reversion of the general's expression to normal. Savage started to call to Stovall, but was afraid of his voice, afraid that it would betray him.

Stovall came back. Now it was his turn to cover his feelings. For he had seen something he had never expected to see. The first chink. The first crack in a piece of human steel.

The lights burned late in Stovall's office. His tie unfastened, his shirt collar open, the ground exec was having an unusually difficult time with a Missing in Action report. Cigarette stubs were piled in his ashtray and a half empty cup of cold, black coffee was at his elbow. Over and over, he shuffled through a pile of Interrogation forms with which the Intelligence officer had supplied him—a summary of eye-witness reports from the crews who had seen Bishop's airplane go down.

Savage wandered in.

"Working kind of late, aren't you, Harvey?"

"Yes, sir." He leaned back and stretched. "Maybe I'm slowing up."

Savage glanced casually over the papers in front of Stovall.

"Need any help?" His voice was still casual, but Stovall knew Savage well enough to detect that it was a little too casual.

"M.I.A. report," he said. "Kind of hard to make head or tail of some of these gunners' accounts." He carefully refrained from mention of the name Bishop. But in the minds of all the men at Archbury, Stovall knew, that name was present, like a flag fluttering at half-mast over the airdrome.

Savage sat down and pulled out a cigar, clipped it and then discovered his lighter was dry. Stovall knocked the ash out of his pipe, sucked it until it glowed red and handed it to the general.

"Thanks, Harvey."

Stovall had barely returned his attention to his work when Savage interrupted him.

"Tail gunners are your best bet," he said. "Off a crew flying wing position." From his tone, he might have been discussing a weather report.

"Yeah, I know," said Stovall, sliding a sheet of paper to

one side. "This guy's got about the only specific information I can use."

After a pause the general stood up and walked slowly past the desk toward the door. But Stovall noticed that Savage's eyes had flicked surreptitiously down at the tail-gunner's name, Hillery, scrawled on the report.

"Better turn in, Harvey," he said. "I'll be over to the quarters soon. Think I'll drop by the sergeants' club. Haven't had a beer with the men for a week."

As Savage's footsteps died away down the hall, the ground exec's eyes dropped their guard, disclosing an expression of profound sympathy and understanding of the other man's suffering.

Savage warmed to the reception which greeted his arrival at the sergeants' club. There was no stiffness or evidence that the men felt their style being cramped by the presence of a general officer. Those with whom he came into contact were glad to see him, and showed it, while the rest went about their business. Sergeants Nero and Coulter steered him to the bar for a beer, pulling rank on him when he tried to pay. After some shop talk about generator failures, Savage inquired whether a gunner named Hillery was present.

"Over there, sir," said Nero. "Shall I get him?"

"No," said Savage. "Just curious. Heard something about him the other day."

"He's a plenty sharp tail gunner," said Coulter. "Got three FW's on the Vegesack mission."

"Of course," said Savage. "That's what it was."

Presently Sergeant Hillery walked over to order another beer. Savage edged along the bar until he was standing next to him.

"Nice going, Hillery," he said.

"How's that, sir?"

"That bag of FW's. Over Vegesack."

"Oh . . . Gee, thanks, General." Hillery was delighted. Entirely without vanity, but with honest pride in an achievement that constituted a high-water mark in his career, Hillery never stopped to wonder how the general knew his name. "Must have closed my eyes tight and squeezed the grips," he added modestly.

Savage laughed.

"Nothing wrong with your eyesight from what I hear, Sergeant," he said. They chatted amiably for several minutes until suddenly Hillery perceived that he had attracted closer attention from the general. The sergeant had just started talking about that day's mission to Oschersleben. He described enemy fighter tactics in detail, continuing to hold the absorbed interest of the group commander. Finally he got around to his version of how Bishop's crew had gone down, noting that Savage's curiosity seemed to relax somewhat.

"No sign of a chute, sir," he concluded. "Straight down into the clouds. Afraid they've all had it, sir."

Savage bought Hillery a beer. He chatted a little longer, then said good night, leaving his own beer half finished on the bar.

Sergeant Coulter stopped him near the door.

"General," he said. "If you've got a minute, I don't think you'll want to miss this."

Following Coulter's glance, Savage saw that Nero had stationed himself alongside an accompanist at the piano. The broad, squat Italian line chief looked flushed and self-conscious, as he loosened his collar with a grimy forefinger.

"Never knew Nero was a singer," said Savage.

"Doesn't sing often," said Coulter. "But when he does, he makes a piker out of Caruso."

In spite of his preoccupation with the loss of Bishop, and his desire to get away, Savage lingered at the door, anticipating the worst, to hear Nero. But the minute the master sergeant's voice rang out, after the introductory chords to "Come Back to Sorrento," the general was gripped with increasing astonishment. Nero's tenor voice, though untrained, possessed startling richness and power.

Shedding his initial self-consciousness, the homely line chief became lost in the outpouring of his voice. Passion was in it—sorrow, defeat, triumph. Savage thought of Bishop—of how Jesse had loved music. Gradually it seemed that the drab room and the weary faces of the soldiers melted away, leaving only a voice that expressed the whole range, heaven high, hell deep, of the experience being shared by all the men who had left their scattered homes in America to join forces in this supreme and terrible effort from rain-swept air bases in England.

Nero concentrated his eyes and his voice directly on the general until he had finished. It was the closest approach Savage had ever experienced to having a man prove to him— without telling him—"I know how you feel."

Savage was at his desk early the next morning, working at top speed, when he heard a knock and saw that Major Kaiser was at the door.

"Come right in, Doc."

"Yes, sir."

The flight surgeon was carrying a large flat carton under his arm. But the general scarcely noticed it, for he was struck by the peculiar expression on Kaiser's face. Savage could have sworn that the man had just been involved in some kind of serious accident.

"May I sit down, sir?"

"Sure. Sure, here's a chair." The general pushed one toward Kaiser, who sat down heavily and looked at Savage with anxious eyes. The general consciously exercised his self-control, forcing his brain into readiness to absorb a new problem for which there was precious little room.

"I'm guilty of a terrible miscalculation, sir," said Kaiser.

"What's wrong now, Doc?" Savage frowned with concern.

"It's Gately. He's over in the hospital. In a plaster cast . . . couldn't even walk to the mess for breakfast."

"Why wasn't I told he was wounded yesterday?" asked Savage sharply.

"That's the hell of it, sir. It wasn't yesterday. Here, take a look at this." He opened his package, withdrew an X-ray plate and stood it up on the desk against the glare of the desk lamp. Savage bent down quickly, staring at the spinal column limned on the glass. Kaiser took out a pencil and pointed to one of the vertebrae.

"Crack of the anterior lip," he said, "of the vertebral body."

"Jesus!" said Savage, beginning to turn pale under his bronze. "You mean he broke his back in that ditching?"

"Not exactly. But that's what it amounts to."

"But . . . but . . . Christ, Kaiser, he's flown two missions since the ditching."

"Yes, sir." Kaiser cleared his throat. "And without complaint, since his original request to be grounded. If he'd reported back to me I might have become suspicious of a more serious condition. Absolutely my fault, sir."

Savage walked slowly over to the window and back again, crumpling up his cigar in his fist until shreds of tobacco fell to the floor.

"I only wish it *were* your fault, Doc," he said in a husky voice. "Or somebody's. But it's *mine!*" He walked back again to the window and turned around.

"What in hell am I standing around here for, Doc? Come on, we're going over to your place."

Kaiser and the general arrived at the hospital in double-quick time, walked down a center aisle connecting several Nissen huts and at length turned off into a round-ceilinged ward filled with Purple Heart cases. Gately, lying in a cast and with weights attached to his feet, looked up from one of the beds at the far end.

Savage approached the bed slowly, painfully aware of a more intense hostility in Gately's eyes than he had anticipated. Meeting those eyes, rejected by them, Savage had to force himself to cover the last few feet until he was standing beside the bed. Now that he was confronted with its occupant, he felt completely at a loss how to begin. He swallowed hard.

"How . . . how do you feel, kid?" he asked finally.

Gately gave him a long, cool stare. He began to wonder whether Gately would answer at all. Then the former air exec raised himself slightly on his elbows.

"Come to think of it, General," he said with bitterness, but without self-pity, making every word count, "I can remember when I've felt worse."

Gately's reply was so cogent, so aptly to the point, that Savage lost track of the words he had come to say. He remained silent a moment, then looked at Kaiser.

"How long, Major," he asked, grasping at any conversational straw, "before he'll be okay?"

"Couple of months, probably, sir. Although one month is possible."

"One month," said Gately, looking not at Savage but at Kaiser, "is more like it, Doc. The sooner you get me out of this iron lung the better."

"We'll do our best, Ben," said Kaiser soothingly.

Savage regarded Kaiser anxiously.

"Are you equipped to give him proper treatment here?" he asked.

"I believe so, sir. But we can move him to a rear hospital if you think it advisable."

"Just leave me here, Doc," said Gately vehemently. "I'm not going anywhere . . . except back to flying duty. Soon as you get rid of this backache for me."

"Nothing to get upset about," said Kaiser. "We'll have you up and around soon enough."

"Okay!" said Gately, making the word sound more like: *See that you do.*

Savage had collected his thoughts.

"Ben," he said, "I'm not much of a letter writer. But I want to write a letter to your father. I'd like to get his address."

Gately stared at him dubiously.

"Why worry him, General?" he asked. "By the time he gets a letter, I'll be out of here."

"What I want to write," said Savage, "won't worry him a goddam bit."

Across Gately's mind there flashed a vivid picture of another occasion and the sarcasm of Savage's voice, saying: "Why don't you cable your father? He'd be goddam proud of you!" Mixed emotions stirred him.

"Care of the Joint Chiefs of Staff," he said coldly. "Washington, D. C."

"Thanks." Savage gave a slight cough. "I'm going to write to him tonight."

He studied Gately's unrelenting expression. And then he found himself also studying the young officer's individual features—the handsome, long-lashed eyes, the sensitive nostrils, the full lips—conscious that he had not taken the trouble before ever really to examine them. It was a stronger face than he had realized, but almost too good-looking. That, reflected Savage, must be what threw me off. Way, way off. He moved a little closer to Gately. He cleared his throat.

"You don't hate me," he said softly. "You just *think* you do." He waited. No answer.

"You never *did* hate me. You hated the things inside

yourself that didn't belong there. You thought you hated *me* when I dragged them out in the open . . . and showed them to you."

Still no answer. Then the general perceived that Gately had begun to look terribly tired.

"I'm shoving off now." He reached out his hand halfway toward Gately's, but the latter, making no move, merely stared up at him blankly. Savage lingered a moment longer, his eyes dropping to the floor. He looked up. "Get some shut-eye," he added gently.

After Savage and Kaiser had gone, Gately lighted a cigarette, blew the smoke upward and regarded the ceiling. He heard footsteps, presently, on the concrete walk outside and recognized the general's voice.

"Pretty painful?" he heard Savage asking.

"Agonizing, General. Bone impinging on the nerve, you know. Long hours at high altitude." There was a short pause. "I know better men than Gately who couldn't have stood that kind of pain for one mission—let alone *two*."

There was another pause.

"You're dead wrong, Kaiser." Gately could hear Savage's voice distinctly. "There *are* no better men than Ben Gately."

For a long time the former air exec stared at the ceiling, as though paralyzed. Everything that was pent up inside him —the humiliation, the hate, the bitterness, the frustration— all at once let go. He turned his head and buried his face in the pillow.

CHAPTER TEN

Widewing

Savage entered the hospital the following morning carrying a small paper bag containing six eggs. Although it was so early that most of the men in Gately's ward were still asleep, Savage found Gately lying awake and listening to a news broadcast, turned down low, from the small radio beside the head of his bed. His eyes lighted up at the sight of the general. He smiled.

Wondering what had come over Gately since the previous evening, Savage held out his hand. Gately took it and the two men exchanged a long handshake. But there was an even warmer handshake in the meeting of their eyes—Gately's clear, Savage's a little misty.

"Morning, sir," said Gately belatedly.

"Morning, Ben . . . how's the back?"

"I'm a cinch, sir. Just give me about a week."

"I'll give you anything you say, Ben."

Gately glanced at his radio, turning it off. "You shouldn't have given me your own radio," he said. "I wish you'd take it back, sir . . . there's a big one over there in the corner."

"Keep it," said Savage. "I never use it anyway."

"Thanks, General."

"Got something else you may be able to use," he said, rolling his six eggs out gingerly on the blanket.

Gately's eyes opened wide with pleasure. "That sleeping pill's still working, sir," he said. "For a second I dreamed I was looking at six eggs . . . on the shell."

Savage grinned. "Sergeant McIllhenny's a pretty fair egg scrounger. Since he got married. He sent these with the compliments of Mrs. McIllhenny."

"Cackleberries," said Gately, picking up one of the eggs and examining it as though it were an emerald. "A genuine cackleberry." His face assumed an expression of frowning calculation. "Now I've got a problem, sir," he continued. "Whether to stretch it out for six days . . . or eat them in pairs for three days."

"Eat 'em all for breakfast this morning," said Savage.

"Not me, sir. I think I'll kind of stretch 'em out."

"More where those came from, Ben. McIllhenny told his wife if any hen fails to make a maximum effort, the bird goes in the pot."

"Seriously, sir, I'd be embarrassed if you brought any more. This is plenty. Hell, I'm rich."

After chatting with Gately a few minutes more, Savage said goodbye, promising he'd be dropping in again soon. On his way out he stopped to talk with a couple of wounded

gunners who were awake, waved again to Gately from the
door and left.

After Savage had made a thorough analysis of the noon-
weather sequence, he gave Stovall a telephone number at
which he could be reached at Lowestoft in an emergency,
changed into his best uniform, drove to the hangar line and
took off from Archbury in a small staff airplane.

It was typical English flying weather—a bagful of visibility
and a couple of yards of altitude—that demanded Savage's
close attention to navigation as identical-looking villages and
fields appeared in the mist beneath the low clouds and sped
by under the nose. In the States, he reflected, you wouldn't
dream of taking off in such weather; in England you had to
or let your airplane rot in storage. Twice, when he was
forced down to chimney height, squinting through his rain-
smeared windshield at shiny wet roofs, he almost decided
to turn back. But each time, the ceiling lifted just enough.
Deep down, he was enjoying his contest with the weather,
a purely physical obstacle separating him from Pamela, and
one that could be surmounted. Actually, the dirty weather
was his friend, for it had enabled him to leave Archbury
with a clear conscience. He found himself wishing that obstacles of the mind and emotions were as readily suscep-
tible to solution. For days he had alternated between giddy
confidence and qualms of doubt about Pamela's ultimate reaction to his proposal.

After landing on a small sod field near Lowestoft just behind another airplane, he met its pilot in the Operations
Office. Captain Heely introduced himself as liaison officer
from Pinetree for RT-Intercepts. On the short drive over to
Pamela's station, Savage was gratified to learn that Heely's
original one-man section had grown to two officers and
eleven enlisted men—a reflection of the increasing importance
General Henderson had been attaching to the work of plot-
ting enemy fighter reaction. Armed with a graphic record of
enemy tactics on each mission, Bomber Command was already doing a better job of guessing what the Jerries would
try next time. It's a damn good thing, Savage reflected, that
I met Pam when I did.

Passing through a dense woods, which concealed radio antennae, their car pulled up in front of a squat, unimportant-looking concrete building. The sentry recognized Heely and motioned him inside, but he stopped Savage to check his identification.

"Right you are, sir," he said promptly. "I have a pass already made out."

The general walked down a long hall, past a large room in which a dozen W.A.A.F.'s with earphones sat in front of radio receivers, and stopped at the open door of a small office. Pamela was at her desk, entering pencil notations on a report. An invisible hand reached its fingers around Savage's throat and choked his windpipe. He stared at her for several seconds before she looked up.

"Frank!"

She jumped up, hurried around the desk and toward him, as he walked forward to meet her. He hugged her against him, his mouth against hers. Presently she moved her head back a little, looking into his eyes.

"About time," she said, "don't you think?" He kissed her again—a longer kiss. Neither of them heard the heavy footsteps behind them until an elderly R.A.F. officer with handlebar mustaches bustled into the room. He stopped dead in his tracks, eyes popping.

Pamela, blushing pink, immediately released Savage, who swung around in confusion.

"I beg your . . ." began the R.A.F. officer.

Simultaneous exclamations from Pamela and Savage canceled him out. The intruder, extremely embarrassed, started to back toward the door, nodding his head awkwardly, but Pamela stepped forward for a fresh start.

"Air Commodore," she said, "I'd like to present General Savage . . . Air Commodore Satterlee."

"Quite," said the air commodore, still backing up. "Delighted." Savage, trying to look calm, merely bowed.

"General Savage," said Pamela, straightening her blouse with one hand and smoothing back her hair with the other, "is . . . my fiancé." Savage's heart leaped at the word.

"Quite," said the air commodore again, acting as though he were stranded like the victim of a nightmare who can't move. "You're a lucky chap, sir. Splendid . . . well . . . God bless."

Bowing, harrumphing and smiling, he backed out into the hall just in time to collide with the hurrying form of a huge W.A.A.F., to whom he apologized hastily and disappeared.

Savage grinned at Pamela.

"Fiancé, eh?" he said. "Don't forget, I've got a high-ranking witness."

Pamela's phone rang incessantly, rendering conversation with Savage, who sat in a chair beside her desk, nearly impossible. W.A.A.F.'s hurried in and out constantly.

"Hello, Eleven Group," she said, while Savage listened more to the lilting, clipped enunciation of her speech than to the sense of what she was saying, "DDI-Four-B here. *Can* you scramble? . . . Have you one missing on your last sweep? . . . Here's a Jerry intercept for you; I believe you'll find your man drifting about in his dinghy in the middle of a ruddy mine field . . . Will you take the co-ordinates? . . ."

He was happy just to sit there, watching her hands and her face, listening to her voice and the occasional trill of her laugh. He felt a little bit the way he once had when, just out of college, he had sat across the aisle of a Pullman from a famous movie actress, whose simplest words and gestures assumed the quality of drama.

Taking advantage of the lull, Pamela explained that her deputy was in the hospital with the flu.

"Double the work for me," she said. "But there's one consolation. I shall be off at sixteen hundred and we'll have a place where we can go and talk alone."

"Jest right," said Savage. "I'm wishing your roommate no hard luck, but . . ."

Pamela laughed. "Not my roommate," she said. "My housemate. We were lucky enough to get a small cottage down the road. I'll make you a spot of tea; you can stretch out in front of the fire in your slippers."

"Great," said Savage, beaming. "Didn't bring any slippers, though. Ought to get back to Archbury some time tonight."

"But you mustn't," she said. "In this weather. There's a bed for you in visitors' quarters."

"Well," he said, "we don't have to worry about that now."

A W.A.A.F. entered with a message for Pamela, which occupied her attention for several minutes. When she was free again, he told her about Gately's hospitalization, about his tremendous respect for the man's guts, his remorse over ordering him to fly with an injury and their reconciliation as of that morning. She let him know, without any hint of I-told-you-so, how terribly happy she was about it. Then her face clouded with sadness and concern when he told her about Bishop's being shot down.

"But you didn't mention it in your letter," she protested.

"I couldn't think of anything else," he lied, "except you, while I was writing." She reached over and squeezed his hand, then frowned as something else occurred to her.

"What day was it, Frank?" she asked.

"February eighth," he said promptly. "Pam, I'm just beginning to notice that your hair . . ."

"Do you remember the time?" she interrupted, in spite of his obvious disinclination to discuss Bishop further.

"1423 hours," he said, "GMT. You know, from a certain angle it's got red lights in it. What do you do to it?"

"Were any parachutes seen?" she persisted.

"Apparently not."

"Do you know the co-ordinates where Jesse went down?"

"Not in my head. Near Oschersleben."

Pamela called in a W.A.A.F. sergeant.

"Bring me the log for February eighth," she said, referring to her note pad, "Oschersleben. I want all the RT-Intercepts within a half-hour before or after 1423 hours, GMT."

Savage sat bolt upright. The W.A.A.F. was gone for several minutes, during which Savage fidgeted in his chair with ill-concealed impatience, thankful that Pamela was busy on the phone. Finally the W.A.A.F. returned carrying a typewritten file, which she placed on the desk in front of Pamela. Savage stood up, leaned over her shoulder and stared at the cryptic entries until she had hung up.

"Now let's see," she said, running her pencil down the margin, reading rapidly. "There were several shoot-downs before 1423 . . . last one at 1418 . . . too early. Nothing at 1423 or 1424." She read further, then suddenly paused.

"Hold on!" she exclaimed. "At 1425. Maybe we've got something." Savage leaned over still closer.

"A shoot-down by flak. *Dickeauto Amerikanische.*"

"That's *right!*" breathed Savage.

"Reported by an Me-109 pilot named *Heinz*. Call sign *Schwarzkopf Acht*."

"Go on!"

"Please, dear, you're in my light . . . Nothing at 1426 or 7. Look, Frank! 1428, same pilot, same call sign . . . he contacted a Luftwaffe airdrome north of Oschersleben . . . Send troops. Farm. One mile east your airdrome. Crash landing. American heavy bomber. Ten survivors scattering south toward woods. Will circle area. Over."

Savage straightened up slowly and sank back into his chair, while Pamela, in great excitement, continued to check through a few subsequent entries.

"The next Fort shot down," she said finally, looking up, "was eleven minutes later and about forty miles west of Oschersleben. Frank! It could only have been *Jesse*!"

Savage, smiling in almost tearful relief, stood up and began taking short paces back and forth in front of her desk.

"All of them okay!" he said jubilantly. "All ten of them!" His eyes shone. He pulled Pamela, wreathed in smiles, from behind her desk and hugged her. "I get magic out of you," he said. "You're wonderful."

"I hope this won't spoil it for you, darling," she said, "but you didn't let me finish. Jesse will be eating out of a Red Cross parcel for a long time. That pilot did circle. He reported the whole crew were taken prisoner."

Savage was still grinning. "So what?" he asked. "I can think of worse places than a P.W. camp." Another thought occurred to him. "How about our headquarters?" he asked. "Did they get a report on this?"

"Of course," she said. "Air Ministry passes it all on to you." She smiled at him archly. "What your chaps do with it after that, I can't say."

Savage wagged an admonitory finger at her.

"Watch your Anglo-American relations," he said. "Remember?"

"I'll do my bit right now," she said. Glancing first at the door, she gave him a quick kiss.

A slanting rain beat in gusts against the windowpanes, but within Pamela's cottage all was snug and warm. She and Savage sat in chairs drawn close together before the hearth. On a nearby table, next to Savage's empty musette bag, lay a heap of the general's burnt offerings: four cartons of cigarettes, two bottles of Scotch, three cans of salted peanuts and two of anchovies, a jar of strawberry jam, a box of Kleenex, some lipstick and a pair of nylon stockings.

They were sipping Savage's brand of tea—in this case, Scotch and soda. For some time they simply sat, enjoying each other's company with small talk, each of them waiting for the other to turn the conversation to the momentous thoughts uppermost in their minds. Pamela was the first to become serious.

"Frank," she said, "if you'll forgive me for talking shop, isn't it about time for them to give you . . . a different post?"

"I've got a pretty good job," he said.

"But it means combat," she said. "Your second tour of combat."

"Yes," he said quietly. "It won't last forever."

She took a deep swallow of her drink. "I should hope not," she said. "Frank, this is the first thing I've ever asked you to do. And it may be the most important." He set down his glass and swung his eyes from the fire to her face. "Don't think I'm cowardly," she continued, "but I'm asking you, for my sake, to stop flying combat just as soon as you possibly can."

"I will," he said guardedly.

"You've got to give me something definite to go on," she said. "How soon, Frank?"

"The minute, the second I know my job is done."

She ran her fingertip around the top of her glass, turning away from him to stare at the fire. When she spoke again, her voice was unsteady.

"I *am* a coward," she said. "An awful coward. But a truthful one, anyway. I've been a coward ever since we met."

Savage took a long drink, then reached for her hand and looked into her eyes.

"I met a war first," he said simply.

Both of them were silent for what seemed to each like a long time. Presently Savage got up and poked at the fire.

"Reminds me," he said. "Better check the weather. May I use your phone?"

She stifled an urge to say no. "Over there," she said.

Savage put in a call to the field, got hold of the forecaster and listened thoughtfully. He returned the phone to its cradle and met her eyes.

"The stuff's lifting," he said. "I can get through." As he walked slowly back to the fireplace, she stood up and went over to him, laying her hands on his shoulders.

"Darling," she said shyly. She reached up and ran her long fingers over his forehead and back through his hair. Through her other hand she felt his shoulders tremble. She led him over to the couch, stretched out with her head on the pillow and pulled him down alongside her. Taking her in his arms, feeling the softness of her against the whole length of his body, Savage was overcome by the turbulence of the deepest bliss he had ever felt. A full minute, during which he believed that he could never let go, passed with their lips pressed hard together. Finally, he forced himself to sit up. He made a visible effort to get to his feet, but turned instead and laid his head in her lap, as Pamela reached a sitting position also.

"Frank, dear?" she asked, out of breath, stroking his hair and regarding his face with eyes that were liquid with tenderness.

"No, Pam. Don't talk."

"I must. Darling . . . I don't want you to go back tonight . . . even if there isn't a cloud in the sky. I want you to stay here. In the cottage. With me."

He stared at her and then toward the rain-swept window, his eyes gradually losing their charge of emotion and longing. His expression altered radically into one of meditation.

"Thinking?" she asked.

He cleared his throat.

"Yes," he murmured. "Thinking."

"Don't," she said.

But he continued to stare intently at the window, as though it were a windshield, looking as she imagined he must look when he was sitting in the cockpit leading hundreds of bombers, weighing the factors of enemy fighters, flak, weather and all the other variables confronting him.

Actually, the old Savage was fighting at close quarters with the new Savage. Where his old self told him, as it had once told Pamela: I don't think a roll in the hay is too important

—his changed outlook told him that any relationship of intimacy with Pamela would be devastatingly important to him. He knew he couldn't take her in his stride and forget about it; he would wind up spending half his time at Archbury wondering how soon he could get back up to Lowestoft again, rationalizing himself into excuses for doing so at the expense of the single-minded concentration demanded of him in his command of the 918th. Had he the right to let himself become more interested in living than in reaching the target? Once he had said to a bunch of youngsters: "Consider yourselves already dead." Didn't that go for him, too?

He lighted a cigarette and inhaled deeply. Finally he stirred, sat up, paused for a moment and got to his feet, facing her. He flicked the cigarette into the grate behind him. His answer was the shortest, and yet the longest, she had ever heard.

"It's no good," he said.

She wanted to argue with him, plead with him if necessary. But his eyes told her that it would be futile, that he had thought it through to a decision and that he would not alter it . . . nor explain it.

She stood up, too. He took her in his arms and held her in a prolonged, breathless embrace. Then, without looking back, he strode to the door, picked up his cap and musette bag, stepped outside into the drizzle and was gone.

Pamela moved to a front window and watched his figure retreating through the gloom.

Two days later Savage was instructed to attend a meeting for all group and wing commanders at Widewing. He felt a novel sense of appreciation as his fellow commanders began filling the conference room. All of their faces were tired. Probably, reflected Savage, at no place in the world and at no time in history could one room have been occupied by so highly select a group of men. These were the main bearings about which the wheel of the air war revolved. Any burned-out bearing here could mean a breakdown of the complex machinery which began with the enlisted technicians at the air bases and spread up to the highest levels of command in Washington. The blank checks written by Roosevelt and Churchill were honored, or repudiated, at the bank window of combat by these leaders. For they functioned just below the precise dividing line between personal leadership and the upper echelons where responsibility became increasingly impersonal and remote from the flesh and blood of human pawns. Savage felt grateful and proud to sit as an equal with these men.

When General Pritchard and General Henderson walked into the room, their faces were unusually solemn.

"Gentlemen," began Pritchard, "I must begin by cautioning you, as emphatically as I know how, that the plans to be discussed at this meeting are for your ears alone. Except for the minimum number of your subordinates who will be directly concerned—of which more later—I repeat that any breach of security will completely nullify the chances for success of the most vitally important assignment yet given this air force." Henderson nodded gravely in agreement.

"It's a tough one," continued Pritchard. "It must be exactly planned down to the last pint of gasoline, the last round of ammunition and the last second of time. Losses in men and airplanes are bound to be heavy. But if this mission is accomplished, the military cost will be cheap. My directive for the mission was worked out by the Combined and Joint Chiefs of Staff. That directive makes it clear that, aside from purely military considerations, grave political considerations, affecting the morale of our Allies and of operations in other theaters, are involved." He paused. "General Henderson will take it from here."

Henderson stepped forward. "First," he said, "if any officer present is certain that he will be required to fly over enemy territory in the next six days, I must ask him to leave the room *now*." Three colonels excused themselves and left. "I will outline the operation briefly. Then we'll go into details." He motioned to a sergeant, who rolled up a screen in front of a huge wall map. Henderson picked up a pointer, but stood to one side for several seconds to allow his audience to absorb the story implicit in the red strings across part of the map. Savage, along with the others, caught his breath.

A single red string stretched from England to a point deep in Germany, then forked. Part of the fork led northeast to Hambrücken, the other ran southeast to Bonhofen, then east to a base in Russia, at the extreme range of a B-17 equipped with Tokyo wingtip tanks. Savage's heart pounded as the skeleton of the plan quickly crystallized in his mind. It was a bold plan, a dangerous plan, he told himself, but it might work. It had the virtues of simplicity and, if properly executed, of surprise.

Henderson waited for the rustle of tense comment among the commanders to subside. Then he reached into his pocket and brought out a shiny round object which he held in his hand so that all could see it.

"Approximately half of these German ball bearings are manufactured at Hambrücken," he said. "Last night, Air Chief Marshal, Lord Charles Portal, handed me this one. I'll repeat what he said to me: 'If you can stop the Jerries from making these things, it's going to be a much shorter war.'" He paused. "General Pritchard and I agree with him. These bearings are essential not only to the production of German aircraft but to equipment critically needed by the nazi ground and naval forces.

"At Bonhofen," he continued, pointing it out on the map, "the nazis have their second-largest factory for the production of the Messerschmitt 109-G. Knock it out and we estimate that thirty per cent of the German single-engine fighter production is knocked out. As to the over-all importance of these two targets, I'm sure that I don't need to labor the point.

"Now for the plan. Its essential features are tactical surprise and saturation of the defenses. We expect you to put every bomber in the air that will get off the ground. Half of the bombers will go to Hambrücken, half to Bonhofen. The Bonhofen task force will penetrate first and will have fighter escort through the German fighter belt—all the fighter support that we and the R.A.F. combined can furnish. This, plus whatever degree of surprise we can achieve by diversionary missions, should hold down your losses. Every airplane in England that isn't going on the mission—medium bombers, fighters, British Bomber Command—will make large-scale feints at other points, timed toward maximum deception. All right. The Bonhofen task force, instead of retracing its course to England against the concentrations of Jerry fighters which will be waiting for them all along the normal route of withdrawal, will continue on past Poland to prepared airdromes in Russia. To complete their shuttle-bombing operation, they will rest up for a few days and then bomb Germany, on their way home to England.

"The Hambrücken task force will follow the same route into Germany as the Bonhofen force. The plan is to time the second penetration fifteen minutes behind the first penetration to catch the enemy fighters on the ground refueling and rearming—flatfooted. After bombing Hambrücken, our bombers will have to fight their way back out from the target until they are met by a maximum force of our fighters, who will give them withdrawal support from the limit of their range." He laid down his pointer and turned again to face his listeners.

"In all probability," he concluded, "as soon as the Luftwaffe wakes up to where we are headed, it will throw everything in the book at us . . . everything they've got. But that cuts both ways. It's a chance for us to break the back of enemy fighter resistance in the air as well as on the ground. If the whole operation is flown as briefed, our own losses may not be excessive.

"Fundamentally, the whole plan hinges on weather. England, the entire continent and western Russia must be clear for twelve hours of daylight. That's a tall order. So we must be prepared to take advantage of the first break in the weather. Meanwhile other operations will be curtailed, so that you can start getting ready; you'll have a minimum of six days. Then the plan will go into effect until the mission is accomplished. Tonight, all of your lead navigators and bombardiers will attend a special briefing at my headquarters.

"And now, one more thing before I turn the floor over to General Phillips, A-3, Eighth Air Force, who will brief you in further detail. I have been advised that many reasons exist pointing to the desirability of our following up the Hambrücken-Bonhofen strikes, at the earliest opportunity, with our first daylight strike on Berlin." A glint of fire flashed in Savage's eyes at mention of the word Berlin. "We shan't go into that this morning. Just bear it in mind; and start getting set."

He motioned to an officer in the front row.

"General Phillips," he said, returning to his seat beside Pritchard.

"You and I," said Pritchard, offering Savage a cigar from the box on his desk, "are overdue for a private bull session, Frank." His smile was warm and sincere. "How's business?"

"We're choppin' and the chips are flyin', sir," said Savage, sniffing the cigar appreciatively. "How about yourself?"

"Rugged, Frank. They're trying to take my airplanes away from me . . . every time I turn around. The build-up's behind schedule. But we're growing anyway. Little by little." He fired up a dirty corncob pipe, for which he had recently forsaken cigars. "But as for you, I'd say offhand you're doing better than just getting by."

"Not complaining, sir."

"You took the worst group we had and made it into the best. Didn't surprise me a bit." He blew out a puff. "Best smoke there is," he continued. "Beats cigars." He crinkled his eyes at Savage.

"I know you hate a desk, Frank," he observed. "You're a fightin' man. But Henderson shares my opinion that there's no sense in your fighting until you get shot down. I'm referring to the job in the States."

"Yes, sir."

"I'm wondering if it isn't about time you took it. Ed says you're reluctant."

"I am, sir. Pretty soon I'll have a couple of boys that can handle the group . . . Gately or maybe Cobb. But they aren't quite ripe . . . not yet . . . with the Hambrücken and Berlin shows coming up. I want to make those two, General. Then the crews will have seen everything. Then I don't care where you ship me."

"I think the time to quit is now, Frank. Before it's too late. I can send Charley Fisher down. Just got here from the States . . . looking for a job."

"Fisher's a good man, sir. But no combat in this Theater. Too green. I wouldn't sleep nights."

Pritchard began to scowl and his jaw assumed a stubborn line which Savage had seen before when the Old Man was in no mood for argument.

"I've tried to tell you the easy way, Frank," he said. "The fact is you're not going on any more missions. I won't approve it."

"I'm just asking for those two, General."

"Nothing doing. I admit you're the best leader we've got. But do you deny that we have others who can do the job?"

"Of course we have, sir. We've got some good group commanders. But I've got the experience. It may make the difference on a strike to Hambrücken or Berlin."

"Others have experience now."

"I've got more. More than anybody!"

Pritchard's scowl darkened.

"I'm not arguing about it, Frank. I'm telling you."

Savage turned a shade paler and stood up.

"Sir," he said, "in all the years I've served under you, and they were the best years I've spent in my life, I've never questioned an order from you. Never thought I would. But on this issue I'm going to have to insist that you let me fly on those two missions."

Pritchard stood up also, and his face was hard.

"You are not in a position to *insist*," he stated evenly.

"I believe I am, sir."

"*What?*"

"Let me put it this way, sir. All you can do to me if I disobey your orders is court-martial me."

"Correct. And I wouldn't hesitate to do it."

"All right. So I tell the public *why* I was court-martialed . . . for insisting on the right to fly a combat mission I believed it was my duty to fly. A general insisting on getting shot at!" He took a step toward Pritchard until his blazing gray eyes were close to the other officer's. "You know, General," he shot out the words, "who would win *that* argument, don't you?"

Savage perceived that he had scored a direct hit. Pritchard squinted at him for a brief moment of frustration, jabbed the corncob pipe in his mouth, swung around the desk, sat down and began visibly to cool off. His eyes strayed alternately between the coal in his pipe and Savage's eyes.

"You win, Frank," he said quietly. "But you had an even better argument. I was afraid you were going to use it." He waited until Savage's curiosity gained the upper hand.

"What argument, sir?"

"On second thought, you had two. Number one: you delivered the goods for me at Archbury and you could have asked anything in my power to grant in return. But I knew you'd never use that one." Again he stopped, but this time Savage also waited.

"I was afraid you were going to read my thoughts and play the ace. I was afraid you were going to tell me that you knew that I *wanted* you to lead those two strikes."

He rose and walked over to Savage, shaking his hand.

"I couldn't have lied to you, Frank," he said. "I've done everything I can to talk you out of it. Now my conscience is clear."

Five times within the next four weeks the Hambrücken-Bonhofen mission was laid on by a warning order and five times the lead navigators and bombardiers were summoned to secret briefings the night before, only to discover upon returning to their stations that the Big Show was scrubbed on account of weather.

A few missions were flown to avoid arousing enemy suspicions, but all of them were planned to conserve strength and rest the crews while keeping them from going stale. Savage, preferring to let the younger men gain experience on easy missions, remained on the ground. He worried constantly about security, for it was obvious that too many people knew something was in the wind, and he missed Pamela terribly. She had not been able once to leave her post at Lowestoft, but her letters were frequent and filled with words which he treasured in his heart for days after reading them. He never ceased to be amazed at the extent to which, having found her man, she went flat out in making it clear that this was so. Twice he called her long distance—an almost impossible feat in the face of the pyramid of official priorities standing in the way of personal use of England's war-burdened telephone system.

Gately dumbfounded everyone, especially the flight surgeon, by recovering sufficiently to leave his bed after three weeks. And within a week of being up and around he persuaded Kaiser and Savage, after a final X-ray, to let him make a mission. There had been no ill effects.

Savage was sitting in his office, perusing a series of weather sequences which led him to anticipate the possibility of the Big Show's being laid on again for the morrow, when Cobb walked in, looking slightly hung-over. The air exec had avoided the club bar faithfully since his first encounter with Savage, until the previous evening, when the general had given him the nod, and with good reason. Cobb was now wearing the silver leaves of a lieutenant colonel. So was Stovall, for a batch of promotions had finally come through.

"Pull up a chair, Joe," called Savage. "Or should I say Colonel?"

"Can't get used to these things," said Cobb, grinning and looking down at his shoulders. He took a seat.

"General," he began cautiously, "I've been wondering. We've got a squadron commander's vacancy. Well, I was wondering if you'd let me take a squadron for a while."

"Tired of being air exec?"

"Oh, no, sir. It's been swell. But . . . well, you know how it is, more or less of a staff job. With a squadron . . . well, you've got a command."

"Like a squadron myself. Always has been and always will be the best job in the Air Corps."

"That's right, sir. That's what I mean. Any chance?"

Savage regarded Cobb shrewdly for a while. "Can't say I have any particular objection, Joe," he said. "If that's what you really want. Your rank's no obstacle . . . new T.O. authorizes lieutenant colonelcies for heavy-bomb squadrons."

"Thanks," said Cobb, genuinely pleased. "Thanks a hell of a lot, General."

"Only one thing, though, Joe. What am I going to do about a new air exec?"

Cobb was prompt with his reply. "What's wrong with the old one? How about Ben?"

Savage reached for a cigar and bit off the end. "Now wait a minute," he said. "Gately'd be fine. But if you're making me a proposition so that I can put him in your place, you're all wet. You're doing a good job."

"No, no, sir. It's nothing like that. I'm not being noble. I've really missed my squadron, General. It's the honest truth."

He studied Cobb closely, with the look of a man who doesn't miss much. "Okay," he said. "*Colonel* Stovall!" The ground exec appeared. "Assign Cobb to his old squadron and reassign Gately as air exec, effective now."

"Yes, sir. Right away." Savage noticed that Harvey Stovall

left with a pleased expression, almost as though it had been his own idea.

Cobb stood up.

"I'll move my stuff out, sir, so Gately can move in tonight."

"No," said Savage. "Don't do that, Joe. I've got a better idea. You stay where you are; but get hold of Gately and tell him to move his bags into my quarters. He can have the spare bed. Tell him that'll save cluttering up my joint when visitors come."

Cobb saluted. "Yes, sir," he said and left.

Not long afterward Stovall came in again and laid a pile of papers, including a postcard, in front of the general. He lifted some papers from the OUT basket, pretending to examine them, while he watched Savage until the latter got around to picking up the postcard. Stovall saw no change in the general's expression as he read it, although when he himself had scanned the brief lines, he had barely been able to stop himself from shouting aloud. It was a card from Jesse Bishop, stating that he and the rest of the crew, none of them seriously injured, were in Stalagluft Nine.

Savage initialed a corner of the postcard, then tossed it in the OUT basket.

"Anything else from behind the barbed wire?" he asked casually.

"No, sir. That's all today."

Savage reached over unconcernedly to his IN basket and lifted out a report.

"More of them we hear from, the better," he said. "You know, Harvey, I figure we'll find out after the war that at least half of the guys that get shot down will turn up okay."

"I certainly hope so, sir. I wouldn't be surprised."

The general concentrated his attention on his report. Stovall returned to his office, carefully closing the door behind him.

Savage tossed the report aside and, his mouth relaxing into a smile, fixed his eyes on an object beyond the window. His reverie continued until he heard a hesitant knock on the door.

"Come in, McIllhenny," he said.

The sergeant stepped briskly forward and rendered his best

Sunday-parade salute. Savage divined something unusual in McIllhenny's manner.

"What have you done this time, Sergeant?" he asked.

"Since the general has put it that way," said McIllhenny, "I'll come right to the point, sir."

"Always a good idea," said Savage, "with me."

"Yes, sir." He reached in his breast pocket, drew out a long black cigar and handed it to the general.

"With my compliments, sir."

"Your birthday?"

"No, sir. At 0930 hours I became a father, sir."

Savage immediately stood up and shook the sergeant's hand. "My congratulations, McIllhenny. That's great. Boy or girl?"

McIllhenny beamed. "Ten-pound boy, sir."

"McIllhenny, that's wonderful! That's . . ." He stopped, at a momentary loss for words. "You're a credit to the 918th, McIllhenny, that's what you are. A boy! Do you realize what a lucky guy you are?"

"I hope I do, sir."

"McIllhenny, this calls for a celebration."

"Thank you, sir."

Savage caught an expectant look in the other man's eyes. "Do you think that boy of yours is worth a stripe, by any chance?"

"At least a stripe, sir."

"I see your point. All right, McIllhenny, you can warm up that typewritter of yours right now with an order presenting you with three additional stripes."

"Comes out just even, sir. *Master* sergeant. Three on top and three below. The general has my deepest thanks."

"You're extremely welcome. I consider that you earned those stripes," he added, "the hard way." He regarded McIllhenny affectionately. "You're a family man, now, Sergeant. No more combat missions for you."

McIllhenny's face fell. "But, General," he protested. "Two more missions and I'm eligible for that Air Medal I've been sweating out."

"Sorry," said Savage, "you're positively through."

McIllhenny stared at his shoes for a moment. "You're not doing me any favor, sir," he said, with a strange, emotional overtone in his voice. "You're punishing me . . . you know, sir . . . I've gotten right handy with a gun. I can pay my way up there with you."

"I know," interrupted Savage, "that you're a good gunner. But that's beside the point."

"The point is, sir, I'd rather take a beating than wait up on the control tower . . . sweating you out. Lot easier to go along."

It gradually dawned on Savage that McIllhenny's words concealed a deeper feeling.

"Nobody likes sweating them out from the ground, Sergeant," he said. "And nobody knows that better than I do. Still . . . I don't know . . ." His voice trailed off.

"General," interposed McIllhenny, "why couldn't we . . . I was thinking, sir, maybe the general and I could kind of finish up combat together . . . at the same time." He watched Savage closely.

"Two more," said Savage finally, "would give you your Air Medal. Okay, just two more, Sergeant. And that's final."

"Very well, sir," said McIllhenny, exhibiting enormous relief.

CHAPTER ELEVEN

Twelve O'clock High!

Savage became wide awake during the two seconds it took him to reach out in the dark and turn off the clangor of his alarm clock. The luminous hands pointed to two-fifteen. In the next bed, Ben Gately sat up and rubbed his eyes.

"Here we go again," he said drowsily.

"Sure hope so," said Savage. He walked to the open window and stared through the blackout. But it was too early for omens of weather. He closed the blackout curtains and switched on the lights.

"Thought I saw a couple of stars through the mist," he said. "But I'm not sure."

"Maybe the stuff is thin," said Gately. "Probably burn off later."

The two men began to dress in silence, each permeated with that inner flood of excitement peculiar to the morning of any scheduled mission. This was extra special. The Big Show had been laid on at last. Today, if only the weather forecast stood up, they would go.

"You know, General," said Gately, reaching for his underwear, "I've been awake for a while—been lying there thinking."

"I can't think till I've had my coffee," said Savage, yawning.

"Maybe I do too much thinking," said Gately hesitantly. "Ever since this show started, I've been trying to sell myself on it. It seems as though for a hundred years I've been getting up in the blackout, like this, and taking off somewhere with a load of bombs." He paused. "Do *you* have to sell yourself on it?"

"No."

Gately waited a moment, but the general did not amplify his statement.

"Well," continued Gately. "One thing I *am* sold on, General. When this is over, after the brains and skill and lives that have gone into it, somebody at the top has got to figure out a better way to run the world—without dictators, and armies and secret weapons." He lit a cigarette. "I know one thing. If there's still any need for an army after this war, old man Gately isn't going to be in it. You'll find me in a pinstripe suit, running for Congress. I'm going to have my say."

"Me," said Savage. "I'm thinking about getting the war won first, before I start sweating about the state of the world."

Savage had begun his ritual of preparation by opening his bureau drawer and taking out a fresh pair of long-handled G.I. winter underwear. As he donned the underwear, clean wool came into contact with clean skin, for Savage had scrubbed himself thoroughly in a hot bath before going to bed. A little thing. But important. He had seen to it, through the flight surgeon, that all combat crews understood the necessity, in the interests of safety, of this detail of personal hygiene. You needed fresh underwear to absorb pre-take-off moisture before the climb to North Pole temperatures, and, more important, to reduce the danger of infecting wounds opened by flak and cannon shells.

Next, he powdered his feet copiously and drew on a pair of silk socks, following them with an outside pair of heavy wool socks. Then he slid his feet into a pair of muddy, heavy-duty, broad-toed G.I. enlisted men's shoes. If a man got shot down, he might have to walk hundreds of miles to escape. Without heavy-duty shoes, he might pull up lame in fifty miles, or, if the shoes were shined, or noticeably different from those worn by European peasants, he would invite suspicion and capture.

He climbed into a pair of light-weight flying coveralls, preferring them to bulky winter flying clothes. Temperatures in the cockpit were not dangerously low, even if the heaters failed. If he had to leave the cockpit temporarily, to assist in some more frigid part of the airplane, Savage preferred to be unencumbered. But at best, it was a compromise that irritated him, whenever he thought of the delays that had deprived the crews thus far of light-weight, electrically heated flying suits, shoes and gloves that could be depended upon to work properly.

After rolling his sleeves above his elbows and zipping his coveralls up the front so as to leave the neck open for coolness on the ground, he went to his washbasin and gave his face a final once-over with a new razor blade, out of deference to the torment sure to result from a tight oxygen mask chafing against unshaven whiskers.

Next he lifted his B-4 bag onto the bed and emptied its contents: a Mae West, a parachute harness and chest pack, an oxygen mask, a throat microphone, a pair of fur-lined gloves, a silk scarf and a small chart board, with large clips, on which to mount his maps and mission data. Deftly he checked the inflation cartridge of his Mae West, insuring that the pin had not punctured it accidentally, and opened the inspection flap of his chest pack to see that the seal had not been broken on the wire leading to the ripcord.

Savage and Gately, who had followed approximately the same procedure, were now ready, although less than ten minutes had passed since the signal of the alarm clock. To both men this pre-mission routine of meticulous attention to detail had long since become second nature.

While Savage had been equipping himself outwardly for the job ahead, inwardly also his mind was undergoing a familiar process of preparation. He counted over a score of important details on his mental fingertips—like Cobb; he must remember to tell Cobb to fly the low squadron a little farther forward today than usual. In addition to miscellaneous items such as this, all of which could be forgotten tomorrow but any one of which might be matters of life and death today, his mind held a photostatic copy of a fantastic mass of details bearing on the mission—details of the route, headings, control times, flak areas, navigation check points, call signs, position of other groups, fighter escort plan and weather data. There might or might not be time to dig these things out from his written data in an emergency. Like other experienced group commanders, he had learned the trick, once a Field Order began clicking out of the teletype machine, of converting his brain tissue into a sheet of carbon-copy paper.

But beneath all of these things, Savage was experiencing the most vital part of his personal preparation. He was donning his psychological armor plate. To some extent it was always there, had always been there, while he was in command of a combat unit. But before each mission it acquired an extra thickness and hardness, shielding him with a profound sense of confidence. Each time, this conditioning left him devoid of fear or weakness when he faced his crews at Briefing.

This morning, he knew, he would need the last particle of strength of mind and heart he could muster. For he was leading eleven groups—the second task force of the Eighth Force—to Hambrücken.

Two hundred and forty combat crew members strained forward in their seats, soaking up every scrap of information during the crackling tension of the long Briefing. When Savage rose at the end to speak, he could have heard an oxygen mask drop.

"Gentlemen," he began, "if you destroy this target, you destroy nearly half of the ball bearings that go into FW's and Me-109's. You fellows know what that means to you personally."

There were a few hollow laughs.

"Furthermore," he continued, "this is the most vital target we've ever gone after. And it is appropriate that we attack it today. One year ago, exactly, twelve B-17's, representing the maximum effort of the Eighth Air Force, took off from Grafton Underwood for a shallow penetration to Rouen, France."

Savage was interrupted by a scattering of handclaps, initiated by Cobb and Gately, which snowballed into cheers and finally an ovation. Not a man in the room was ignorant of the fact that Savage had led that first mission. The general was taken completely unawares. He held out his hands, helplessly, motioning for quiet. But the cheering only increased. Finally it was too much for Savage's self-control. He turned around, pulled a handkerchief from his pocket, blew his nose, got a grip on himself and once more faced the crews. Gately helped quiet the room down.

"Thanks," said Savage, fighting to hold his voice steady. "Thanks all of you. Better save the cheering for tonight, though. Let's see . . . where the hell was I? . . . the anniversary. As I said, a year ago twelve B-17's was a maximum effort! Today we're going to put thirty times that number of heavies into the air—half to Hambrücken and half to Bonhofen, both of them deep in the guts of the Reich." He stopped. His face brightened into the kind of smile he might have worn if all of them had been going to a ball game.

"Good luck!" he called simply, and jumped down from the platform. After the crews had begun to file out, Savage walked over and complimented the Intelligence officer on an excellent briefing. Then he led him over to the map.

"Always been curious about these prison camps," he said. "Know where Stalagluft Nine is?"

"Yes, sir. Right here . . . about twelve miles north of course today."

Savage studied the location carefully. "Thanks, Captain," he said.

At 5:30 A.M., fifteen minutes before taxi time, a jeep drove around the five-mile perimeter track in the semidarkness, pausing at each dispersal point long enough to notify the waiting crews that poor local visibility would postpone the take-off for an hour.

Savage, sitting in the grass with his pilot, Rexall, received the news with a scowl. Timing, he knew, was everything. Suppose the weather permitted the other task force, whose bases were in East Anglia, to get off on schedule? An hour's delay for his own force would give the enemy fighters time to re-form between thrusts.

"Notify me instantly," he said to the officer in the jeep, "when the Bonhofen air division takes off."

The minutes crept by painfully. Rexall got up and gave the Piccadilly Lily another once-over, with especial attention to the oxygen—human fuel, as important for this mission, he knew, as gasoline. Gunners field-stripped their .50-calibers again and oiled the bolts. Master Sergeant McIllhenny lay in the grass with his head on his chute, feigning sleep, sweating out his fourth start.

Forty-five minutes later the jeep drove up at high speed and advised Savage that the Bonhofen force had just taken off. What was worse, the 918th had received an order for further postponement of an hour. Savage lost his temper.

"Jesus *Christ!*" he said. Calling to Master Sergeant McIllhenny, he entered his car, drove to his office and waited impatiently while Stovall tried to get a call through to General Henderson.

Gately came in.

"Hell, General," he exclaimed, "they've got to scrub us. Another half-hour and southern England will be fogged in . . . none of our fighter escort will be able to take off."

"I know, I know, Ben . . . I'm trying to get Henderson now."

With growing impatience, Savage waited for over ten minutes before Stovall succeeded in getting through to Pinetree. Savage grabbed up his phone.

"How about it, Ed," he asked, "are we scrubbing? . . . What's that? . . . But my God, Ed, the timing's all shot. Surprise is out the window. The plan's failed! . . . You really mean that? . . . Okay . . . Willco." Wearily he hung up, turning to Gately and Stovall.

"It's still on," he said. "Says there's a chance our fighter escort can still get off. And maybe the Jerries will get too badly scattered in the first show to meet us in strength." He throttled his urge to express his own opinions. "Come on, Ben," he added. "We'd better get back to our ships."

At his hard-stand, Savage began looking at his watch two and three times a minute, burning up valuable energy in his frantic anxiety to get started before it was too late. Every fifteen minutes of postponement meant just that many more cannon shells waiting for his crews.

A few minutes before the revised start-engines time, his eyes lighted when he saw the jeep once more approaching. But his hopes plummeted as soon as he saw the operations officer's expression.

"Set back another hour, sir," said the captain. Savage threw down his cigar and trampled it with his heel. Once more he drove back to headquarters. Again Stovall struggled to get a free circuit to Pinetree, without success.

"I'm afraid, sir," he said, "that every group and wing commander in the air division is trying to get hold of General Henderson at the same time."

"I know damn well they are, Harvey." Savage stood up, looking at his watch.

A clerk hurried out of the adjutant's office. "Long-distance call for you, sir. From Lowestoft."

"I'll take it," said Savage, hurrying back to his desk. Pamela was on the other end. Her voice was urgent.

"Frank," she said, "I've got to talk in the clear. Can you hear me?"

"Shoot!" he said.

"Frank . . . Captain Heely is on his way to Pinetree with the intercepts. But he may be too late. You've *got* to scrub!"

"Give it to me fast as you can, Pam!"

"The Jerries put up everything in Germany against your first show. Their fighters have already landed, refueled and rearmed. They're sitting on their airdromes along your whole route . . . waiting. Waiting for your other people to come back out. You'll run right into an ambush. It's suicidal. You've *got* to scrub!"

"God bless you, Pam. Goodbye!"

He slammed down the receiver and sprinted out to his
    McIllhenny set a new record from Archbury to Pine-
        ticipating correctly that Henderson would be in the

brand-new underground Ops Block up on Daws Hill, Savage left his car at the entrance to the tunnel and rushed along the subterranean corridors until he came to Henderson in the Ops room.

"Is it still on?" he asked, without preliminaries, breathing hard. Henderson glared at him, passing a hand through rumpled hair.

"Yes," he said. "What are you doing up here, Frank?"

"Got a call from the R.A.F. Latest RT-Intercepts. Do you have them?"

"No. But I'll have them soon."

Savage repeated quickly what Pamela had told him. Henderson showed his alarm at the intelligence, but he showed annoyance even more.

"There will be no more postponements," he said firmly. "In forty minutes we go. You'd better start back."

"But, Ed! You can't mean that! They're laying for us right now! We'll catch hell coming and going!"

"Look, Frank. I'm sick and tired of having everybody trying to talk me out of this strike. They'll *go!*"

"Just to celebrate an anniversary? To buy a lousy headline with blood?"

"YES!" roared Henderson, with more conviction than Savage had ever seen in the man. "Exactly! To buy a headline we need! To buy the politicians! To buy the skeptics who don't believe we've got the stuff to hit a tough target in spite of hell! To buy the airplanes the pressure groups will send somewhere else if we let a thin fog stop us from hitting the most important target they ever gave us! *Now do you understand?*"

Ignoring the question and calling upon every bit of persuasiveness at his command, Savage stepped closer to Henderson.

"Thin fog!" he said. "That's a laugh! It's thick enough so we'll need jeeps with spotlights to find the end of the runway for us! Thick enough to cost us a bunch of airplanes colliding in the soup before we even get assembled!"

"You're exaggerating!"

"Am I? You've already scrubbed this show *twice* when the weather was better! Hambrücken will keep . . . till another day and better weather! Ed, it's a foolhardy waste of men!

And planes! For *what*? Is an anniversary, or another star, worth *that* to you?"

"Savage, there are a lot of things you don't know! I still make the decisions here! And I don't give a good goddam *what* you think! They'll GO this morning . . . even if we don't get one airplane back!"

Savage held Henderson's gaze for a long moment. His reply consisted of two words. But they were the two words which win wars.

"*Yes, sir*," he said in a voice like ice.

His brakes squeaking as the B-17 crept along the perimeter track in fits and starts, Savage glued his eyes to the red halo of the light on the back of the jeep a few feet in front of the nose. The red light was all that he could see through the dense fog which had rolled over Archbury. Cursing the delay, inwardly, he sweated out the slow journey to the head of the runway, praying that a wheel would not roll off the edge of the narrow strip and mire his ship in the mud. At the runway he ran up his engines.

When the jeep had lined him up on the correct heading of the runway, only twenty yards of which Savage could see in front of him, he focused his eyes on the Directional Gyro, gradually advanced the four throttles until their manifold pressures were exactly equal, released his brakes, rolled forward gathering speed, holding the Gyro on dead center with his rudder pedals, and completed his instrument take-off without seeing the ground. Climbing slowly on instruments, he wondered in the back of his mind how many B-17's from Chelveston and Molesworth, nearby, were milling around fighting with him for the same piece of air. The LaGuardia Field control tower would have its hands full if a score of transports were stacked up over the airport at one-thousand-foot intervals; how would they like a couple of hundred ships at unknown altitudes, overloaded with bombs and gasoline, crowding the sky in their immediate vicinity? Savage recollected the helpless moments he had spent in the Archbury control tower, listening to the desperate call of a caught just after a take-off on instruments with the ded of emergencies—failure of an engine from a or turbo. Fifty feet off the ground, too heavy

to climb, unable to see to land, the pilot's dilemma was
classic—and often fatal.

At 9:00 A.M., heaving a sigh of relief, Savage broke out of
the cloud tops into the glare of the sun. Beneath the Piccadilly Lily, the fields of England lay still blanketed in the
undercast from which other B-17's were surfacing, and
from which many, colliding in mid-air, never emerged. The
Lily continued to climb slowly, her broad wings shoulder-
ing a heavy load of incendiary bombs in the belly and a
burden of fuel in the main and wingtip tanks that would
keep her afloat in the thin upper altitudes for many hours.

From his window on the left hand side of the nose, Savage anxiously watched the white surface of the undercast,
where his pilots were puncturing the cloud deck, rising clear
of the mist with their glass noses slanted upward for the
long climb to base altitude. Savage fired a green-red flare to
identify himself to Cobb, of the low squadron, and to Gately
of the high squadron. Five Forts had already tacked onto Savage to form the lead squadron. Soon Cobb pulled into position with a cluster of six and Gately joined up with his clutch
of nine. The group was assembled, intact.

The sky over England grew heavy with the weight of
thousands of tons of bombs, fuel and men being lifted four
miles straight up on a giant aerial hoist to the western ter-
minus of a twenty-thousand-foot elevated highway that led
east to Hambrücken. At intervals, arcs of sputtering red,
green or yellow flares shot across the deep-blue backdrop as
group leaders identified themselves to wing leaders. For
nearly an hour, still above southern England, the bombers
climbed, nursing their straining Cyclone engines in a three-
hundred-foot-per-minute ascent, forming three squadrons
gradually into compact group stagger formations—low
squadron down to the left and high squadron up to the
right of the lead squadron—groups assembling into looser
combat wings of three groups each along the combat-wing
assembly line, homing over preassigned splasher beacons by
radio compass, and finally cruising along the air division assembly line to allow the combat wings to fall into place in
trail behind Savage's lead group.

Formed at last, each flanking group in place one thousand
feet above or below its lead group, Savage's fifteen-mile pa-

rade moved east toward Lowestoft, point of departure from the friendly coast. He looked down for a last glimpse of Lowestoft, a speck in the curving coast line of another world, and gave a little wave of his gloved hand. Unwieldy, but dangerous for fighters to fool with, the bomber stream moved with stately purpose out across the North Sea.

In the copilot's seat of one of the last B-17's in the long procession, General Ed Henderson watched the show with the breathless suspense of a man on only his second combat mission, coupled with the knowledge of backing a terrible gamble with his own life, voluntarily. From Henderson's perch, the task force resembled huge, anvil-shaped swarms of locusts—not on dress parade, like the bombers of the Luftwaffe that died in droves over Britain in 1940, but deployed to uncover every gun and permit maneuverability.

The English Channel and the North Sea glittered bright in the clear visibility as the 918th left the bulge of East Anglia behind it. Savage knew that his force was already registering on the German RDF screen, and that the fighter controllers of the Luftwaffe were busy alerting their *Staffeln* of Focke-Wulfs and Messerschmitts. He stole a glance back at cloud-covered England, hoping to see some sign of friendly fighters on the way to the rendezvous. But all he could pick out were a dozen Forts, which had followed Savage's force to fill in for any abortives from mechanical failures in the hard climb, gliding home to base.

Savage fastened his oxygen mask a little tighter and looked at the little ball in a glass tube on the instrument panel that indicated proper oxygen flow. It was moving up and down, like a visual heartbeat, registering normal, as he breathed.

Already the gunners were searching. Occasionally the ship shivered as guns were tested with short bursts. He could see puffs of blue smoke from Cobb's squadron close below him, as each gunner satisfied himself that he had lead poisoning at his trigger tips. The coast of Holland appeared in sharp, black outline. He drew in a deep breath of oxygen, consulted his map and saw that the navigator was going to hit the enemy coast right on the nose.

108, Savage crossed into Holland, south of The Hague. drecht, at 1117, he saw the first flak blossom out light and inaccurate. A few minutes later Mc-

Illhenny called from his waist-gun station: "Fighters at ten o'clock low." Savage saw them, climbing above the horizon ahead of him to the left—a pair of them. For a moment he hoped they were P-47 Thunderbolts from the missing fighter escort, but he didn't hope long. The two FW's turned and whizzed through the formation in a frontal attack, nicking two of Cobb's B-17's in the wings and breaking away in half-rolls; Savage got a good look at one of them when it flashed past at a six-hundred-mile-an-hour rate of closure, its yellow nose smoking and small pieces flying off near the wing root. The guns of the 918th were in action. The pungent smell of burned cordite filled the cockpit and the Lily trembled to the recoil of nose and ball-turret guns. Smoke immediately trailed from the hit B-17's, but they held their stations.

Here was early fighter reaction. Earlier even than Savage had expected. There had been something desperate about the way those two FW's came in fast right out of their climb, without any preliminaries. The interphone was active for a few seconds with brief admonitions: "Lead 'em more" . . . "Short bursts" . . . "Don't throw rounds away" . . . "Bombardier to left waist, don't yell. Talk slow."

Three minutes later the gunners reported fighters climbing up from all around the clock, singly and in pairs, both FW-190's and Me-109G's. The fighters Savage could see on his side looked like too many for sound health. No friendly Thunderbolts were visible. From now on, Savage knew, the group was in mortal danger. His mouth dried up and his buttocks pulled together, but he was used to it. His brain, clear as a bell, was able to ignore it.

A co-ordinated attack began, with most of the fighters diving out of the sun head-on from twelve o'clock high, the nine and three o'clock attackers approaching from about level and the rear attackers from slightly below. The guns from every group in the combat wing were firing simultaneously, lashing the sky with ropes of orange tracers to match the chain-puff bursts squirting from the 20-mm. cannon muzzles, blinking red in the wings of the Jerry single-seaters.

Both sides got hurt in this clash, with the entire second element of three B-17's from Cobb's squadron falling out of formation on fire, with crews bailing out, and one B-17 from Gately's squadron disappearing in a brilliant, explosive flash. Several fighters headed for the deck in flames or with their pilots lingering behind under the dirty yellow canopies that distinguished some of their parachutes from those of the Americans.

Savage swallowed hard against his dry throat. Already, in the first brush, he had lost four airplanes as against none in twenty-three previous combat missions. He ordered Gately and Cobb in closer for mutual support. One thought was uppermost in his mind: Wütz Galland's finally getting smart! He's going to concentrate on shooting the entire lead group out of the sky! If he gets *me,* he knows it's worth two groups farther back.

He glanced over at Rexall. It was freezing in the cockpit, but sweat was running from the copilot's forehead and over his oxygen mask, although the ship was on automatic pilot and neither man was exerting himself physically. Savage pulled the side of his oxygen mask away from his mouth, leaned over to the boy's ear and yelled: "They don't like us!" Rexall returned a ghastly grin.

Savage checked with the navigator. They were still on course and on time. He felt considerable relief during the brief distraction from sitting there and watching fighters aim between his eyes. Every alarm bell in Savage's brain and heart was ringing a high-pitched warning, but his nerves were steady and his brain calm. He knew that the largest and most ferocious fighter resistance of the war was rising to stop his formations at any cost.

A few minutes later the bomber stream absorbed the first wave of a hailstorm of individual fighter attacks that were to engulf it clear to the target in such a blizzard of bullets and shells that many a copilot closed his eyes. At 1141, over Eupen, Savage looked out the window after a minute's lull and saw two whole squadrons, twelve Me-109's and eleven FW-190's climbing parallel to him as though they were on a steep escalator. The first squadron had reached Savage's level and was pulling ahead to turn into him. The second was not far behind. Several thousand feet below him were many more fighters, their noses cocked up in a maximum climb. Over the interphone came reports of an equal number of

hazard. Savage began to worry whether or not they would run out of .50-caliber slugs before reaching the target.

Henderson glanced out of his window and watched dreamily while a B-17 turned slowly out to the right, its cockpit a mass of flames. The copilot crawled out of his window, held on with one hand, reached back for his chute, buckled it on, let go and was whisked back into the horizontal stabilizer of the tail. Henderson figured that the impact must have killed him. His chute didn't open.

Henderson looked forward and almost ducked as he watched the tail gunner of a B-17 ahead of him take a bead right on his windshield and cut loose with a stream of tracers that passed a few feet overhead on their way toward an enemy fighter attacking from the rear.

Still no letup. The fighters queued up like a bread line and let the Forts have it. Each second of time had a cannon shell in it. The strain of being a clay duck in the wrong end of this aerial shooting gallery became almost intolerable to Savage; as on previous missions, he felt an impulse to grab a flare pistol—anything—and fight back. The Lily shook steadily with the fire of its .50's and the air inside her was wispy with smoke. Savage checked the engine instruments for the hundredth time. Normal. No injured crew members yet. It seemed a miracle. Maybe he'd get to that target yet, in spite of the 918th's reduced fire power. The four airplanes he'd lost meant forty-eight guns.

Now a new problem arose, calling for a decision—one of those decisions that mean success or failure of an entire mission. A decision easy to make on the ground, but, as bitter experience in the Eighth Air Force had repeatedly proved, weirdly difficult for a man to make, with thousands of lives at stake, alone in the milky never-never world of the frigid sub-stratosphere, sucking at an oxygen mask, eardrums aching from the maddening splinters of static and enemy radio interference, cramped and acutely uncomfortable physically and taut with the stress of the mortal anxiety that subjects a man under enemy fire to a sensation akin to having a pair of ice tongs hooked into his guts.

The navigator had just informed Savage that the winds aloft, blowing at 120 miles per hour, had suddenly shifted to the opposite direction. Should this condition still obtain when the target was reached, it would mean that the bombers must approach Hambrücken *upwind* from the assigned I.P. (Initial Point), adding minutes of vulnerability to the bomb run and presenting the German flak defenses with a beautiful, slow-moving target.

Savage began formulating his decision with the painful concentration of a patient trying to solve a crossword puzzle while the dentist is drilling a tooth.

Fifteen minutes from target time, after a breather of several minutes, a new wave of fighters bore in on the 918th. Battle damage overtook the Lily with a rush. A 20-mm. cannon shell penetrated the right side of the cockpit and exploded beneath Savage's armor plate, peppering him only slightly about the shins, but damaging the electrical system and cutting the top-turret gunner in the leg. A second 20 mm. entered the radio compartment. A third 20-mm. shell entered the left side of the nose, tearing out a section about two feet square, damaging the right-hand nose-gun installations and injuring the navigator in the head and shoulder; he called to Savage that he was okay. A fourth 20-mm. shell penetrated the right wing into the fuselage and shattered the hydraulic system, releasing blood-colored fluid all over the cockpit floor and creating a fire hazard. A fifth shell punctured the cabin roof and severed the rudder cables connecting with one side of the rudder. A sixth shell exploded in the No. 3 engine, which caught fire.

Instantly Savage reached up, hit a red knob marked "3" and trimmed the ship for three-engine performance. The No. 3 propeller slowed down as the blades rotated to a full-feathered position—edge-on to the slipstream. The fire reduced itself to a thin stream of smoke. Unfastening his seat belt and ordering Rexall to take over, Savage grabbed a small walk-around oxygen bottle and made his way aft to the radio compartment, feeling his strength ebb swiftly from even this small exertion at high altitude. He saw at once that the radio operator, with his legs severed above the knees, had already bled to death. He turned his attention to a fire on the bulkhead, smothering it with a hand extinguisher. After the gunners in the waist waved to him that they were okay, Savage returned to his station and made a check of the rest of the crew over the interphone.

Advancing the throttles for still more additional power, Savage maintained his air speed and pressed on toward Hambrücken. In view of fire in an engine nacelle, partial loss of control, structural damage and injured personnel, he did not know whether he could make it. There was every justification for abandoning ship, a thought which had begun to obsess the rest of the crew. Rexall pleaded with him repeatedly on the interphone.

"Christ, General! We've had it," he finally called, hysterically. "Let's bail out while we still can!" The others, listening to the copilot's voice, caught the panic and several began preparations to bail out—order or no order. Savage looked across and saw that Rexall had gone completely to pieces. He pressed down his mike button.

"You son of a bitch," he enunciated distinctly, *"you sit there and take it!"*

The psychological effect of these cold-blooded words, coming in the nick of time, had an immediate and magical effect on the crew and averted a crisis. The Lily kept on.

At last the fighters, their fuel exhausted from the long chase, diminished their attacks on the 918th to almost nothing. Even the Me-110 executed a 190-degree turn and disappeared from Savage's view. The 918th was approaching the I.P., directly south of the target.

Savage called the navigator, who told him the wind was still blowing hard from the north. Instantly Savage discounted the possibility of bombing upwind from the designated I.P. and weighed the alternatives. If he selected a new I.P. north of the target, the bombers would benefit by a fast bomb run, with minimum time of exposure to enemy flak. But the new flight path would lead the bombers directly over the densest concentrations of the flak positions which the briefed route had been carefully planned to avoid. Secondly, the fast bomb run might be too short, with a tailwind, for accurate bombing. Third, the delay in flying upwind to a new I.P. would upset the timing of the rendezvous of the bombers with their fighter escort on the withdrawal. Hours later, the friendly fighters, at the limit of their fuel range, would be waiting to meet them, but they wouldn't be able to wait long; minutes, even seconds, could be decisive.

Savage quickly discarded this alternative in favor of bomb-

ing cross wind, from an I.P. about ten miles west of Hambrücken, since an I.P. east of the target would take him
farther into enemy territory and prolong the mission.

"Savage to navigator," he called. "How's the visibility
west of the target area?" To the navigator, the general's cool
voice gave the casual impression of a man asking what was
playing at the Bijou.

"Navigator to commander," he called back. "Hazy west of
target. No undercast."

"Roger." Savage consulted his map. "Savage to tail gunner.
How close is the next combat wing?"

"Tail gunner. Right behind us, sir."

Savage breathed easier. He wouldn't have to break radio
silence to divulge the change of plan to the commanders following him.

"Savage to navigator. Set a course for Halstuben. That is
your new I.P."

Firing an orange flare to alert the bomber stream in his
wake to change of plan, Savage swung smoothly around 70
degrees into his new heading. He fired another flare over
Halstuben, as the Lily turned again into its bombing run.

"Okay, Roby," he called to the bombardier. "You take
it on in from the I.P. Everything okay?"

"Roby to commander . . . Hell of a cross wind, General.
But I think I can hold the target."

To himself, Savage prayed almost tearfully that his decision
had been the right one, that, as he phrased it in his mind,
"some poor bastard wouldn't have to go back another day and
do it all over again."

The 918th proceeded on its bomb run. The bomb-bay doors
opened. A red light appeared on the instrument panel. Up
ahead, Savage watched ugly, black puffs of smoke appear
level with the nose. Flak. Plenty of it. Enough to get out
and walk on. But a lot less, he knew, than there would
have been north of Hambrücken.

A black burst mushroomed so close in front of the Lily
that Savage could see the red heart of flame in the center of
the smoke. Simultaneously there was a metallic crunch and
he felt a jar, as a heavy fragment of steel punctured the nose
compartment below. Over the interphone, he heard the single
word from Roby—"Bombs . . ." But the word "away" did

not come. The red light blinked out. The B-17, relieved of its bomb load, surged upward.

The navigator called frantically: "Roby's hit bad! Let's get the hell out of here!"

Savage moved the wheel into a left turn away from the target, looking down to see that Joe Cobb, on the inside of the turn, didn't overrun the formation. In the next second Savage was appalled to see a burst of flak catch Cobb directly in the tail, severing it. Cobb started straight down, but almost immediately the airplane exploded into a thousand fragments no bigger than a man's fist. Nor was there a trace of any chutes. Cobb's instant death registered on Savage's eyes, but not on his brain. He pressed his mike button.

"Able leader to Charlie two and Charlie three, tack on behind able squadron!" he called sharply. The two survivors of Cobb's six-ship low squadron dropped back behind Savage.

Calling on the bottommost depths of his self-control, Savage set course for home. He sent Rexall below to check up on Roby. Then he looked back toward the target. Pillars of smoke rose from the vicinity of the Aiming Point at the ball-bearing plant. And above it, boring in through dense barrages of smoky flak, the other groups were raining down their bombs. The mission had succeeded.

Breaking radio silence, Savage called Gately on VHF.

"Able leader to Baker leader, over."

"Baker to Able."

"My radio operator is dead, Baker. Can you send the strike report to headquarters for me?"

"Roger. Willco. Baker out."

Hundreds of miles to the west, at Lowestoft, this conversation was monitored by a W.A.A.F. who immediately carried it into Flight Leftenant Mallory. Pamela's brain reeled with relief: Savage was still alive. The sending of the commander's strike report indicated that Savage was still alive. It was the first intercept from the Americans. All the rest had been German. And all of them portents of disaster, spearheaded by an intercept from Wütz Galland indicating that he had landed to refuel before resuming the chase. She hid her face in her hands.

When Rexall returned from the nose he gave Savage an incredible report. An instant before bombs away, Roby, crouching over his bombsight, had been struck in the chest by a piece of flak which hurled him back six feet to the rear of his compartment. He had crawled forward, released his bombs and dropped dead over his bombsight in the middle of the sentence: "Bombs away."

Savage gradually hypnotized himself into a sort of coma, in which his mind, grasping like a drowning man at a straw, clung only to the one thought—*stay on course; get home.* The death of Cobb, of Roby, of the radio operator, and even the overwhelming fact that he had successfully bombed Hambrücken, receded dreamily into his subconscious. There was still the eternity of the long journey to base. Thank God that engine fire had finally gone out.

Occasionally the sky again became mottled with fighters. But their attacks were sporadic. The Jerries, too, had fought themselves out. Suddenly Savage glanced down at his map, then called the navigator.

"Pass Control Point eight at twelve miles north of course," he said. "Got it?"

"Twelve miles north of course at Control Point eight. Roger." There was a pause, then the navigator called back. "That's right over Stalagluft Nine, sir," he said.

"That is Roger," answered Savage.

A half hour later Jesse Bishop, sitting on the steps of a barracks at Stalagluft Nine, heard a deep, low rumble in the sky. Slanting his eyes upward, he made out a long column of black specks—fifteen miles of them. His eyes shone and his lips parted.

"Hundreds of 'em! Must be hundreds of 'em!" He turned to a pilot standing next to him who was also staring upward. "It's Savage!" Bishop cried. "I *know* it's Savage."

Twenty thousand feet above Stalagluft Nine, Savage, having kept his promise, prayed that Bishop had seen the B-17's.

One hour later, and feeling like a man recovering from ether, Savage heard the navigator call out happily: "I can see the coast, sir." It was true. Savage caught a glimpse of sunlight flashing on an expanse of water in the distance. The gunners, surrendering to the reaction from the long hours under strain, began to chatter excitedly. Savage calmed them down, cautioning them to stay on their toes, for the friendly fighters, fog-bound at their bases in England, had been unable to keep their rendezvous.

Ed Henderson, despite the altitude, surrendered to his unbearable craving for a smoke by taking alternate puffs from a cigarette and his oxygen mask. The English Channel appeared. At last they were leaving the enemy coast. Savage nosed down into the gradual descent toward England. And then the voice of McIllhenny shot a final squirt of adrenalin into Savage's weary bloodstream with the warning: "Four fighters at five o'clock low!" Savage immediately called the other group leaders and alerted them. This was just the kind of thing that could be fatal. More than once, fighters had shot down B-17's, whose gunners were already removing their barrels, when they were almost home.

The unidentified fighters finally came into Savage's field of vision—three FW's and the same red Me-110. They were climbing above the horizon, far ahead. Suddenly they turned and headed directly for the 918th out of a dive. With nose guns shot out, the Lily had only its top turret guns with which to reply as the fighters swelled into close range, apparently aiming right into Savage's cockpit. In another second, with the leading edges of their wings blinking tiny flashes of light, they breezed head on through the 918th's formation.

No. 1 and No. 4 engines immediately quit, leaving Savage with only one engine. He shoved the wheel forward and dove straight down toward the water. There was no longer any doubt in his mind that somebody, probably Wütz Galland, was out to get him, personally.

The tail turret called.

"Keep agoin', General. Them bastards are tailing us!"

Savage gradually pulled out of the dive as close as he dared get to the water, praying that the B-17, relieved of the weight of nearly all its fuel and ammunition, might reach the English coast on one engine. It had been done. He ordered the ball turret chopped loose and everything on board jettisoned except guns, ammunition and ditching equipment. The air speed slowed down from 250 in the dive to 150, then to 100, finally to 90. Pulling maximum manifold pressure, the No. 2 engine rapidly overheated and began to lose power.

Savage looked out and saw that the fighters were circling, unable to attack from below and apparently reluctant to take the chance of diving and pulling up too late to avoid hitting the water.

"Stand by for ditching!" ordered Savage. "Acknowledge." The men called back from their station one by one. Just above wave-crest level, Savage cut off his last engine. "Here we go," he called. "Get set!"

The B-17 settled into the waves in a cloud of spray and decelerated violently to a standstill, tail high, with the cockpit partly submerged. The eight survivors of the mission, acting automatically from the habits instilled in ditching practice drills, scrambled from their escape hatches, released the two yellow dinghies from the top of the wing, clambered aboard and shoved off from the water-logged Fort.

"LOOK OUT!" screamed a voice. A second later a stream of bullets stitched a series of foaming puddles across the water a few feet from Savage's dinghy, followed by the roar of the red Me-110 as it pulled out of its shallow dive. The three FW's had disappeared. Only the Me-110 had lingered for the kill.

Without hesitation, Sergeant McIllhenny dove from Savage's dinghy and swam with powerful strokes back to the B-17. He climbed up on the wing, which was already awash, before Savage, who was watching the Me-110, knew what was happening.

"Hey! McIllhenny!" yelled Savage. "Come back! Do you hear me? Get the hell back in this dinghy . . . *quick!*"

But McIllhenny paid no heed. He began lowering himself through the cabin roof, pausing only for a glance at the Me-110 which was maneuvering into position for another pass at the stranded men. McIllhenny disappeared for a moment. Then Savage could see his head emerge in the blister of the top turret, which, except for the tail, was now the only part of the airplane above water.

Over his shoulder Savage saw the Me-110 begin its approach, but his attention was still on McIllhenny, to whom he and the other crew members were still frantically calling.

McIllhenny held his fire until the Jerry was within safe range. Then his twin .50-caliber muzzles spouted streams of lead. As the B-17 began settling rapidly toward its final plunge, the water rose above the top turret until only the muzzles of the guns, still smoking, showed above the surface. Then they too disappeared beneath the waves.

The Me-110 roared past. This time it was trailing smoke. Before he died, McIllhenny had gotten a piece of it. Wütz Galland had had enough. He turned and faded south toward France.

Twenty minutes later an Air Sea Rescue launch of the R.A.F. hove to alongside the two dinghies, in which they found six men who greeted them with cheers and a weary general who looked up at them with eyes like those of a dead man.

CHAPTER TWELVE

Threshold

No mission was scheduled, but Savage and the combat crews were wearing flying clothes when the latter walked briskly into the Briefing room two mornings later at 10 A.M.

Even to the men in the front row, the general did not appear to be suffering any ill effects from the strike on Hambrücken. He was freshly shaved, his eyes sparkled and his whole manner exuded drive and energy, by contrast with most of the crews, many of whom were suffering a reaction that had left them hollow-eyed.

"Well, fellows," said Savage. "We've got a job in front of us. I want you to start looking ahead . . . not back . . . at what happened day before yesterday. We lost a few. Other groups lost more. For a day on which the Eighth Air Force as a whole lost sixty-six bombers, we got by fairly light. But we still lost too many. The bombing should have been better. That's what I want to talk to you about." He glanced down, organizing his thoughts, extemporaneously, as always. When he looked up, the men experienced that familiar illusion that he was talking to each one of them individually.

"We have a good group," he continued. "We've got to make it better, though. I'm not satisfied. Half of our low squadron was taken right out of the play yesterday on the first pass. Better gunnery might have prevented it. So—" he was speaking sharply now—"we're going to have better gunnery. After the Briefing, when you gunners check your bulletin boards, you'll find that when you're not eating, sleeping or flying, you'll be sweating out your time on the gunnery trainers and at the target range. No one present will leave the station until further notice.

"*Pilots.* We're going back to school, men. Practice missions. Fundamentals. Our formation flying isn't perfect . . . *yet!*

"*Navigators.* Frankly I am fairly well satisfied with navigation. But some of you weren't so hot with your nose guns yesterday. What I've said about the gunners goes for all of you too. You're going to fire a lot of practice rounds.

"*Bombardiers.* All lead bombardiers will drop at least one practice bomb a day up at the Walsh until further notice. That means you must stand by in cockpit readiness, when the weather is doubtful, in order to take advantage of even an hour and a half's break in the weather. *Understood?*

"Gately!"

"Yes, sir."

"I'll hold you responsible for the lead crews."

"Yes, sir."

Savage looked at the floor again, unhurried, thinking.

"One more thing," he said. "I don't want any of you getting the idea that the Old Man is bearing down on training all of a sudden just because he's got some kind of a wild hair up his butt! I don't want anybody merely going through the motions! It's no secret that you'll walk in here some morning before long and see a string stretching to Berlin." He paused.

"Now's the time to start getting ready. Dismissed!"

During the next few days, Stovall marveled at the way the general, always tireless, drove himself and all of the men at Archbury. Savage, he reflected, had the resilience of a rubber ball. The harder you slammed him against the wall, the harder he bounced back. No combat missions were scheduled,

but the station seethed with such a constant uproar of training activity that only a hardy few showed up at the club any
more before hitting the sack early.

Twice Pamela had called. On one occasion the general had
been in the air. On the other, after a messenger had interrupted him lecturing a group of new replacement crews, he
had sent word that he could not come to the phone. Even
General Henderson, who had called to notify Savage personally that higher headquarters had just approved a Distinguished Service Cross for his leadership of the Hambrücken
mission, had to wait for more than an hour before Savage
could be located.

Savage was at the wheel of a jeep, with Gately sitting beside him, as they drove toward Savage's hard-stand. Stovall
shared the rear seat with the flight gear of the two fliers.
Shedding red light across the airdrome, the rising sun filtered
through thin wraiths of mist. It was Tuesday. Pamela had
wired that she would get home today for a week's leave.
Resolutely, Savage thrust the thought from his mind, for it
had the sting of salt in an open wound. With an equal effort
of will, he had previously dismissed McIllhenny from his
thoughts, except for a brief minute in the office, when he had
signed two papers. McIllhenny had missed his Air Medal by
only one mission of the five usually considered a minimum.
So Savage had signed a recommendation for an Air Medal,
anyway—in addition to his recommendation for a posthu-
mous Congressional Medal.

Savage was concentrating on the larger thought.
BERLIN.

This was the day he had lived for. This was the culmina-
tion of seventeen years of training as a military pilot and
commander. Furthermore, he believed that this day would
mark the beginning of the end for Adolf Hitler and his blood-
smeared henchmen.

Harvey Stovall stole a look at the general's face. The eyes
looked calm, but dangerous. The features had the solidity of
granite. Stovall knew that he was looking at a man living the
supreme hour of his life. He felt profound confidence that
all the minions of hell could not stop the general from

leading the Eighth Air Force to Berlin and getting home safely on this day.

"Six minutes before start-engine time," said Gately, after they had unloaded the general's gear at the hard-stand. "Time for a smoke, sir." He lighted a cigarette with a steady hand. Savage drew a few more puffs on his cigar before throwing it down and stepping on it. He stared for a moment at his brand-new B-17, sinister-looking and complacent, squatting heavily on her fat tires.

"Might as well get started," he said, smiling at Gately. "Luck, Ben." Then he winked at Stovall. "I'll try to get home this time, Harvey," he said, "without getting my feet wet."

He picked up his chest chute and strode purposefully toward the Fort until he was standing beneath the nose hatch. He tossed his chute inside, then gripped the edges of the hatch to hoist himself up, his biceps standing out bare below his rolled-up sleeves.

And then, Gately and Stovall, watching him, saw a strange thing. Savage did not pull himself up, but continued to stand with his hands gripping the hatch, his arms straining. The two men walked over. Savage's face was an ashen gray. Sweat poured copiously down his face. Invisible to them, sweat was also streaming down his shoulder blades and down the back of his legs. His body shivered and his teeth chattered. His eyes, still fixed upward toward the nose hatch, were stricken, despairing, struggling like those of a drowning man. He made another effort to pull himself up against the unseen weight of some crushing load.

As Gately and Stovall hurried to his side, scarcely able to believe their eyes, both men understood in a flash what was wrong. The incredible had happened.

Frank Savage had broken down.

Too many missions. Too many near-misses from flak and cannon shells, buried too long in the subconscious. Too many drains on the adrenalin discharged into the bloodstream to enable a man to cope with dire emergencies. Too many hours spent sitting helplessly, unable to retaliate, against the airborne firing squad of the Luftwaffe. Too many sleepless hours spent staring at the ceiling of a bedroom under the pressure of responsibility. Too incessant and excessive a demand on the physical resources of even the strongest human body, when deprived of the opportunity for recuperation. Too much emotional stress from the perpetual denial to himself that he and his men were flesh and blood, with a right to live. Too long a residence in the halls of the living dead.

But even in this final crisis, Savage's heart and mind had not failed him. All the old determination was still there, exposed nakedly in his eyes. And all to no avail against the paralysis of nerves and muscles. Glowing with false brilliance in the days since the Hambrücken mission, like a light bulb just prior to burning out, his faculties had failed him simultaneously under the nose hatch. The body ignored the command of the brain. He was literally incapable of climbing into that airplane again.

Fighting to compose his features, the general turned to Gately with tortured eyes and leaned a hand on his shoulder. He spoke barely audibly.

"You take it, Ben," he said.

Without a word, Gately reached out and gripped Savage's arm, and then quickly hoisted himself up through the nose hatch.

Like a drunken man, head lowered, Savage staggered back to the jeep with Stovall, who was too stunned to utter a syllable. Savage climbed in and slumped back exhausted into the seat. Leaving him there, wondering whether he ought to summon the flight surgeon, but feeling instinctively that the best thing was to leave Savage alone, Stovall hurried over to the operations jeep which always stood by until the general had taken off.

"Get a pilot, right away, from a spare crew and send him over to take Colonel Gately's airplane," he ordered curtly.

"Okay, sir." The jeep sped off down the perimeter track.

Stovall walked slowly back to Savage's jeep and climbed in beside him, just as Gately's engines began exploding into life. Savage was staring straight ahead, unseeing, until Gately taxied out. Then he turned his head wearily and watched the long procession of bombers jockeying along the perimeter track toward the head of the runway behind Gately, like a clumsy herd of elephants, head to tail. A red flare streaked out onto the grass from the Control Tower.

Gately's B-17 began to roll, accelerated slowly with its overload of gasoline and bombs and finally, after covering almost the whole length of the runway, separated itself from the ground and roared straight ahead in a flat climb with its wheels curling up into the wing roots. At thirty-second intervals a new B-17 was airborne, until all of the bombers had cleared the airdrome. They circled at one thousand feet, assembling with the precision of veterans into their squadrons, and then into a single group.

Returning directly across the field, with the group closed up in solid battle order, Gately rocked his wings three times.

Then the 918th Bombardment Group set course for the wing assembly line, to assume the lead of the Eighth Air Force, and rapidly faded from sight.

Savage watched until the last speck was invisible, dropped his eyes and fumbled in his pocket with shaking fingers for a cigar. Silently, Stovall struck a match and gave him a light. His eyes, if Savage had looked at them, would have startled the general with the sheer anger that glowed in them. For the ground exec was more deeply angry than he had ever been in his whole life. Angry with something for which he could not have found the right name—unless the word was "war." At last Stovall found his voice.

"Frank," he said, "I know what you're thinking. You think you chickened out. I'll tell you how chicken you are! I'll tell you what a failure you turned out to be!" His voice became impassioned.

"You think you aren't leading the group to Berlin today, don't you? Well, who in hell do you think *is* leading it then? A no-good loafer you pulled out of the wastebasket and turned into a *man!* A combat leader. A better one than you are, for all I know. But if he is, *you made him!*" He stopped for breath.

"*He's* just *one!* What about the rest? Goddamit to hell, Frank, you're riding up there right now at every crew station. In every cockpit. So they don't need you any more. They're young, they're tough, they know their jobs . . . and they're going to win this war."

Savage still did not meet Stovall's eyes.

"Don't you see?" Stovall rushed on. "You *are* through! You've had it! But you were fighting after the bell! You were still running blindly after you had broken the tape! Can't you understand that you've already *won?* You've *won! The fight's over!*"

Savage, still looking down, remained silent for a long time.

"Thanks for trying, Harvey," he said at last in a broken voice. "I—I'll be okay tomorrow—"

Stovall, without arguing, started up the jeep and turned into the perimeter track. Neither man spoke. Now that he had discharged his outburst from his system, Stovall was beginning to feel awed. He felt humble in the presence of greatness. For all these months he had thought of Brigadier General Frank Savage as a superman. Now he knew that Savage was not a superman . . . that he never *had* been. Rather, he saw Savage as a man who had made a superhuman effort. A man capable of giving everything that was in him . . . and then giving some more. Furthermore, he knew that it would be useless to try to tell Savage that he was not a failure. Men like Savage would always be failures . . . in their own eyes, always short of the level of attainment toward which they strove.

Finally Stovall, who saw with relief that color was returning to Savage's face, ventured a suggestion.

"Maybe Doc Kaiser ought to have a look, Frank."

"No. Just drop me at my quarters."

When he had stopped the jeep at the door of the quarters, the ground exec started to get out with Savage, but the latter motioned him back.

"Better stick around headquarters, Harvey," he said. "I'll be over later." He walked heavily to the door and closed it behind him.

Savage stood for several moments leaning with his back against the inside of the door, as though to shut out a tempest raging on the other side. Once more a trembling seized him, then passed. His eyes fell on a bottle of whisky on the table. He walked slowly across the room, picked up a glass, raised the bottle to it unsteadily and poured out a straight drink. With the glass halfway to his lips, he paused and stared at the liquor intently.

"Davenport . . . Keith Davenport," he muttered aloud. He set the glass down so abruptly that some of the whisky spilled. Taking out his handkerchief, he methodically wiped up the wet spot.

Then he went into his bedroom and returned with a pair of boots dangling from one hand and his dog bone in the other. He poked up the fire in the grate before sitting down, with his back to the room, near the curling blue flames.

Mechanically, he commenced to hone the toe of one of the boots, rubbing the same patch of glistening leather. It was quiet in the room, save for the occasional hissing of the coal fire, the rumbling of a truck on the road outside and the ticking of the noisy alarm clock in the next room, whose hour hand completed two circuits of the dial before the man sitting alone in the easy chair beside the fire interrupted his work with the boot and the bone.

Major Kaiser, his troubled face thrust hesitantly inside the door, knocked and cleared his throat.

"Anything I can do for the general?"

Savage looked up blankly.

"No . . . no thanks, Doc."

The flight surgeon waited uncertainly for several seconds, but Savage had returned his attention to stroking the boot in his hand. Kaiser withdrew.

Another hour passed before there was again a knock on the door, followed by Stovall, who carried in a tray of hot lunch and placed it on the table.

The general did not even look up.

Stovall stealthily withdrew, hoping that the aroma of the food would speak for itself. As he stepped outside, his cheeks were wet.

Early-afternoon shadows crept across the bare floor; still Savage remained in his chair, his eyes fixed on the fire, his body motionless except for the slow movement of his hands as he polished the second boot.

Shortly before twilight, Savage suddenly stood up. In the distance he could hear the vibrations of engines. He strode to the window and stared out, while the rumble of a formation swelled to thunder directly over the field. His eyes lost their blank look, and his lips moved, as he counted. "Twenty-one," he said distinctly. Warm red blood mounted to his cheeks. He walked over to his whisky bottle, standing beside the tray of cold food, and then he noticed a slip of paper on the tray. His eyes burned with fire as he read the message: "Strike report. All combat wings bombed primary visually.

Visibility hazy, two-tenths cloud cover. Results good. Gately."

Savage poured a stiff drink and took a deep swallow. Then he picked up his phone and called General Henderson.

"Ed," he said calmly. "Frank Savage. You can go ahead and cut that order on me. Yes . . . that's what I said." He hung up, while Henderson was still talking, and finished the whisky in his glass at a gulp.

Savage turned his jeep off the highway ten minutes later and started up the winding road to Desborough Hall, riding, with the windshield down, beneath arching elm trees. He still saw the trees and fields about him in the dead, gray hues in which they had registered on his eyes for months. And then, gradually, subtly, he began to see color. In the fading sunlight, he saw the green of early spring on the hedges and at the tips of tree branches. He heard the tinkle of a cowbell. He smelled the fresh pungency of the earth and detected the scent of wood smoke.

That tiny stone bridge, across a creek; he had never noticed before how beautiful the moss was, growing from the cracks. That doe, with two fawns trailing her; he had never observed that there were deer in Desborough Park. That flock of pheasant, with their brilliant, shiny plumage, ignoring the jeep's approach as they leisurely crossed the road; why hadn't he seen them before?

Dimly, Savage commenced to realize that the world of living things about him was transforming from black and white into technicolor. His senses of sight, hearing and smell were awakening from their long hibernation into acute awareness. Almost physically, Savage's burden began to grow lighter by the second.

His bronzed features broke out into a smile that mirrored the sense of almost intolerable relief that suddenly buoyed him. Three lines from an old Northumberland fighting song, which he had memorized on a convivial evening at a British bomber station, crossed his mind once more:

> *I am hurt, but I am not slain.*
> *I'll lay me down and bleed awhile,*
> *And then I'll rise and fight again.*

Savage gripped the wheel tighter, pressed down harder on the accelerator and opened his mouth wide to gulp the rushing wind. In a cloud of rising dust, the jeep vanished around the next bend in the road.

About the Authors

BEIRNE LAY, JR. and SY BARTLETT both saw service in the United States Air Force in World War II. One of the original members of General Eaker's 8th Air Force staff, Beirne Lay saw combat as Commander of the 487th Bomber Group, was shot down over France and evaded capture for three months until liberated through the efforts of the French Underground. Sy Bartlett, as Aide-de-Camp to General Carl Spaatz, was one of the first to arrive in the European Theater. Assigned to Operations on the staff of the 8th Bomber Command, he engaged in many combat missions with both the United States Air Force and the Royal Air Force. Later, as a member of Brigadier General Frank Armstrong, Jr.'s B-29 crew, and as Chief Intelligence Officer of the 315th Wing, Bartlett saw action in the Pacific and flew on every other mission over Japan until the surrender.

GROUP #2 IN THIS HIGHLY PRAISED SERIES . . .

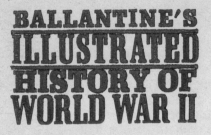

BALLANTINE'S ILLUSTRATED HISTORY OF WORLD WAR II

Four new titles have now been added to this important new series of all-original BIG SIZE war histories—each book measuring 8¼" by 5½" and profusely illustrated with approximately 150 rare photographs, combat maps and detailed drawings:

STALINGRAD: the turning point,
by Geoffrey Jukes

AIRCRAFT CARRIER: the majestic weapon,
by Captain Donald Macintyre

BASTOGNE: the road block,
by Peter Elstob

PANZER DIVISION: the mailed fist,
by Major K. J. Macksey

"An auspicious start . . . Emphasis is on photographs, some of rare vintage, yet the text in each case is solid and authoritative, written with spirit. Readers who continue to be fascinated by the manifold aspects of World War II, the largest single event in the 20th Century, will find these books a bargain, not only because of their price but also their contents."

—Martin Blumenson, former Chief Historian,
U. S. Office of Military History

Each book is priced at $1.00—or you can order all four books delivered postage free to your home by sending $4.00 to

BALLANTINE BOOKS, 101 FIFTH AVENUE, NEW YORK, N.Y. 10003